THE
WALKER
CLAN
SERIES

THE WALKER CLAN SERIES

BOUND FOR HORSESHOE BEND
ANTHONY THORN

TATE PUBLISHING
AND ENTERPRISES, LLC

The Walker Clan Series: Bound for Horseshoe Bend
Copyright © 2013 by Anthony Thorn. All rights reserved.

No part of this publication may be reproduced, stored in a retrieval system or transmitted in any way by any means, electronic, mechanical, photocopy, recording or otherwise without the prior permission of the author except as provided by USA copyright law.

The opinions expressed by the author are not necessarily those of Tate Publishing, LLC.

This novel is a work of fiction. Names, descriptions, entities, and incidents included in the story are products of the author's imagination. Any resemblance to actual persons, events, and entities is entirely coincidental.

Published by Tate Publishing & Enterprises, LLC
127 E. Trade Center Terrace | Mustang, Oklahoma 73064 USA
1.888.361.9473 | www.tatepublishing.com

Tate Publishing is committed to excellence in the publishing industry. The company reflects the philosophy established by the founders, based on Psalm 68:11,
"The Lord gave the word and great was the company of those who published it."

Book design copyright © 2013 by Tate Publishing, LLC. All rights reserved.
Cover design by Rodrigo Adolfo
Interior design by Jomel Pepito

Published in the United States of America

ISBN: 978-1-62994-489-0
Fiction / Westerns
13.11.20

Dedication

To my wife, Joanne, who taught me love.

Contents

Prologue 9
Background 11
Characters 13
Ernest Walker 15
Sylvia López (Red) 20
Irish Meets Basque 23
Coffin Ship 30
Ship Survival 34
Port Side 38
Thugs 42
Wagon Train 48
Boston Harbor Thugs 54
Late-Winter Storm 60
Storm Recovery 65
Crossing the Creek 70
Indian Attack 73
Their Own Wagon 78
Wolves 82
Buffalo Stampede 88
A New Life 93
Resupply 97
Civil Unrest 101
Battlefield 108
Confederate Soldiers 113

Battle Scars	118
Unionists	122
Going Home	126
Rocky Mountains	131
Elk Mountain	137
Camp Meat	143
Bringing It Home	147
Tomcat	153
Utah Territory	159
Ute Land	164
Black Bear	170
Nancy Walker	174
First Christmas	179
Daniel Clark	184
Springtime	190
Mormons	193
Black Hawk War	196
Eviction Notice	199
Leaving Home	202
Idaho Territory	205
Oregon Trail	207
Homesteading	210
Surveying	213
Nez Percé	217
Cabin Building	220
Horseshoe Bend Sawmill	223
Nez Percé Camp	227
Claymore Walker	231
Mustanging	238
Carie	244
The Letters	250
Afterword	256
Note from the Author	259

Prologue

This book tells a story that begins with the event that pushed so many immigrants from Ireland to seek newer and better places to live. Ireland was going through a tough time. Their inhabitants were suffering from starvation. They depended on their potato crop that became diseased with blight. Since potatoes were their mainstay for both food and trade, they had nowhere to turn. The landlords let their workers go, but the peasants could not find work and became desperate. The New America had opened up and offered new hope to the Irish. The entrepreneurs of the seas took advantage of the time and loaded their ships full of both cargo and immigrants leaving Ireland. Most ships were ill equipped, poorly managed, and many lost up to 50 percent of their passengers from disease. America, however, was also struggling with an internal Civil War. America sought freedom of all its people and fought to maintain that right. When the federal government looked at the situation in the south, they saw slavery as the violation of human rights. No man should be another man's slave. The south depended upon a slave workforce. The slaves did not receive a wage but just forced into free labor in a foreign land. The immigrants fleeing from Ireland landed to come face-to-face with the American transition. Ernest and Sylvia found many friends as well as enemies as they pushed their way from Ireland to the promises the west had to offer. They became instruments of this great nation that opened up the pathway for others to follow.

Background

Thomas Malthus published an essay on the *Principles of Population* in 1798. In this essay, he claimed that the population in Britain was growing faster than their food supply. He predicted that many would starve unless something changed. His essay brought awareness to this overpopulation and starvation issue, creating panic at the highest levels in the British government. The United Kingdom of Great Britain included Ireland, England, Wales, and Scotland, which came together to merge their resources. A new flag, the Union Jack, flew over these united countries early in the 1800s. The entire United Kingdom was under the London parliament rule. The Irish could no longer make their own laws but had to rely upon the British in London. The main staple in Ireland was their potato production. Land was scarce, and they relied upon their potato crop most exclusively. However, a fungal disease called potato blight wiped out a major part of their crop. This disaster hit the rural areas hard, and as Malthus had predicted, many lost their jobs, starved, and died as a result. The British government began to panic and stepped in to give aid by importing thousands of bushels of maize into Ireland from the New America, but the continuing fungal problem exhausted potato supplies. Typhus, scurvy, and dysentery ran rampant in the rural areas of Ireland to further annihilate and frustrate them. The British attempted to help with soup kitchens, but this only helped slightly. The rich Irish proprietors evicted peasants who could not pay their rent because they had no potatoes to sell. The unrest caused thousands of Irish to cut their losses and set sail to the new promise land called America. The panic sent a wave of residents streaming to the ships sailing to America. These ships were so overcrowded that many died along the voyage. These ships, known as *coffin ships*, sailed from Ireland.

Characters

Ernest, Sylvia López (Red), Nancy, Claymore Walker: Irish-Basque Family

Shane, Bridget, Patrick, Ernest, and Carieanne Walker: Irish Family

Thomas Malthus: Author

James Lenny: Scout

Raul: Dock Thug

Jason and Julia Hicks: Merchants

Joshua Barker: Wagon Master

Lester, Margret, Daniel Clark: New York Wagoners

Mark: Lester's Brother

John, Shirley, Mary, Harry, Edward, Joseph Reynolds: Wagoners

Freda and Husband: German Wagoners

Quantrill: Bushwhaker

General James Lane: Jayhawker

Louis Woods: Confederate

Raymond Leigh: Wounded Confederate

Sergeant Nettles: Union Sergeant

Bear Claw, Blue Sky, and Running Dog: Ute Neighbors

Sees Far, Mare-ah, and Perl: Ute Neighbors
Antonga Black Hawk: Southern Ute Chieftain
Julio, Lillian, and Jeremiah Martinez: Basque Neighbors
Tye Parker: US Marshal of Idaho Territory
Gray Elk and Babbling Brook: Nez Percé Neighbors
Daisy: Cow
Ole Blue, Sissy, and Hank: Mules
Ole Shep: Sheepdog

Ernest Walker

Shane and Bridget Walker, Irish peasants, struggled to keep from starving. They were tenant farmers in Dublin, Ireland, who rented their plot of land from a rich proprietor with power and resource. The Walkers were dependent upon the potato harvest for survival, their one and only farm crop. It was their mainstay. They had many good years of farming, but when their only crop failed, they starved. The potatoes just turned black and rotted from the inside out. They called it potato blight. Since the crops went bad, the farmers had to turn under their crop before harvest and wait another season to replant. Year after year, the potato crop failed, not only on their farm, but also throughout the country. They blamed everything—the weather, insects, or something in the wind, but could not pinpoint its source. The blight spread to their seed crop, so they could not even count on their next planting. Nothing seemed to work.

They suffered in these perilous times, and the future did not look bright for them or their children. The great famine ravaged their countryside, forcing thousands of them out of work with no substance to live on. The ruling British's feeble attempt to solve the problem did not seem to help. The peasants turned to rebel against their British rule. They fought the British with any tools they could find, only to be bitterly defeated.

The Walkers were a typical family and had three children, two sons and a daughter. When their older son, Patrick, died in one rebellious act at the hands of the British, they were heartbroken and decided to take drastic action to save their other son, Ernest. Bridget thought that their only daughter, Carieanne, could help her as a servant girl at one proprietor's house. Shane looked over to Bridget, who was about to cry. "Our unscrupulous proprietor has already removed many of his tenants who are now penniless. He has just issued me a Notice to Appear. The local barrister will pronounce judgment on us next week. As head of this family, he will have me thrown in jail for owing him back rent. Unless we can find another place to stay, we will be living in the streets like most of our pauper neighbors have been. Bridget, I just cannot let them do that. We have to take some action now, or we will be begging in the street next week. Ernest cannot stay here. He is a strong young man, and if he stays, he will more than likely follow his brother's footsteps, and the British will kill him. I talked to many at the pub, and they said that the New America held many promises. Many sent their children to America aboard one of those sailing vessels leaving the harbor and heading across the Atlantic Ocean. I think that we should send young Ernest to America. At least there, he will have a fighting chance of survival."

"If you do that, we will never see him again. We already lost one son, and I do not want to lose another. I just love our children and want them where I can hug their necks occasionally and watch them mature."

"I know, my dear, but if he stays here, we will watch him starve and possibly lose his life fighting the British. He is strong and has good morals. I am confident that if anyone can survive, he will be able to. If I were a young man, I would love to cross the sea to that new land of opportunity. If we were able, I would recommend that we all cross over and take part in building that virgin frontier. I am sure that he can find happiness there, and after all, isn't that what we want for our children?"

When they lost their home and saw no future for their only living son in their impoverished country of Ireland, brokenhearted, Ernest's parents scraped together all they had and paid the captain for Ernest's passage, gave Ernest a little extra money, then prayed for his survival as they squeezed him aboard an overcrowded ship. Immigrants climbing aboard had to prepay for passage on a ship heading to the New America.

The captain noticed a burly young man traveling alone and addressed him. "Would you be willing to help the ship's first mate with sailing this vessel? I am a few sailors short and can use a strong man like you to help with the cargo and rigging. I will pay you back for some of your passage once we get to America."

"Aye, I do not see why not. I am not traveling with anyone, and it will help me out when I get to the new land."

"Good." The captain nodded to the husky young man. "Many of my sailors hop off the ship as soon as we dock, and after having too good a time at the bars and brothels that line the ports, they head back for the next voyage broke and many times beat up. Sometimes they do not even make it to the ship in time and leave us shorthanded as we are now. Just talk to the first mate, and he will direct your activity."

Ernest found the first mate staring down in the cargo hold. He was tall and had big, muscular broad shoulders like himself. Ernest introduced himself. "My name is Ernest Walker, and the captain asked me to find you and report to you for work."

"Great! You can start by helping the dock workers fill the cargo hold with the pallets of cargo we are carrying. The cargo is our payload as well as the immigrants. Those derricks will pick the pallets up from the dock and swing them over into this cargo hold. I want you to climb down into the cargo hold and help the men place those pallets on top of one another. After the supplies are loaded, help the sailors rig the sails and release the cables from the dock. Just ask one of the workers what you can do to help."

It was hot down in the hold. Derricks swung the loaded cargo pallets into the hold. The pallets had ropes dangling from them so that they could steer the pallet to their resting spot. "Grab that line, the worker pointed it out to Ernest. "Pull it over so that it may set squarely on top of that pallet while the derrick driver lowers it. Watch out and don't get caught under one of those pallets, or they will flatten you like a bug."

Sweat poured off the ones in the hold. There was no breeze, just hot and stale with no air moving. Throughout the day, they worked filling the hold with cargo. At the end of the day, it was full and ready for departure. "Whew!" Ernest reflected on the hot, muggy hold in the bowels of the ship. "It seems to me like this ship will sink from carrying that much weight."

"No problem." The operator of the derrick laughed. "I have seen the time when we've held a little more. We not only used to fill the cargo hold but loaded the upper deck full as well."

There was no way to predict the weather, especially toward the tail end of winter. There were days when suddenly, strong bitter-cold winds and high waves would rip and tear the sails to shreds, and then days and days of calm winds that would not even fill the sails. After the huge early-season storms, Ernest and some of the other sailors climbed up fifty or sixty feet to the rigging to pull down any ripped sails. A sailor sitting on the deck would sew through the many layers of canvas to repair the sail using his thimble, needle, and thread from his mending kit. After mending the sails, the sailors would climb back up the tall rigging and set the sails in place again. To Ernest, this seemed to be the routine after every big storm. It was very strenuous work and required much stamina. He thought he was in very good shape but found muscles he did not know he had.

After the first few days of bucking the waves of the storm, most of the passengers began to get seasick. They returned to stay in their bunks after leaning over the rail on the deck. The greenish salty water of the ocean mixed with the smell on board and the constant rocking and rolling of the ship was enough to gag a veteran. The passengers got so sick that they would not even go to the rail. They would just lean over their bunks and cut loose with the vomit. It would drip down through the bunks on the passenger below them. The stench in the sleeping quarters became unbearable. The sick would go to the wooden water barrels and dip out water and splash on their faces. Others following them would do the same, causing whatever sickness they carried to spread.

Ernest slept in a hammock with the other sailors on the port side or left side of the ship. Even as icy cold as it was, he liked the open air on the deck, so he found a spot next to the wheelhouse and slept outside as long as the weather permitted. When the weather was too bad to stay outside, he would go into the galley. Since the ship sailed across the ocean twenty-four hours a day, Ernest was on call to mast the sails on the yardarm at anytime of the day or night. During the stormy weather, there was no time for resting. The calm days allowed him to weave his way along the deck and talk to the immigrants.

Sylvia López (Red)

Sylvia López's parents had no country. Being a Basque family, they roamed from one land to another as gypsies in a covered wagon. They made their living by serving others. They were good sheep herdsmen and lived out of their wagons. They owned no land and were not residents of any country. They had their own secret language (Shelta) and lifestyle. Like the Walker family, many Basque families became homeless due to the potato famine. Her parents perished from the resultant diseases of the famine, leaving Sylvia an orphan. She was a bright young woman and knew how to speak several languages. Her mother also taught her how to heal the sick with many herbs and spices found in and around the hillsides.

The other gypsies in their troop used her family's money to bribe and beg her passage to the new land on a ship preparing to leave port. They felt that the virgin land would be her best option; otherwise, they would have to sell her to the highest bidder. They knew that to sell her meant that she would spend a lifetime in some parlor house and no doubt would perish at an early age from some contacted disease. Since they could not pay for her entire passage, they sold her service for the remaining cost of that passage. They arranged through an immigrant agent, who referred to her as an indentured or bondservant. Her contract required her to work with the galley staff until they reached America. As with so many passengers, she was frightened but could make the best out of what she received. She heard the horror stories about the ships and their death toll. Basques were independent survivors, and Sylvia was at the top of her class. She took a couple of deep breaths, steeled herself, and marched right into the galley to start her serving job.

"Where do you want me to start?" She spoke to the man sorting through the crates and putting the supplies onto the shelves.

"Just help me stack that food on the shelves so that we can grab what we need. Since these poor Irish have brought little food for their own journey, we will have to feed them. The law mandates us to bring one pound of food per day for these immigrants. They have not specified what kind of food, so we have purchased what we could find. Our cook will heat some of it on our brick fireplaces. Your job will be to distribute whatever he gives you equally to all the passengers. We don't have much room, so we have just piled up what we have here in the galley's storeroom. Try not to smash the produce because it has to last us at least a month. When you get that done, move two or three of those water barrels into that closet. If we leave all of those barrels out on the deck, the passengers will pollute it within a week. We have a limit on the amount of fresh water we can store. It is the first thing that seems to go bad. We have to protect some of it to help those that get sick. Be very careful whenever you use it. Always make sure that you keep it clean. Your life will depend upon it."

"It sounds like you have been on many of these voyages. Are there many bondservants that work here? What kind of problems usually arises during the voyage?"

"I don't have time for any of this chitchat. Just follow my instruction, and we will get along fine. Now, get to work and tend to business."

Sylvia learned quickly that her boss was a no-nonsense type of person. He gave the orders and expected them followed just as he had given them. The servants quickly found out that he meant what he said when he said it. Sylvia went right to work and did not wait around for any more instruction. She had learned that when faced with tyrants, you just bowed your neck and went to work. Those who did not, suffered all kinds of mistreatment during or after their shift. While under these conditions, she knew from experience that it was best just to focus on ones own work.

When the cargo hold was fully loaded with pallets and over three hundred immigrants packed tightly onto the decks, the ship set sail in mid-February from the Ireland port heading toward the New America. Passengers assigned tiny cots, hammocks, and bunks lined up side by side to make maximum use of space. Men, women, and children were all crammed together. There was very little privacy. The latrines were just holes cut in the bow of the ship where the pollutant waste just fell into the greenish-brown sea.

Passengers were instructed by the captain as he bellowed into a bullhorn. "Attention, passengers, be very conservative with your eating and drinking. What we have on this vessel is very limited and has to last us our entire voyage. Watch your children, and keep them away from the rails. You brought them aboard, so they are your responsibility. Do not expect any of our staff to take care of your kids for you. If you failed to provide decent food for your family, you will have to eat what we have available in the galley. As we sail, we will hit days of some rough weather, then days of very calm weather. If you get sick, just lean over the side and clean up your own mess. The crew will be busy with their duties. Do not cause your sickness to spread throughout the rest of this ship. If you have any problems, see one of the members of this crew. Thank you."

Some of the passengers heard what the captain said. Most passengers, however, never heard or paid any attention to what he warned. There was too much noise, so they were on their own.

Irish Meets Basque

As Sylvia was carrying a tray of food to the ship's guests, a large redheaded burly young man turned a corner too quickly without looking and ran headlong into her. The food flew from her tray, and they both slipped on the food and sprawled on the deck in a tangle of arms and legs. Ernest, the large Irish boy, was red-faced and started apologizing to her. Then he tried too quickly to stand back up and again slipped on the deck and fell on top of Sylvia. The passengers roared in laughter at their expense. When Ernest had slipped the second time, they both began laughing themselves silly. As they became untangled, Ernest tried to wipe the food off Sylvia, which made an even a bigger mess.

"Please stop trying to help me, ya big clumsy Irish galoot. Go get yourself cleaned up. I will clean up myself and this mess ya made." She told him.

"I am so sorry, Red." He tried to appolozize slipping and sliding on the food. *What a fool I made of myself,* he thought as he headed away. *That Irish gal sure was spunky, I will give her that. I really made a bad impression on her. At least, she laughed instead of cursing me. Maybe if I clean myself up and watch where I am going, she will see me again and accept my apology. She sure was a pretty little thing with that long red curly hair. She didn't seem to take offense when I called her Red.*

What a big, clumsy, but handsome galoot, Sylvia thought. *I wonder who he is and where he came from. I hope that I can see him again. He was polite. I even like the nickname Red he gave me. It was kind of cute. If I had met someone like that in Ireland, maybe I could have stayed there instead of traveling clear across this ocean.*

Sylvia picked up the tray and the leftover food. Then she returned to the supply room. The food manager came over to her, scolding and shaking his fist. "I am going to charge the expense of the food to you. If you don't pay for this mess, I will sell your contract to someone else when we reach the new land. Clean yourself up, then get a mop and finish cleaning up this mess."

Sylvia bit her lip to keep from telling him what she really thought, tossed her apron in the corner, flipped her red hair, grabbed another apron, and hurried out with a mop and bucket to clean the deck. When she finished her shift, she headed to her room and turned the corner just to run into Ernest again.

"Please stop trying to run me over," she said.

"I am so sorry, lass." He managed to say grabbing at her to keep her from falling. "I guess I just haven't found my sea legs yet. I need to introduce myself to you. My name is Ernest Walker, and I am from Ireland. My parents put me aboard this ship, so I hired myself out to work with the other sailors aboard this ship."

Sylvia stared up at the big redheaded galoot looking down at her with his large, soft, pleading green-blue eyes. She demanded, holding out her hand. "I am not Scottish, so do not call me lass. You owe me two dollars for the food I had to pay for. I just got off my shift and hope that they don't extend my labor contract, no thanks to you. By the way, I thought you were Irish. What sort of a name is Walker? I thought all Irish had names like O'Hare or O'Malley or O'Something, but not Walker."

Ernest reached into his pocket, produced two dollars, and handed them over to her. "Not all Irish have the *O* in front of their surnames. Some are just plain, like Walker. I will have you know my original surname was Walkyr, but my grandparents changed the *y* to an *e* to be more consistent. The Walkyrs initially came from England's northernmost country of Northumberland in England. Some say my great-great grandfather purchased Shakespeare's house."

"Oh, so you are an old English poet who moved to Ireland. My name is Sylvia López, and I hope you find your sea legs and what you are looking for." She relented, showing a bit more compassion. "López is a common Spanish surname. My family changed the spelling of the *ó* and just used the old-fashioned *o*. Sometimes I like the sound of the old way of pronunciation better. I have no idea how my ancestors came to Ireland from Spain, but I guess they must have. I am Basque, and we are notorious for being wanderers. Now, I am heading to America aboard a big, overcrowded ship working for my passage and getting crushed by overpowering poetic Englishmen claiming he's Irish."

"Aye lassie, ya mind taking a wee walk with me? Maybe if we walk side by side, we won't run into each other."

"Laddie, get this straight. You ran into me. As long as you don't trip and push me over the rail of this ship, I will walk with you. The fresh air will feel good after spending time down in the galley."

"If I do knock you over, lass, I assure you, I will jump over the rail myself and try to rescue you. I sure would not want to try to swim that far though. This ship will travel almost three thousand miles, and with a nonstop pace at five miles per hour, it will take us over a month to get to America. When we arrive at the port in Boston, what are your plans?"

"I haven't got any specific plans yet. In talking to some of the help, when we arrive in port, apparently, many greedy con men will swarm aboard to grab our bags and try to con us into taking a room at their facilities and then extract an outrageous fee for their services. Their attempt is to make us bondservants to them. The families who have lost loved ones are the most vulnerable, especially the widows and single girls like myself. Once they get their hooks into us, they will exploit us any way they want. I don't want to become a slave to anyone. To trade one poverty-stricken land for another is not any dream of mine. So to answer your question, laddie, my first priority is to head inland away from the port."

"I agree. I would like to migrate west into this New America's frontier of untamed lands. I think it would be exciting to work lands that have never been touched. I enjoy working with my hands, and I don't want to be beholden to anyone either. From what I hear, the American interior is very dangerous where they have natives who can be quite hostile. Some even take scalps. I'd sure hate to lose my hair to one of them."

"I wouldn't like to lose my hair either. I like your thinking though." Sylvia turned, looking directly into his eyes. "My heritage is being nomadic. Basques are known as great sheepherders and always traveling in wagons. I think that someday, I would like to live in a cabin of my own in the mountains, beside tall green pines, meadows of wildflowers, and a little stream with fish. I love nature, the smell of fresh air, and animals, both tame and wild. I have traveled in a wagon most of my life. It was not too bad, but I am looking for a solid foundation under me."

"It sounds like our dreams are a wee bit similar. We both are young and single, not afraid of work, and don't want to be enslaved by anyone. Ah, here is your room. We need to have more walks like this, keep our ears and eyes open, and find out as much as we can about migrating into the interior of this new land. I hope you don't mind if I look you up again darlin'. I'd like to know more about your dreams and expectations."

"You can find me anytime you want. I will be either hauling out food or in my room. Just try not to run into me again while I am carrying food. My boss is already threatening to sell my contract to someone when we reach America."

"Oh, so ya be a bondservant too?"

"Aye, but just until we reach America. Then I have met my obligation, 'less of course, if some big galoot keeps causing me to run up my bill."

"You're never going to let me forget that, will ya lass?"

"Nope. It was good for a laugh though, was it not?"

"It sure was. I still find myself laughing at your antics. Good night."

Their friendship continued to grow throughout their voyage. They were from different backgrounds, but they did not see that it would make any difference in this new land when they met on board the ship. They were both very young but strong-minded with similar interests. The crowded ship's voyage was long, and the young couple found they needed each other's strength to cope on the voyage. On one of their walks, Ernest asked the young red haired Irish lass. "Have you heard anything of the stability in this new land we are going to?"

"Aye, I know that slavers have imported black slaves, not only men, but women and children as well, from Africa and its neighboring communities. They have been doing this in Europe and this New America for over a hundred years now. Slavers haul slaves by the shipload to the southern end of America. Slavers are selling these men and women to work on plantations. These imported slaves are similar to indentured servants or bondservants, just as I am aboard this ship, only they cannot regain their freedom no matter how long they work. I have heard that if these black slaves behave, they survive fairly well. There are some mean owners, of course, that whip and beat them into submitting to their will. Many die from the harsh treatment."

"That is pretty much the same as it is throughout Europe too. I think that the treatment in Europe is harsher than their English colonies though. Indentured servants have been around for a long time. It is nothing new. If someone owes anything to someone else and have nothing to trade for it besides labor, they become their bondservant until their debt is paid off."

"That is exactly why I am working in the galley serving this food. I am just working for my passage to America, only I am not black."

"The black slaves are a little different though. They did not owe anyone anything. Slavers just hunted them down, bound them hand and foot, and then shipped them off to auctions in America for cheap labor. The slavers kill many in the process of capturing them and leave their families to fend for themselves. The slave's inhuman treatment is worse than the treatment of sheep and cattle. The captured are just hauled away to the markets and sold at auctions to the highest bidder."

"There are a lot of talks that the north end of America is trying to free the slaves. I heard there is unrest and fighting going on now between these two factions. It seems to have created an armed conflict in America, the northern half against the southern half. I sure hope we don't get caught up in their conflict."

"I am sure it will affect us one way or the other. I have seen enough fighting and don't want any part of it. I lost my brother, Patrick, in a rebellious uprising and felt the pain it causes. There are always injustices on both sides of any conflict. Most of them start political, and then they recruit their armies when they cannot or will not reach a verbal agreement. The armies then just face off and shoot each other until one side has slaughtered more and subdued the other."

"I am sorry to hear about the death of your brother Patrick. Do you have any other siblings?"

"Aye, a sister named Carieanne. She is the apple of my parents' eye. My deifiúr is vivacious and fun-loving. She would never leave Ireland as long as our parents are alive."

"I'd love to meet her. I am sure that she could tell me a lot about you and what you were like growing up."

"Carieanne and I have always been close. We laughed and played together. I sure do miss her. Patrick, however, worked with Father tending the fields. He was always working and was very serious."

"I am sorry. I should not have brought them up. I am sure that you miss your whole family. It sounds to me like you were a very close family."

"We were."

One chilly evening as they walked across the deck, Sylvia was shivering a little. He took off his coat and wrapped it around her. She looked up into his kind, warm, inviting eyes and thanked him. As their hands touched, they did not let go. Hand in hand, they continued their stroll. When they came to her door, she handed him back his coat and kissed him on his cheek, sending chills down the length of his body. He wrapped his arms around her and kissed her gently on the mouth. She did not pull away but hungrily kissed him back. Then she turned and scurried into her room, tingling down to her toes.

Ernest stood outside her door, letting the moment surge through his body and fade back out. He somehow felt it was a pivotal moment in their lives.

Neither could get their minds off the moment throughout the next day as they worked. When her shift ended, she anxiously looked forward to their meeting. As the days followed, they never went anywhere without holding hands or leaving without a kiss. The kisses became longer and warmer with each parting.

Coffin Ship

Since there were no dining rooms, they ate the food wherever the passengers congregated. Servers carrying large trays throughout the crowded deck distributed the food from the galley. Not all the food was good for eating, especially after the first few weeks as it began to become moldy and sour. Water was another issue. The ship carried a limited supply of barrels of fresh water strung throughout the ship, but the open barrels soon became contaminated as people dipped water with any container that was on hand. Additionally, they would wash their faces and hands directly in the barrels. Disease spread from the contaminated foul food and water supply. There was no hospital or medical staff present, and the sick spread disease to the others. Death was imminent, and soon, many succumbed from their ailments. The first mate directed the disposal of the dead and had them tossed overboard to prevent disease from spreading. Families were left alone crying and mourning their loss. When a husband died, the window and her children were vulnerable and left to the perils of the strong and ruthless that awaited them. Many families aboard were traveling alone with no one else to lean on.

While Sylvia was serving food, a crying woman stopped her and painfully complained, looking for someone to help. "My little girl is so sick that she cannot stop heaving. I don't know what is the matter with her. Please have a look at her and see what is wrong."

Sylvia looked at the young girl and gave in to compassion, asking the girl, "What have you been eating and drinking?"

"I have been eating the food that you've brought and drinking the water out of the barrel."

"Show me the water barrel."

She looked into the water barrel, sniffed, then gagged and looked at the girl's mother. "This water is putrid. Just look at what is floating on it. She is suffering from diphtheria and dehydration. You cannot drink that stuff. It is loaded with bacteria and so foul that it stinks. Anyone would get sick drinking that stuff. We need to talk to the captain and see if we can dump this slime over the side and replace it with clean water."

Sylvia and the girl's mother found the captain and told him the trouble. He looked at the two with dominant arrogance. "I told you passengers that you needed to keep the water clean. If you did not, then it is your own fault. This ship is limited on the amount of water we can haul. Just find another barrel and use the water that is in that barrel."

They looked all around the ship and found that almost every water barrel was so putrid that it would not be long until the entire ship would be nothing but sailing dead. They approached the captain again and tried to explain to him. "Every water barrel is so contaminated that it could float a cannonball. Here, see for yourself." Sylvia responded boldly as she handed the captain a jar of putrid the water she had filled from one of the barrels. "Furthermore, not only is the water contaminated, but the food is also mostly rotten and not fit for a hog to eat."

"Just filter the stuff out of the water, and it will be fine. Sort the food, and it should last the rest of the voyage. It is that or let the passengers go hungry and thirsty."

"If it is good enough for us to drink, Captain, show us how by filtering and drinking it yourself. If you don't get sick, we will do as you say." The mother growled with disgust shoving the jar into the captain's hand.

"Don't test or get smart with me, you two. Passengers contaminated the water, so you are stuck with it until we get to port. Sylvia, if you stir up any more trouble, you will find yourself thrown off this ship and set afloat. Now get out of my sight, else I will lose my patience."

"I am so sorry." Sylvia painfully but passionately responded to the child's mother as they were going back to where her daughter lay. "I can help you out a little by bringing you a jar or two from an uncontaminated barrel from the galley, but you can't say anything about where you got it, or there will be a run on the galley. There is not enough good water for everyone. If the captain finds out, he will set me afloat. I know the captain was very serious when he threatened that he would throw me over the rail."

"Just help us any way you can."

"When I came aboard in Ireland, I brought a bag of some herbs and spices. I can take some dandelion, hyssop, and lavender and boil it in clean water to make her some tea to drink. It will help strengthen her stomach so that she can hold down the good water and food. Be sure that she drinks at least a full cup every two hours."

Sylvia took the jar of putrid water they had given to the captain, cleaned the jar, and filled it from the hidden barrel of fresh water she had in the galley. She made sure that no one saw her. "Here is some uncontaminated water. Drink it sparingly. I will bring some good food later, but your daughter is just in need of some good water."

Whenever Sylvia and Ernest walked the decks, Sylvia would cry and hug Ernest. "I feel so bad about the dying. I have talked to the captain about the deplorable conditions of the foul food and water, but to no avail. The captain just wants to ignore the problem. He feels the contamination was a problem the passengers created themselves. That the water was good, as was the food, when we left Ireland, and there was sufficient quantity to last the time it would take to reach America. I wish that the passengers would have a mutiny and take over this *death ship*. There are so many sick and dying that only about half of the ship will survive this trip."

"You saved that little girl from death by whatever concoction that you fed her along with the good water and food you have been sneaking to her. I know that her mother was very grateful that you helped her."

"Aye, I think she would have died from dehydration and malnutrition if I hadn't been a thief. I just wish there was something more I could do to save those that are suffering."

"I know. I have helped many with the sickening job of tossing the dead into the sea. Listen, we are only a week out from port. Even if there were a mutiny, it would not help. We just have to do the best we can until we reach land. I heard that they lifted the fifteen-day quarantine that they used to impose on ships coming from Ireland. I will be so glad to get off this death ship. I don't know what we would do if we had to spend another two weeks aboard this ship while docked. Not long ago, the harbor authorities required ships to drop their passengers off on Grosse Ile, a two-mile-long island in the St. Lawrence river, for a fifteen-day quarantine. The island contained a small medical facility, but it was quickly overburdened by immigrants. Many immigrants died while waiting in line to get treatment. I guess you could say that we are lucky that they lifted the quarantine."

Ship Survival

Ernest and Sylvia were survivors and kept each other alive and sane. Ernest looked for a deck that Sylvia was serving and would wait for her. They would meet at the end of her shift and walk the decks until it was time to go to bed. One evening after her shift, Ernest looked for her at their regular spot, but she did not show up. He searched around the galley and down the lower deck where her sleeping quarters were. He heard someone struggling, and then he heard her muffled scream in one of the cabins. He stepped back and slammed his shoulder into the locked door, breaking it down. Two sailors were trying to molest her. She was fighting them off but showed little chance of succeeding. One sailor had his arms wrapped around her and was trying to force her to the deck. The other sailor was trying to work around her flailing feet, looking for an opening, when Ernest flattened him with a roundhouse right swing. "Now, mister, let her go." He warned the one wrestling with her.

"Get out of here, mister. This is no affair of yours. Ouch! Stop biting me!" he screamed out in pain as Sylvia clamped her teeth down hard on his arm, drawing blood. He released her and swung his hand, preparing to backhand her.

That gave Ernest the opening he was looking for; he lunged for the sailor and shoved him away from her. The sailor tripped over Sylvia's outstretched foot and reached out to stop his fall as Ernest slammed into him and bore him to the deck. Ernest fell on top of the sailor and jammed his knee into his stomach. While he was down, Ernest pounded his head onto the deck until his eyes rolled back into their sockets. The other sailor started getting back up when Sylvia kicked him right between the legs then brought up her knee to meet his chin as he bent over in pain. His eyes rolled up into their sockets, and he hit the deck and did not rise again.

"Wow! You pack quite a punch yourself, darlin'. Are you okay?" Ernest asked, smiling as she wrapped her arms around his neck, trembling.

"Aye, now that you arrived. They grabbed me when I left the galley and dragged me down here. I thought I was a goner until you showed up. How did you find me?"

"I could not find you after your shift and started looking for you when I heard you screaming and struggling."

Ernest tied them up and went to find the first mate. When he found him, he told him what had happened. "I have tied 'em up in their room, and if I ever see 'em again or they touch Sylvia again, I will kill 'em. You had better keep 'em tied up and turn 'em over to the authorities when we dock."

"I will take care of them. Do not hurt them again, or I will turn you over to the authorities also. I will just leave them tied up until we will get to the port the day after tomorrow."

Ernest walked with Sylvia around the deck to quiet their nerves. She just did not want to let go of him; it had been a harrowing experience. When they arrived back at her room, she rose up on her tiptoes and kissed him solidly on the lips. He did not pull away but pulled her head toward his and returned her affection. "I really don't want you to leave." She pleaded with her eyes.

"I know. I don't want to leave you either. I do not know what I would have done if anything ever happened to you. I just find myself thinking about you all the time. We are getting very close to America and will be disembarking in a day or two."

"I feel the same as you. I do not want to lose you. I have never felt as safe as being around you."

"Well, ah, I guess we should just get married or something. That way, we would always be together."

"Excuse me, but did you just ask me to marry you ?"

"Ah...yeah, I guess I did. Well, it is hard to take that back. So what do you say, will you be my wife?"

"I have not thought of anything else since I first met you. Of course I want to marry you, and I want to spend the rest of my life with you. We should ask the captain to marry us tonight."

"That would be great, except I have to handle rigging the sails tonight. We'll talk to the captain tomorrow."

"I don't know if I can wait that long." She courageously invited as they bodily embraced, sending chills up and down both of their spines.

Since Ernest and Sylvia decided to unite in marriage while aboard ship, the next day, they approached the captain. "Absolutely not. I will not marry anyone while they are working for me on this vessel. I hired you both to work, not fraternize. If you do not have something to do, I can find something to keep you busy. Now, both of you need to get back to work."

"We are only a day out of port, so we will just have to wait until we disembark. Besides, I don't think our first night or two would be very pleasant here on this ship as crowded and sick as it is."

"I am disappointed, but you are right. We need to wait to be married on the new continent. I will be glad to get off this death ship. I have hated dispensing food that was so rotten the rats would not even eat it. I have tried to help so many folks, but there just was not any good water, food, or medicine to help them. After the first week, the water on the deck started stinking. I could not even force myself to wash my hands in it. There just was no control over how people used the available water. I am so glad that I found that barrel of fresh water and protected it from everyone. I used it to help some of those that were sick. I think we would have both been sick as well if we had not have used it for ourselves. We are completely out of clean water and decent food. If we do not make it to port tomorrow, the captain will become really enraged when he finds nothing to eat or drink himself."

"I know you feel bad about hiding that water, but what choice did we have? We could have suffered like the rest or protected ourselves. At least you were able to save some of the children by giving them the fresh water. I know that you tried your best to talk the captain into putting out some controls on dispensing both the water and the food, but he could not care less. All he wants is to make all the money he can on this voyage. I am surprised that this ship stays afloat as loaded down as it is with both cargo and people."

It was hard to leave what homeland they had and venture across the ocean alone. Their family and friends had simply placed them on board the vessel and wished them well. They had given them what money they could spare, but it was up to them to see themselves through. Well, they were going to make it and create their own way. They knew that their family and friends that they left behind had loved them and were just looking forward to giving them a new life away from the corruption and starvation of their old country. They had grown up with calluses on their hands and knew that if one was willing to work hard, no obstacle was too great to manage.

Port Side

As they arrived in port at one of the large bays in the Boston Harbor in mid-March, Ernest was busy mooring the ship to the crowded dock. Ships at the port lined up, awaiting delivery of their cargo. Derricks were working back and forth, carrying pallet after pallet to stack along the crowded dock. The weather was cold and windy as the oak, maple, beech, and hickory trees barren of leaves blew in the wind. The musty smoke-filled air from the coal-fired furnaces mixed with the salt drifted along the seashore. Carts pulled by long-eared donkeys bounced along the cobblestone path carrying supplies and passengers. The Taconic Mountains of the Appalachian range majestically appeared in the distance.

Just as they tied off the ship and the gangplanks dropped to the dock, men streamed aboard to help the immigrants depart. Their ulterior motive was to steer them toward their employers' lucid businesses. The immigrants, though, just wanted to get off the diseased vessel with all their family and belongings intact, and any help seemed appreciated. Many were unaware that bondsmen, who wanted nothing more than to sink their talons into this new resource, were steering them toward their demise. Those traveling alone were the most targeted, but couples and families were not immune. Most immigrants were vulnerable as they had looked toward the riches the new land promised.

Sylvia finished picking up the trays and returned them to the galley. She tossed off her apron for the last time and turned to go when her boss caught her. "Sylvia"—he smiled menacingly—"I'd like you to meet Raul. He is the new owner of your contract."

"What do you mean?" she shockingly questioned. "My contract terminated when we docked. You can just tear it up."

"That is not true. You have accumulated additional expense during the voyage and now can either pay for the five years that you owe, or go along with Raul and work it off."

"I don't owe you five years and have no more money to pay you. I completed my contract. I am leaving this ship."

"All right, you are coming with me." Raul grabbed and twisted her arm, pushing her toward the dock. She struggled and beat her small fists against the very large chest of this man. Frantically, she screamed for Ernest, who was on the port side gathering his belongings and could not hear her cry for help on the starboard side where they were pushing their way along the crowded gangplank of departing passengers. All was to no avail as Raul dragged her down the long gangplank. She tried to break away, kicking and screaming for help from anyone. The passengers were just sick and exhausted. Even though the departing passengers heard her screams and saw her fighting the big man, they had no strength or wish to intervene. They just wanted to get off the death ship as fast as their legs would carry them.

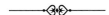

Ernest looked up the first mate and asked for the return of the money his family had paid for his passage, board, and room as they had agreed. The first mate laughed at Ernest. "What agreement?" The first mate grinned. "Let me see what this agreement says."

"You never gave me a contract."

"Well, if you have no contract, so how is it that I owe you anything?" He smiled. His smile left his face as the young man looped a roundhouse haymaker right onto that smile, plastering it all over his face. The first mate was a big man, but Ernest's work-hardened fist fell on the first mate like a sledgehammer.

It flattened his lips and caused him to stagger back. He did not go down, but he had to shake his head to get the bells to stop ringing. He did not have time to set himself because Ernest's left fist burrowed into his stomach, causing a gush of foul air to leave his smashed lips. As he was leaning over, trying to get his breath, Ernest brought his other fist up from the lower deck to meet his chin. It popped his head back, and he flew backward off his feet to hit the rail of the ship, unconscious. Ernest reached into the first mate's jacket and took $50 from his purse. "Thanks. Since I am not a thief like you, you can keep the rest." He shoved the purse back into his pocket and pushed the unconscious man back onto the deck.

Ernest worked his way toward the gangplank from the port side, looking around for Sylvia. *I wonder where she is. She told me she would meet me here at the head of the gangplank.* Then he caught a glimpse of her as she was fighting and struggling, being carried one-handed by a very large thug. The gangplank was so crowded that he could not work his way down until Sylvia disappeared. Ernest panicked and looked around for any other way that he could get off the ship. A derrick was dangling a lead rope down to the dock from the cargo hold. He climbed the rail and leaped over the water, grabbing the line. He slid down the rope and swung toward the dock, landing hard. He rolled and just caught sight of the thug pulling Sylvia around the corner of a bar. Pushing and shoving his way, he ran to the corner. "What is going on, Red? Why is that man rough-handling you?" He shouted and ran, pushing through the crowd toward where he had last seen her.

He could not spot her anywhere. There was an entrance to the back of the bar, but otherwise, the alley they had entered was a dead end. "Red, where are you?" he hollered again. Then he listened. There was so much sound coming from the inside of the bar and the passengers leaving the ship that he could not hear anything from her. The only place they could have gone was into the door in the back of the bar, so he tried to open it. He pounded upon the locked door. There was no response. Then he put his shoulder to it, broke the door lock, and started inside, looking for Sylvia.

The interior was dark where he had entered a storeroom. There was a path between cartons tacked around the room. It led toward the back entrance to the bar. As he started that direction, two thugs who looked like bar bouncers came in from the bar and pointed. "You cannot come in here tearing up the place. Get out before we throw you out."

"Where is my fiancée?" Ernest shouted angrily.

"We told you to get out, and we don't know where you lost your fiancée."

THUGS

The two bar bouncers were huge, even towering over Ernest, who himself was very largely built. Each bouncer wielded a pair of brass knuckles. He looked around for an equalizer and found a pipe about two feet long next to the door he had broken. He grabbed the pipe and charged the pair blocking him. "Get out of my way if you are not going to show me where she is."

As he started forward, one bouncer threw a roundhouse right. Ernest ducked under it and brought the pipe sharply across the man's knee. He heard a snap, and the big bruiser went down hard, screaming in pain and holding his right knee as he went. The other bouncer charged him. Ernest brought the end of the pipe up and punched him right in the solar plexus. The pipe buried itself all the way to his backbone. As the brute bent forward, Ernest swung the pipe again and smashed it to his forehead. The man's eyes rolled up in his head, and he toppled over on top of the man groaning and holding his knee. Ernest turned and smashed the pipe over the other one's head. He quieted his groaning. The man just sat there then toppled over.

Ernest pushed through the door leading into the bar. It opened at the back end of the bar where the bartender was pouring watered-down drinks. When he saw Ernest, he reached under the bar and grabbed his sawed-off shotgun. As he turned to level it on Ernest, Ernest brought the pipe down hard, breaking his arm. The shotgun fell to his feet. Ernest picked up the shotgun and shoved it under the bartender's nose. "I am only going to ask you this once. Where is the redheaded gal that was just dragged through here?"

"I can't tell you that!" He cried out in pain. "He'll kill me."

Ernest cocked the shotgun. "Tell me or you can die right here, right now."

The bartender motioned with his head. "They went in two doors down on the right."

Ernest smashed the short double barrels on the side of his head and pushed past the bartender. He broke in the second door on the right, charging in like a raging bull. The thug had a hold of a rope and was trying to tie Sylvia's hands to a worn rail that looked like it had been well used by other captives. Sylvia screamed as she struggled to get free. "Ernest! Get him off me!"

"Mister, let her go."

The man shoved a chair at Ernest, knocking him down. He dropped the pipe and the shotgun but jumped back up in an instant. The thug had to let go of Sylvia as he met the angry young man charging at him. Ernest's momentum and flying tackle knocked them to the floor. The thug was cat-quick and jumped back to his feet and tried to stomp Ernest's head. Sylvia charged him and blocked his kick. She paid the price as he knocked her to the ground. Her interaction, however, allowed Ernest to get up and square off with the thug. They circled each other, looking for an opening.

"I have paid for this legal contract." The thug grinned with a smirk, rattling a piece of paper in front of Ernest. "And she is now my bondservant for the next five years."

"I already told you that I fulfilled my contract!" Sylvia cried.

"Let me see the contract." Ernest demanded.

"No." The thug glared and jammed the contract back into his breast pocket. "You have no right to interfere with my rights."

"I am her fiancé and have every right." He informed the brute and continued to circle, looking for an opening.

The thug swung a pile driver fist that Ernest blocked, returning a short jab that connected, flattening his nose. The nose had been broken before, and the thug threw an onslaught of fists, knocking Ernest back. Ernest lost control and charged at the thug, swinging with his left and right. As the thug backed up, Sylvia caught the thug's leg with her right foot. The thug's left foot buckled, bringing him down to his knee. Ernest landed on top and hammered his head into the floor with blow after blow until he felt Sylvia pulling him off. He reached down, searched for the contract in the thug's pocket, and stood up from the bloody mess.

While he searched for the contract, Sylvia grabbed the shotgun and the pipe and then wrapped them up in her jacket. Together, Sylvia and Ernest headed through the bar and out to the street with the rest of the passengers. They walked inland away from the port, leaving the chaos behind.

"Thank you." Sylvia recovered, flying into his arms and wrapping her arms around his neck, hugging her burly fiancé.

"No problem. I love you." Ernest passionately responded. "You know that I now hold your contract, and you are my bond now." He smiled.

"Aye, of course. For the rest of my life, I will be your loving servant."

It was late when they found a boarding house to spend the night well away from the port. They had left what little belongings they had on the ship, which were very few, and needed some provisions. They asked the matron of the house, and she told them where they could find a mercantile and the livery stable in the morning. Exhausted, Ernest slept on the couch while he let Sylvia sleep in the bed. After breakfast the next morning, Ernest and Sylvia found the livery and inquired about purchasing two riding horses.

"Sure, I have a whole corral full of them. Just go out back and pick out the ones you want."

"You can ride, can't ya darlin'?" Ernest asked Sylvia, smiling.

"Of course. I practically grew up on a horse."

"What do you think about those two bays next to the watering trough?"

"I like them." Sylvia admired and made her way over to them to inspect them more closely. "They seem gentle." She commented and stroked their manes.

Ernest peeled back their lips to look over their teeth. "They look to be about three years old and in good health." He lifted their legs and inspected their hocks. "Let's go back inside and negotiate for these."

"You seem to know your horses." The stable owner complimented the young redheaded couple who were obviously in love. "I will let you have them for $60 apiece."

"No." Ernest argued. "We'll give you $40 for the pair, saddle blankets, saddles, and bridles."

"Now, sir, you have asked me to give these to you for less than I have in them. We are in a Civil War here, and good horseflesh is hard to come by. There is a high demand for them, and I cannot buy any deadbeats for what you are offering. You look like a nice couple. I will give them to you for $30 each and throw in the equipment."

"Done." Ernest concluded and peeled out $60 and handed it to the man. They rode over to the mercantile, tied their mounts to the rail, and went inside.

The owner looked up while stocking merchandise on the back wall. He looked and acted like a nice honest man. "You two look a little bewildered. Can I help you with anything?"

Ernest and Sylvia looked over the store piled high with everything from boots to coffee. They looked at the kind man, and Ernest took the lead. "I am a little hesitant to show too much, but we just came in from a harrowing trip on board a death ship from

Ireland. When we arrived, dock thugs tried to make bondservants out of us. Yesterday, we had to leave what little belongings we had on the ship and fight our way through them. We are a little worried that they are looking for us. We would both like outfitted with some suitable riding clothes, boots, a tarp, bedrolls, and a rope. We would also like coffee, a side of bacon, some trail rations, and I would like to look at a rifle and a handgun."

The merchant shook his head. "The rabble at the dock has shanghaied many who have come off those ships. That gang at the dock has given this country a bad name. Do not worry about us giving you away. We are here to serve, not to get into any conflict. I am sorry that you had such a terrible welcome. Remember, they are not representative of the general populous in this great new country." The merchant commented and looked across the aisle at a young girl. "Julia, my daughter, can help your wife and you with your riding outfits. I will get the rest of your traveling supplies."

"Oh, we are not married yet, but we will be shortly." Sylvia smiled.

"Well, congratulations." Julia looked admiringly at her. "Come on, I will show you some things you are going to love." As the girls went arm in arm over to some stuff Ernest would be embarrassed looking at, he turned his attention to travel supplies.

The owner showed them his supply of rifles and handguns with ammunition. "I will also need some shotgun shells for this chopped-down greener that I inherited from a bartender at the dock trying to ventilate me. I am quite limited on my funds, so if you have used guns that shoot straight, that will be sufficient. Also, could you help us locate a group heading west that we could trust and join?"

"Well, young man, with the recent conflict between the north and the south, the waterways are a dangerous place to travel. You will be wise if you join a wagon train of pilgrims heading west. You might be in luck. There is a wagon train ten miles from here of immigrant families heading west. I am not sure if they have left yet, but I helped provision them, and they are preparing to leave. Just tell the wagon master that Jason Hicks sent you. We've known each other most of our life, and he is as honest and trustworthy as they come."

They rode out right after they tied the supplies behind their saddles on their horses, with Ernest taking the lead. He had a growing concern that Raul and his thugs might be looking to get even with him for taking Sylvia and her contract from him. Raul did not appear to be the type to forget about a five-year bond, especially with a beautiful young girl. She could make him a lot of money in so many various ways.

They followed the Connecticut River west. The ground was rocky, and plowing it would be next to impossible. The rock formations along the river, however, reminded him of Ireland. Sylvia was glad that she had purchased each of them a warm coat to fend off the March chill. They saw white-tailed deer bounding into the trees as they passed while Peregrine falcons soared overhead.

Wagon Train

They followed Jason's directions to Pioneer Valley and located the wagon train. Ernest found the wagon master and introduced himself. "I am Ernest Walker, and this is my fiancée, Sylvia, or Red as I call her. Jason Hicks, the owner of a mercantile where we purchased our provisions, sent us over to see you. We just arrived here from Ireland on a ship. We want to travel west. Jason told us that you were going that direction, and we were wondering if we could join up."

"Yes, I just did a great deal of business with Jason. My name is Joshua Barker. Do you have a good, strong wagon and mules to pull it?"

"No, sir. We have just purchased two riding horses and a few provisions that will hold us over for a few days. We did not have enough money for anything else."

"I am sorry, young man, but we are not a charity organization. We travel in wagons that have families in them. We do not approve of young unmarried couples traveling together."

"I understand. We just got off the ship, and since we were working on the ship for our passage, the captain refused to marry us onboard. We want to get married, and as a wagon master, Joshua, you could solve that problem by performing the ceremony. Listen, we are strong, young, and willing to work our way west. Surely, you are in need of some help to move this many wagons west."

"I do not know. How are you with animals?"

"I grew up on a farm in Ireland, and Sylvia, or Red as I call her, is a Basque and practically lived her whole life in a wagon. On our voyage here, I worked as a sailor, and she worked out of the ship's galley. We kept healthy and strong. We are willing to work hard. We are willing to work for our passage doing whatever is necessary."

"Hmm. All right, Ernest, I will have you help with the livestock, and your fiancée can help with the cooking. You will have to obey my orders, and if I catch either of you loafing when there is work to do, you will have to find your own way back. You are lucky you caught us. We were preparing to leave in one hour, so we had better get started. It is almost noon, and the first day will be short. When we camp for the evening, I will take care of hitching you two together. The livestock you will be working with include Missouri mules, Belgian, Percheron, Clydesdale, and Morgan draft horses, oxen, and riding horses. I expect you to keep the livestock healthy, well fed, watered, and secured. You will need to help the travelers hitch and unhitch their teams. Sometimes these teams can be a handful. If you need anything, just call on one of the other men to lend you a hand. Remember, you are working not only for me, but also for every wagon on this train. Sylvia, I will depend on you to help manage the supply wagon. Keep it well stocked and inform us whenever a necessary supply is running short. I will even have you drive the wagon. You will need to begin breakfast long before sunup and finish the evening cleanup long after the sun goes down. When the wagons are ready to roll out, I expect you to have everything packed back up and ready to move out."

"Fair enough. You will not be sorry you took us on."

That evening as the travelers gathered around the campfire, Joshua Barker stood at the side of the campfire before Ernest and Sylvia. He took out his notes looked at those gathered for the ceremony and began the vows. He turned to Ernest. "Do you, Ernest Walker, take Sylvia López, or Red as you call her, to be your lawfully wedded wife, to have and to hold from this day forward, for better or for worse, for richer or for poorer, for sickness and in health, until death do you part, so help you God?"

"I absolutely will do as you say, love and honor her all the days of my life."

Joshua turned to Sylvia. "Do you, Sylvia López, take Ernest Walker to be your lawfully wedded husband, to have and to hold from this day forward, for better or for worse, for richer or for poorer, for sickness and in health, until death do you part, so help you God?"

"I will, and furthermore, love and honor him all the days of my life."

"Then by the power invested in me as wagon master, you two are now husband and wife. Ernest, you may now kiss your bride."

Ernest looked down at Sylvia, smiled, and leaned down and kissed his wife in a long, loving embrace. She wrapped her arms around his neck and pulled herself up on her tiptoes while he held her waist.

"Okay, okay. Now that is over, you can release her. Everyone, I would like to introduce you to Mr. and Mrs. Ernest Walker."

With that, the travelers applauded, and Freda, an older German wagoner, struck up a tune on her guitar. She sang:

> Sylvia my darlin' your brawny laddie did say,
> Come with me, and let's travel west this way.
> Don't ya run and don't ya hide,
> Oh Sylvia, come an' be my bride.
> Oh my Sylvia, come let's join this train,
> I can't deny how ya have lit my flame.
> We will laugh and we will cry,
> but together we will surely fly.

Freda and her husband had just joined the wagon train from the upper New York area where they had owned a dairy farm. Since many new farms had sprung up in the area, they decided to look for fresh soil. They sold their farm where they had lived for many years and learned the English language. She loved music and played the guitar singing wedding songs she made up for the new couple. She also was very fluent on German love songs and ballads. As her husband sat on a log puffing on his pipe and watching her play the guitar, his leg bounced up and down in tune with the music. They were excited about rolling west into the new frontier. The immigrants danced around the campfire, slapped Ernest on the back, and kissed his bride. The women gathered around Sylvia and gave her words of advice.

One woman about the same age as Sylvia told her, "I'm so excited that you have joined our group of pioneers heading west to begin a new life. It is so beautiful to have another strong young couple join our adventure. My name is Margret, and this is my husband, Lester Clark. We were married just a few weeks ago ourselves near Albany, New York. We immigrated here from England a few years back. I had been living with my aunt, and Lester has been living with his older brother Mark and his wife. Since we had been talking of immigrating west, my aunt and Lester's brother gave us this wagon as a wedding gift and a little travel money to let us follow our dreams. If there is anything that we can help you with, just let us know. We are all from different backgrounds merged into this family of travelers. I hope you will consider me as your sister as we travel together west."

"Thank you. Everyone here has been so helpful and kind that this is beginning to feel like a real family. Both Ernest and I have traveled all the way from Ireland alone and need a good support group. I hope that we can be like sisters too." Sylvia hugged her new kindred sister, Margret.

"Congratulations you two." A middle-aged woman greeted the newly married couple. "My name is Shirley Reynolds, and this is my husband, John, and our four children. Mary and Harry are twins and sixteen years old, Edward is twelve, and Joseph is eight. We have been looking forward to this trip for a long time.

I told John that eastern America is getting too crowded, and we need to move west. Well, we are now following our dream and moving to a new land."

"What was it like in Ireland, and how did you get here? How did you meet? Wasn't it frightening to be away from your family and friends?" Mary asked as she and her three brothers gathered around the newly married couple.

"Now, children, leave them alone. You can ask all the questions you want later. I am sorry." Shirley apologized and glared at her children. "They are very inquisitive and want to know everything."

"That is all right." Sylvia laughed. "That is just the nature of children. In the next few days, we can get to know each of them and answer all their questions. I love children and someday hope to have a few of our own."

"Ernest, I haven't introduced myself to you yet. My name is James Lenny. I am the scout for this wagon train. I am sure glad you came aboard. We are in need of strong young men like yourself. Those two bays that you bought from the stable near Jason's mercantile are fine-looking animals. I looked them over before we left and wanted to buy them myself. They have a lot of bottom to them. Maybe you will ride with me after you get settled in and do a little scouting and hunting for us."

Joshua spoke with his booming voice to all the wagoners gathered around the campfire in the center of the circle. "We are heading out early in the morning, and we need to give this new couple some time on their own. They can bed down over in that grove of hardwoods. Everyone needs to hit the sack. The morning is only a few hours away. James and John, I would like you to take the first shift of guard duty. Just circle around the wagons and make sure that none of us is disturbed. Keep an eye on the livestock. We can't afford to lose any of them."

That evening, the young couple found a place at some distance from the wagons to bed down on their first night as a real couple. It was well away from the circle of travelers, but close enough that they could call for help if they raised their voice in alarm. Ernest hung the tarp up between two trees and made a bed of pine needles to set their blankets on. "At least we are on solid ground, and this ship isn't rocking and rolling under us."

"It is a little bumpy, and the rocks are hard." Sylvia smiled at her new husband as she smoothed the blankets down and pulled some rocks out from under their tarp.

"I don't think that I will notice any rocks or bumps tonight." Ernest smiled a luring smile at his new bride as he stripped down and crawled under the blankets. The night was peaceful and filled with quiet nightlife, discovery, and sounds of love.

Boston Harbor Thugs

Early the next morning, while eating breakfast and preparing to leave, a half a dozen tough-looking men rode up into the circle of wagons. "We need to speak to the wagon master." A burly man with a bandage wrapped around his head named Raul demanded.

"My name is Joshua Barker, and I am the wagon master. What can I do for you?"

"Do you have a young single redheaded gal here by the name of Sylvia López? She belongs to me. I have a five-year bond contract on her. The roughneck that was with her stole $50 from the first mate on the ship they were traveling on."

Joshua walked over to Lester and gave him instructions. "Go tell Ernest and Sylvia that a man by the name of Raul is here with a contract demanding her return. Tell both her and Ernest to stay where they are at and don't come over, but find out what this is all about." To Raul, Joshua asked, "Why did not you send a constable out to get them? Let me see your contract."

"Ah…that is the reason we came out ourselves. Her fiancé attacked and stole it from me. Additionally, he attacked the first mate and stole some of his money from him. I demand to have her, her contract, and the $50 returned."

"I see. So it is only your word that you do have a contract, and you want us to give this girl up to you. Tell me why he only stole the $50 from the first mate. Are you saying that he could have stolen more?"

"That is right, he took the contract I had with her. I do not know why he only took $50 from the first mate and left the rest. If they are here, you had better turn them over to us, or we'll tear this wagon train apart."

"Let me get this right. You don't have a contract in your possession, nor can prove you ever had one. You want me to give a girl to you so that you can make a bondservant out of her? If I don't comply with your demands, you will tear my wagon train apart and possibly injure me or my ward. You also say that this roughneck took only $50 from the first mate and left him the rest. Is that about the size of it?"

"That is exactly it. You will give this girl to me and have the brute pay $50 back or suffer the consequences. Is that plain enough for you?"

"Tell me again, how did you lose this bond contract, and how did you get it in the first place?"

"The gal contracted with the captain of the ship that brought her here from Ireland to pay for her passage. She accumulated a lot of expenses on the way and upset the passengers by interfering with what the captain ordered. The bond is for five years and has not been paid. I bought the contract from the captain, and she is now under my bond."

"How did she interfere with the captain's orders?"

"She demanded that he drink the putrid water that the passengers used and stole water from his private stock to feed those malcontents. She also refused to feed them the food that was aging a little and stole the food from his private stock to feed some sick kids. She practically incited a mutiny. That would have been punishable by death, but the captain was generous and just added time to her contract."

"I see. Those are some pretty foul things that she did. So you are telling me that she attempted to find clean water and good food to give to the passengers, disobeying orders. So now what do you plan on doing with this gal once you get her back?"

"Mister, that is none of your concern. I will do with her whatever I so want, but I will tell you that she will pay for running away, that's for sure. Now give her up. I am tired of your questions!" Raul raged as the veins stood out on the side of his neck.

Lester approached Joshua and told him what he had found out. "She told me that she fulfilled her contract, which was working in the galley from Ireland to America as partial payment of her voyage. She further stated that they must have forged the five-year bond on the contract after she had signed it. Ernest said that he took $50 from the first mate because he refused to pay him that amount as promised for working as a sailor on the ship. The first mate told him that they had not written a contract and thus did not owe him anything for working."

"Tell the men of the wagon train to get their guns out quietly and prepare to engage this scum." Joshua told Lester. He walked back over to Raul, who was enraged and pacing in a circle near his horse.

"Mister, we do not have anyone by the name of Sylvia López here and have no idea what you are claiming. It seems that you cannot prove anything you say. Now, if you don't mind, please leave while we prepare to finish breakfast and hit the trail."

"I do not believe you, mister!" Raul shouted as he stepped his horse closer. "You had better give her up, or we will begin looking into every wagon here."

"I do not think so. Leave now. I told you there is no one by that name here. If you come another step closer, we will blow you back where you came from." As he was speaking, seven men holding rifles emerged out from the circle of wagons.

"You think a bunch of farmers scare me? We will be back, Mr. Wagon Master. You can count on that. And we will tear this train apart."

"It will be the last thing that you try. If I ever see you again, I will personally blow you out of your saddle."

The men from the Boston harbor jerked their horses around and headed back toward the port.

"All right," Joshua instructed, "the fun is over. Now load up, and we are moving out."

He strode over and poured himself another cup of coffee as Ernest walked up to him holding the shotgun. "Thank you. I am sorry that we brought trouble to this wagon train. We were trying to leave those brutes behind. I did take $50 from the first mate who promised me that amount if I worked as a sailor on the ship. I did work hard day and night throughout the voyage without complaining , but he refused to give me what we agreed. We fought, and I took only what he promised and left the rest of his money. I started looking for Red and spotted a thug dragging her down the end of the crowded gangplank and disappearing around the back of a bar. I jumped on a lead rope from the ship's derrick and pushed my way through the crowd. I had to battle my way into their bar to find her. They tried tying her to a rail in the back of their bar. I was lucky and overpowered them. I am sorry that I did not tell you sooner that I did take her and their contract from them. Here, Joshua, is the document. See for yourself what the contract says."

"I see here where they handwrote that last statement after the signature with a different pen. Let me take care of that issue for you." Joshua crumpled up the contract and tossed it into the fire. "Now there is no contract. Sylvia's last name is now Walker, not López. We can resume our journey. Besides, I have heard of that scum and their trick tactics before." As he turned to go, they heard Sylvia scream. Ernest and Joshua turned and ran toward where he had left Sylvia. Two of the harbor brutes were fighting to load her onto the back of one of their horses when Ernest reached them.

Raul saw him coming and lifted his rifle from his scabbard. Ernest leveled the shotgun at Raul and spoke authoritatively. "Drop that rifle now, or I will blow you out of that saddle."

Raul lowered the rifle back into its scabbard and dismounted. "You stole $50 from the first mate and came into my establishment and stole my property from me, and now you are going to pay."

Ernest handed his shotgun to Joshua, who was directing Raul's thugs to let Sylvia go. As soon as Ernest handed Joshua his shotgun, Raul charged at Ernest and knocked him to the ground in a waist-high tackle. They were evenly matched in both height and weight. As Raul made a grab for Ernest's head, trying to pound it into the ground, Ernest twisted away and bucked in the middle, throwing Raul off to the side. Ernest, free of the weight, rolled to his right and sprang to his feet. They stood and faced off with one another. "You don't have a pipe now to hit me with, do you, farm boy?"

"I don't need one to handle scum like you. You tried to steal my fiancée, and ya came here trying to steal my wife. Now you are going to pay for it."

Raul threw a right jab that Ernest ducked from and took the blow on his shoulder. While he was offset, he snapped a left that flattened Raul's nose and made a bloody mess out of his face.

It was not Raul's first fight, and he shook it off then charged at Ernest. Ernest stepped aside and brought down both his fists on the back of Raul's head as he passed, driving him to the ground face-first. Ernest made a dive to land on the center of Raul's back, but Raul rolled to his left and drove a booted heel to the side of Ernest's head, stunning the Irishman. With a roaring bellow, Raul twisted around and tried to kick Ernest again in the side of his head, which would have ended the fight. Ernest grabbed his ankle and twisted hard, sending Raul to the ground again. They both sprang to their feet and began to slug it out toe to toe.

Raul's thugs were cheering him on as the men of the wagon train were encouraging Ernest. Joshua continued to keep the thugs covered. Sylvia had scrambled over to Joshua's side and was now holding the shotgun and shouting at Raul.

Ernest knocked Raul to the ground with a work-hardened fist to the jaw. As Raul started to rise, Ernest brought up his fist from the ground and hit Raul under his jaw. Raul flew backward and landed on his back. Both men were breathing hard. As Ernest was bent over catching his breath, Raul crawled over to his horse and grabbed its stirrup to pull himself up straight.

"Now, get on your horse and get out of here. You tried to cheat me and steal my wife. The next time I see you, I will kill you."

Raul pulled himself up into his saddle, wiped the blood off with his sleeve, and turned to leave. As he was facing away from Ernest, he slipped his gun out of its holster and twisted around to shoot Ernest. Sylvia saw Raul's gun come out and brought the shotgun up and feathered the trigger. Raul flew backward off his horse as did another of the men he had with them, scattering blood and gore all over the two sitting on their horses next to them.

"Now go and pick up that trash off the ground, then get out of here. That woman is my wife, and you'll not touch her again."

The double-barrel shotgun in Sylvia's hands looked mighty big to the four who were left. "Ma'am, if you just lower that thing, we will leave. We were just following Raul's orders."

Sylvia ran to Ernest and wrapped herself around his neck as the scum lifted what was left of Raul and his partner onto the back of their horses and rode away.

"I do not think they will return," Joshua grinned as he stood next to Ernest holding his pistol. "All the bluster faded from them when they lost their boss. Now maybe we can get the wagons moving down the trail again."

"That was some battle." Lester smiled as he helped Ernest over to his wagon. "You found quite an Irish gal there. Remind me never to cross her. She did not hesitate to blow that thug out of the saddle when he had you dead to rights."

The Boston thugs had left, and no one expected them to return. Their boss was dead with plenty of witnesses to attest to it being an act of self-defense. There was no contract to show that Sylvia owed anything. She and Ernest were now free of the threat that had lingered over them.

Late-Winter Storm

Long and trying days followed as they slowly crawled their way along the trail following the path that many other immigrants had traveled. The trail followed a path leading through the hardwoods. The hardwoods were so thick with underbrush that was practically impregnable. Ernest and Sylvia slept on the ground, generally under Lester and Margret's wagon. They worked from before daylight to well after the sunset. Ernest worked with the livestock, unhitching them, taking them to feed and water, then rehitching them to the wagons in the morning. He worked hard and kept the livestock safe, well fed, and watered.

Sylvia was always up early and had the fire going under a tripod to boil coffee and cook breakfast. She practically ran back and forth, keeping the wagon crew fed. Joshua assigned her the responsibility to manage the supply wagon and to alert him whenever they were running low. They soon learned that Sylvia was also a good nurse. Whenever someone got hurt, she was the one that directed the first aid, providing medical care and nursing them back to health. The travelers treated the new couple with respect. Margret worked alongside Sylvia whenever they stopped. They chatted away as they worked. Whenever they stopped for a day of rest, Sylvia took Margret and Mary into the woods to help her gather herbs to help healing and ailments. Margret had given her a bag for her collection of herbs, tree bark, and spices. Sylvia taught Margret and Mary what to look for and gather. They learned the names of the herbs and how to use them from Sylvia.

Some were for teas, others for poultices, and still others were to give food a better taste. They gathered heather, bilberry, hemp, and lavender for use as antiseptics and controlling bacteria. They also gathered some catnip, cowslip, hemp, chickweed, willow, ivy, hawthorn, elder, oak, nettle, and mistletoe to help relieve pain and other miscellaneous ailments. Other items like garlic, apple, dandelion, and parsley she received from other members of the train. It was not enough, but it would help. She could add to her collection whenever they stopped and had more time to hunt. Different seasons and locations would provide other herbs and spices she would like to have. She labeled what they found and separated them as she placed them in the bag. She also wrote in a little notebook what herbs and spices to use for different ailments.

The children on the train would laugh and play games that the two young wives devised. Sylvia was a gifted artist and had learned to play a guitar as a young girl. She borrowed a guitar from Freda and played for the children, singing the old Irish songs to them. The young boys followed Ernest and Lester around, helping them with their chores.

Ernest practiced with his rifle and handgun. He did not have much powder or lead and did not want to waste a shot. He learned to hit what he aimed at. Both his muzzle-loader rifle and handgun were single shots, and he had to reload them after each shot by pouring sixty-three grains of powder down the barrel and tamping down a wad containing a lead ball. He made his own lead balls by heating lead to liquid and pouring the hot lead into an iron mold. He would file the sludge off to make a smooth round ball that would fit smoothly down his rifle barrel.

"Hey, you're getting pretty good with that ole rifle." Sylvia complimented her new husband.

"I have practiced a little, and the scout, James, showed me a few tricks."

"Maybe I should learn to shoot as well."

"I don't know. It seems a little dangerous to me to have a little fiery redheaded gal like you packing a firearm." He teased, provoking a response.

"Hey! I handled that shotgun quite well, did I not? I have been watching you, and I think I can shoot that long gun as good as you with a little practice."

He handed her the rifle and held it up to her shoulder. She snuggled the butt to her shoulder and put her left hand out on the hexagonal barrel. Ernest let go of the rifle, and she staggered and toppled forward. She would have fallen had Ernest not reached out and caught her. "Wow! That thing is very heavy. Maybe I should try the pistol instead."

"That is a good idea." Ernest smiled as he traded her rifle for the pistol.

"It is a little heavy too, but I think I can handle it." She took it in both of her hands. Ernest showed her how to sight the pistol at a target, slowly and gently squeezing the trigger. He also showed her how to load both the pistol and the rifle.

"Someday you may need to load one or both for me if we are ever attacked by hostiles."

On the first shot, the pistol kicked up and back unexpectedly, surprising her. She looked over at Ernest, who had a big smirk. "Wow! That thing kicks like a mule." She complained, rubbing her sore wrist. After she shot the pistol a couple more times, she began to hit what she was aiming at.

"That's not bad, but we had better save the rest of the powder and ammunition. You need to keep the pistol, and I will keep the rifle. That way we will both have some protection whenever we have need. I will keep the shotgun wrapped up with our belongings behind my saddle. We need to keep all the guns loaded and ready to use. Since we will keep them loaded, we will need to keep them away from the children. One never knows when hostiles will strike us, so we must prepare ourselves."

The next evening, a late-winter storm tore through their camp. Cold blowing wind, a few snowflakes, and then a blind whiteout with a raging wind tore at the canvas tops covering their wagons. They covered their faces with scarves, exposing only their eyes. Joshua told James, his scout, "Find us immediate protection against this storm. We can't survive much longer exposed to the elements like we are."

James led them into a ravine that gave them some protection from the howling winds. Joshua had them circle the wagons into a tight circle, move the livestock into its center, and double hobble them. The animals turned to face away from the wind and huddled together. There was no chance for them to start a campfire. The men and women worked together, braving the storm to try to hang tarps between the wagons. They gave up after one ripped loose and went flying away to the seven winds.

"We just have to crawl into or under the wagons and hunker down until this thing blows out!" Joshua shouted, trying to carry his voice above the noise of the storm. "If we can keep the canvas on our wagons, that will be the best we can do."

"Lester, can you help me tie this tarp on the underside of your wagon? Red and I will bed down there, if it is okay with you."

"Sure, that is no problem. C'mon, Sylvia, crawl up into my wagon while Ernest and I try to wrestle this tarp."

Lester worked with Ernest tying the tarp around and under the spokes of his wagon wheels to give Sylvia and Ernest some protection from the elements. When completed, Sylvia crawled back out of the Clarks' wagon and then ducked under it where Ernest had laid a tarp under their gear. Lester brushed off the icy snow caked onto his trousers and boots, crawled up into the back of their crowded wagon, and slipped under the blankets with Margret.

"Brr, this is so cold." Margret shivered, watching Lester remove his clothes to snuggle next to her for warmth. "I will bet everyone on this train is shivering as bad as we are though. This is the worst storm I think I have ever seen. I wonder how Sylvia and Ernest are doing under our wagon."

"I don't think you have to worry about those two. They are strong, tough, young people and will snuggle together and keep warm no matter how cold it is outside. Besides, they are newly married. Ah…honey, so are we." Lester grinned and wrapped his long arm around Margret, snuggling in closer for warmth.

Storm Recovery

The next morning, the storm had blown itself out, but they sat beneath three feet of wet drifting snow. Sylvia looked around under the wagon and chuckled. "Ernest, it is beginning to get warm under here. Look, we cannot move these wagons through these drifts. We should just stay snuggled under this nice little shelter in our cubbyhole."

"It sure is nice in here, but I need to check on the livestock, and you, young gal, need to start breakfast. I am getting hungry."

Ernest pulled on his boots and coat and began to dig his way out from under the wagon.

"Hey, that's cold!" She complained as a big ball of snow went down her back.

Ernest broke through the crust that was even with the bed of the wagon. "Hey! You two in there, are you going to sleep all day?" he teased as he rattled the canvas of Lester's wagon.

"Go away!" Lester shouted. "There is nothing we can do today except get cold and wet. All right, all right, I am coming out." As he opened the flap at the back of the wagon, a large overhang of snow fell down in his back. "I told you this was a bad idea." He murmured. "We should just stay under covers."

Ernest could not keep from laughing. "You'll live, ole boy. Come on, and I will brush you off. It looks like we are going to be here a couple of days at least. It will take that long for this stuff to melt. After it warms up and dries out the ground, we can move out of this ravine."

"You need to pull some of the wood out from under the belly of the supply wagon we stored to keep it dry and start a campfire for Margret and Red. I will try to make a path to the center of the wagons."

Ernest lumbered over the snow and finally made a path to where the horses had been standing. The horses had stomped down the snow. It was muddy, but at least they could build a fire on the ground. He gathered the horses and led them out of the circle into a grove of trees where they could forage on the exposed grass. It had been a chilly night and now a wet miserable morning.

Once the fire was warming the circle, Sylvia and Margret set out a pot of water to boil. When the aroma of coffee drifted around camp and a pot of stew was boiling under a tripod over the campfire, the travelers began to join them around the fire. They had thirty wagons in the train, and everyone was cold and wet. They started several more fires in the center of the circle.

Joshua looked up into the sky and watched as the snow blew and plastered the trees with layers of thick, white, and wet snow. The trees bent with the weight of their heavy load, and many were breaking. "This is one of those late-winter storms. They seem to be the worst and wettest, but they normally dry rather quickly too."

By noon, the wind started up again. It was slightly warm though as the sun rose into a clear sky. The snow began to recede.

As the day waned, Joshua approached Ernest and Lester. "While James is out scouting, you boys need to saddle a couple of horses and see if you can bag us some camp meat. We are getting a little low, and some venison would sure help the moral. Take a couple of pack animals with you to bring back the meat."

"We'll get right on it." Ernest looked around and waved at Sylvia. "Red, we need to refresh our meat supply. James asked us to go out and see if we can find any game. Lester and I are going out. I think that Joshua has an extra rifle that he may use."

Sylvia gave them some jerky and canteens filled with good water. Shortly, they rode out of their campsite in the ravine looking for deer signs. The snow was knee-high on the horses, and they had to lunge through the drifts. Under the trees, the snow was just ankle deep, and they had little trouble riding. Two hours later, they came across some deer tracks that led from a tree line into some tall brush alongside a creek. Ernest motioned for Lester to work his way to the end of the brush, and he would drive the animals to him.

He secured the two pack animals, waited until Lester positioned himself on a little rise above the end of the brush line about five hundred yards away, and then started into the brush with his horse making noise. It was not long before Lester saw movement in the brush coming toward him. A big buck scurried from the brush and then stopped to look behind him. At that moment, Lester feathered the trigger and brought down the buck. He quickly loaded another shell into the rifle Joshua loaned him. He brought down two more deer before Ernest emerged from the brush. Just as Ernest appeared, another buck bolted from his side of the concealment toward the creek. Ernest downed him from the back of his mount.

"You can't have all the fun." Ernest told Lester, smiling as he reloaded. "We have enough meat to take back. I thought we would have more trouble finding them. They must have hunkered down in this brush seeking shelter."

They dressed them out and loaded them onto the two packhorses they brought with them and headed back to the ravine. It was getting dark when they arrived. James had been watching Ernest and Lester from a nearby ridge as they flushed and killed the deer.

Sylvia and Margret were proud of their husbands when they brought in the needed camp meat. "I am so proud of you two for bringing in meat. We sure needed it to sustain us." Margret told the two hunters. Sylvia had to laugh at them as they strutted around, explaining how they had tracked and made their kill.

The next morning, the sun came out and began to melt the snow. By noon, it was a muddy mess, and Joshua approached, sloshing through the thick mud. "We need to stay the rest of the day. It should frost and harden the ground tonight, so we will move out of this ravine at daybreak. We will hitch two sets of draft animals and pull one wagon up out of here at a time. When we have all the wagons out, we will rehitch the animals to their own wagons and hit the trail again. I don't expect we will be able to make it too far, but James will try to find us dry ground on which to travel. It'll be better than just sitting here."

By noon, the wagon train was again following the western trail. It was slow going as the animals had to pull the heavy wagons through the mud, but at least they were moving.

James asked Ernest and Lester to help scout occasionally. They were quick learners and began to read signs almost as proficient as their scout. James showed them where a group of unshod horses had been kept and where its group of the Indians had camped. They rode together and discussed where the most likely ambush sites were in the terrain. James, along with Ernest and Lester, worked out the best route for the wagon train to take. They looked for hard or rocky ground to keep the wheels from sinking down into the mud. That evening, they had to stop by a creek that was overflowing its banks. The wagon train circled next to the creek and made camp.

Joshua looked out over the raging stream. "James, in the morning, you should follow the creek upstream, and Ernest, you go down the creek and see if you can find a better place to cross. We may have to wait here a day or two to let the water subside before crossing. I would sure hate to lose a wagon by being in too much of a hurry."

It was noon when both James and Ernest returned. "We had better just set up camp here. Neither Ernest nor I could find a more suitable place to cross. The banks are steep, and the water is raging both above and below us. We just need to wait for this melt to runoff."

Crossing the Creek

At noon the next day while looking over the creek, Joshua talked to Lester, John, and Ernest. "Boys, I have been studying the water. I don't think that the water will subside for at least a week. I have decided I want to cross this creek, and no matter how long we wait, we will have a difficult time. We need some logs cut and trimmed the length of the wagons to help support their weight. We will have to float the wagons across. Therefore, I want you two to take some of the men, go into the woods, and bring back six large logs to float the wagons. Meanwhile, I will gather rope from the wagons to tie the logs on. We need to be ready to cross by noon tomorrow. It will take us the rest of the afternoon to cross."

By evening, they had the logs cut and trimmed next to the creek. "Lester, I want to take your wagon across first, since yours is the lightest. Once we get yours across, we will bring the logs back and begin pulling the next one across. In the morning, I want you to pull your wagon next to the creek. We will tie one log on each side of your wagon. With two ropes tied on each side of your wagon, James, Ernest, John, and I will cross over the creek on horseback with the other end of the ropes. When I give the word, Lester, I want you to slap leather against those big Missouri mules of yours and drive your wagon into the creek while we pull your wagon across. You will drift downstream a little, but I think we will make it okay."

"Sounds like a good plan to me. I will sure give it a try whenever you are ready."

The next morning, Lester had his wagon pulled next to the creek. Margret was wringing her hands when Sylvia walked up to her and took one of her hands. "It will be just fine." Sylvia consoled Margret. "Your husband and belongings will make it across just fine. I have no doubt about it. Let's just say a little prayer to keep the men safe and to give them a helping hand."

"Hee-haw!" Lester yelled as he slapped the reins against the big mules to get them into motion. They were hesitant to jump into the icy-cold rushing stream but reluctantly did, making a big splash. The four men on the other side of the creek had pulled all the slack out of the ropes, and their horses dug into the mud, pulling hard on the ropes. The wagon rolled into the water while the mules still had good footing. The mules' heads were bobbing above the water as they pulled in their harnesses. The wagon began to float and twist down creek. The men on the opposite bank pulled even harder on the ropes.

"Don't let up until the wagon finds the bottom again!" Joshua hollered. The mules began to emerge on the other side of the creek when the wagon finally touched its wheels to the creek bottom again. They pulled the wagon clear out of the creek before they released the ropes and untied the logs. Margret and Sylvia jumped up and down, screaming in delight, as they saw them clear the creek, cheering them on. Next, they pulled the supply wagon across. Sylvia and Margret crossed on horseback between Ernest and Lester so that they could build up a fire and start coffee and a meal. It was a long, tiring afternoon, but they succeeded in pulling all the wagons across without any mishap. They sat down exhausted on the far side of the creek. Freda and her husband, who usually rode drag, was the last wagon that made the crossing. Everyone cheered as they cleared the bank on the opposite side.

Joshua pulled a bottle of rye whiskey out of the supply wagon. "Men, I don't hold with much drinking, but a nip now and again can relax us after the stressful day we have had. We keep a bottle or two in the wagon for medicinal purposes, but our success at this creek crossing deserves a celebration." He handed the bottle around to the men, who took just a slug to quiet their nerves.

Freda pulled out her guitar and began playing an old German tune while the children danced around the campfire. Freda's folk songs were songs called trinklieders. These folk songs centered on German pubs and their brags. Having sung many, she passed the guitar over to Sylvia who played an Irish tune named "Brennan on the Moor." It told a story of a brave young highwayman named Willie Brennan in Ireland. He had a wild career beginning in the Kilworth Mountains and causing many of the wealthy to shake with fear. Several of the pioneers danced around the campfire with the music, celebrating the coming of spring.

Indian Attack

After two months on the trail, the last wagon was pulling a steep grade a few days out of Pittsburgh along the Monongahela River where it converged with the Allegheny River to the north. Maple, oak, and cherry hardwood trees lined the river's steep banks. Dogwood, hemlock, rhododendron, and black willow scrub brush ran along its bank with limestone rock outcroppings. At least a dozen yipping Delaware Indians looking for an easy score burst from the line of trees bordering the trail and attacked the wagon train from the rear. The Delaware Indians were generally peaceful, but two white trappers that had stolen an Indian maiden and had assulted and killed her had stirred up this renegade group. The leader, betrothed to the maiden, was on a warpath of revenge when they spotted a slow moving wagon train.

Joshua quickly took control and yelled at the wagon drivers. "Get those wagons on top of that ridge and circle them up quickly!"

When the attack came, Ernest had his rope tied to his saddle horn, with the other end tied to the last wagon, helping to pull it up the steep hill. Lester also had a rope tied to the other side of the wagon. The Indians shot the German immigrant couple that were in the wagon riding drag, pulling the hill. Ernest quickly let go of his rope, pulled his rifle out of its scabbard, and raced back down the hill to deflect the attack, which killed the older couple driving the wagon. He got one shot off and downed one of the Indians in the lead. He jumped from his horse onto the driverless wagon, moved the bodies out of the way, and grabbed the reins.

An Indian raced his horse up to the back of the wagon and jumped aboard while the rest of the attackers backed off. Out of the corner of his eye, Ernest saw the Indian as he made his way toward the front of the wagon. Just as the Indian reached him with his knife poised to strike, Ernest swung the barrel of his rifle, striking the Indian across the side of his head. He felt the bone-crushing impact as the Indian fell over the side of the wagon, bouncing under its wheels. Lester continued pulling double duty on the wagon with renewed effort. They finally reached the crest of the hill, and the wagon rolled into the circle with the other wagons.

The outriders had found a spot on top of the hill and had directed the wagons to build a circle with their wagons to fend off the attack. Once they had made a tight circle, Ernest arrived, climbed down from the wagon inside the circle, and found Sylvia, where they fought side by side. Ernest did the shooting while Sylvia reloaded as Ernest had instructed her. They worked well together as a team.

John and Shirley were also fighting together while their four children huddled low in the bed of their wagon. When John rose up to shoot one of the Indians circling their wagons, he felt a sharp blow hit his chest by an in-flight arrow. Shirley let out a scream and caught him as he dropped down onto her lap. Lester and Margret were hunkered under their wagon. Lester had his rifle poked between the spokes and was shooting at the yapping Delawares. An arrow glanced off one of the spokes to penetrate his shoulder. He sagged back and handed Margret the rifle. The pilgrims fought the hostiles off, but Freda and her husband, the older German couple that was riding drag, were shot and killed.

The Reynolds children ran to find Sylvia. "Our papa is shot in the chest, and it looks real bad." Mary and Harry told her in unison. "Please hurry, it does not look very good."

Ernest jumped up and followed the twins to where John lay. He pulled him out from under the wagon and laid him on a tarp near the fire. Sylvia grabbed her bag and went over to administer aid. Edward and Joseph, the youngest of the Clarks, stood to the side, hanging on to Shirley as Sylvia bent over John.

Margret hollered at Ernest for help as she struggled to carry Lester toward the fire. Ernest raced to grab Lester under the arm and laid him next to John on the tarp.

Sylvia bent to the task to patch up John and Lester. The arrow that was still protruding from John's chest had to come out. "I want you two men to hold John down while I work on him." Sylvia instructed James and Ernest.

"Is he going to be okay?" Shirley asked as she wrung her hands, fearing the worst.

"He is in bad shape." Sylvia told her. "I will do everything I know how, Shirley. If I try to pull the arrow out, its head may come off, or worse, it will break off inside him. I think the best way to get it out is to push it on through. He was lucky that it had not hit any vital organs. He is not frothing from the mouth, so his lungs have not filled with blood. I can see a bulge in his back where the arrowhead is protruding. If I drive it on through, I should be able to get it out intact. I will need to remove the feathers to keep them from coming off inside him though."

With a knife, she sliced partway through the arrow and broke it off just below the feathers. John groaned loud when she tried to push it on through. She did not have the strength needed. "Ernest, find something that I can use to pound this thing on through with. Margret, cut a piece of leather off one of our bridles and bring it to me. John can clamp his teeth on it while we pound the arrow through."

Ernest picked up the heavy rock and brushed it off. "Here, will this rock do?"

"Aye, but wash it off first. I can't have the dirt falling into the wound."

Ernest quickly washed the large rock off, wrapped it in a cloth, and handed it back to Sylvia. With Ernest's help, she pounded the arrow on through John's body with the rock. With every hit she made, John screamed. After removing the bloody arrow, Sylvia was relieved. "Margret, pour alcohol into the wound, plug both the entrance and exit holes with clean cloths to stop the bleeding, and then bind them to his chest with cloth strips." Sylvia instructed.

The second man was Margret's husband, Lester. An arrow had grazed his shoulder. While Margret cleaned and wrapped John's wound with the help of his wife Shirley, Sylvia cleaned Lester's wound, helped Margret pour alcohol on it, and bound it with clean cloths.

"Hey! That burns." Lester painfully complained. "I am not passed out like John."

"You will live. Quit your whining. Maybe next time ya'll duck." Sylvia grinned, putting away her tools after cleaning them with the alcohol-soaked rags.

"Thank you." Margret hugged her with hands still shaking. "You did a splendid job patching them up. I had never done anything like that before and hope to never do it again."

"I have never had to pound an arrow through a body before either. I sure hope I did not do any more damage to John. I have worked on some wounds before back in Ireland, but never arrow wounds or any wounds this severe." Sylvia confessed to Shirley and began to shake after realizing what she had done.

"Well, we have done the best we could. I did not see anyone else jump in to do the job. I am sure that we will have to do many things for the first time as we journey on. John and I both thank you, even though he cannot say it right now. I know you have done your best, and that is all anyone could ask. I cannot say how much I appreciate you and Ernest. You two have been a godsend to us and have helped all of us in so many ways."

Ernest and a couple of the other men helped Joshua dig a hole at the top of the crest overlooking a little meadow, wrapped the fallen German couple in a tarp, and laid them in the hole. Joshua looked around for anyone who would like to speak. "We need to say a few words over this couple before we finish the burial. I guess I will do the honors. This fine German couple placed their lives into my hands when they signed onto this trail heading west. They talked me into leading this group. I am very saddened that they did not make it to their destination. They were hardworking without any complaints. I will always remember them, the support they gave, and encouragement that they offered." They bowed their heads as Joshua read the twenty-third Psalm from an old Bible he carried in his saddlebags:

> The Lord is my shepherd; I shall not want. He maketh me to lie down in green pastures: he leadeth me beside the still waters. He restoreth my soul: he leadeth me in the paths of righteousness for his name's sake. Yea, though I walk through the valley of the shadow of death, I will fear no evil: for thou art with me; thy rod and thy staff, they comfort me. Thou preparest a table before me in the presence of mine enemies: thou anointest my head with oil; my cup runneth over. Surely goodness and mercy shall follow me all the days of my life: and I will dwell in the house of the Lord for ever.
>
> Psalm 23 (KJV)

Lester stepped up and bowed his head. "Dust to dust, ashes to ashes, may God have mercy on their souls." Lester concluded the burial ceremony. They filled in the hole with the dirt, and one of the passengers placed a wooden cross next to their graves.

Their Own Wagon

After they buried the couple, Joshua Barker asked the Walkers if they would take over the couple's wagon rather than abandoning it. "I know that if they had the chance, that they would want you two to have their wagon and its contents. They told me how happy they were at having you two along to help with the journey."

"What about its belongings?" Ernest asked. "Shouldn't they be sent to their relatives?"

"As far as I know, that family did not have any relatives. If there are some things that you don't want, set them out of the wagon. Someone else may need them. If no one wants the stuff, we will simply leave it beside the trail as others have done before us. We don't have time to do anything else. If you do not want the wagon, we will divide their belongings among the other wagons and leave the wagon beside the trail. I noticed that you only had an old black-powder musket and cap-and-ball pistol. You helped a great deal fending off the attackers during the fight. If you look under the wagon seat, you will find they left a decent rifle. You might want to practice using it so that you may help us better repel the next attack." Joshua advised the young couple.

"I sure hope there is not another attack. It will be an honor for us to take their wagon. Ernest and I will sort through it as quick as we can. Freda was a good friend, and I feel that I am invading their privacy by taking all they have. If anyone else needs anything that the couple had, please let them know that they are welcome to it. You are too generous. We will share whatever we have with anyone on this train." Sylvia responded to Joshua.

"Good. We will be moving out in one hour. I do not want to be exposed out here in the open with hostiles around. Not only are there Delawares out, but the Ottawas, Chippewas, and Shawnee have moved into this area as well."

"Red and I will be ready to move this wagon as soon as you give the word."

"Sylvia, since you will not be driving the supply wagon anymore, I think that Harry can handle it. I will ask John if he minds letting his son handle the supply wagon while you handle this one. I think I would like Ernest to help James on that bay of his. That leaves you to handle this wagon after you get used to it."

"Oh, that is not a problem, Joshua. I can handle it, and I know that Harry will be able to handle the supply wagon too. He helped me at times with it already and is a good driver."

The young Irish couple quickly crawled through the wagon and decided that they would take it all, just the way the couple had left it. They would take their time to look through the boxes in the wagon later. Maybe, she thought, they could find something that would identify Freda's relatives. They felt that they were indebted to the family that had perished, so Sylvia did the only honorable thing she could think of and laid fresh-picked wildflowers onto the freshly dug graves.

Ernest and Sylvia climbed back aboard their wagon, offered up a prayer of thanks, kissed, and took up the reins of their own wagon to fall in line with the rest of the train. That evening while making camp, Sylvia found a pistol in one of the boxes and gave it to Ernest. He cleaned it and reloaded it with cartridges from a box they found next to the pistol. She found the guitar that Freda had played and pulled it to her chest. *I will always remember you, Freda. We were just getting to know you and your husband. If I find anything in your belongings that show me who your relatives are, I will see that they get this and any other memento they might want. I will forever remember you whenever I touch these strings. I will even learn a few of your German ballads, even though I will never be able to sing the words with your accent.*

"Red, I think we should give Lester and Margret our older guns since we have these newer ones."

"Aye, that is a good idea. They have worked so hard and helped us out so much."

Joshua and Ernest rode into the settlement outside of Pittsburgh. They approached the wharf and asked if there was a doctor in the area. A man pointed to a little clapboard store that had the doctor's sign nailed to it. "What can I do for you?" the doctor asked.

"We have two men injured in a battle and was wanting you to ride out with us to look them over where they were stabbed by arrows. We removed the arrow that was stuck through the injured man's chest and cleaned up the wound but wanted you to look him over." Joshua reported to the doctor.

"Well, I will go with you as soon as I get my bag. Why don't one of you go over to the stable and hitch up my horse to the buggy. Just tell the stableman that I am in a hurry." The old sawbones hurried inside and gathered what he needed, then hurried over to the stable and crawled on the buggy's seat. Joshua led the way back to the wagon train where the pioneers awaited their arrival.

When they arrived back at the circle of wagons, the doctor climbed down from his buggy and walked over to the wounded man that was lying down. The doctor knelt down and opened the man's shirt, pulled the bandage off, and inspected the redness around both the entrance and exit wound. "You are very lucky. If the arrow had entered a quarter inch either way, it would have hit a lung or heart. I am surprised that it did not hit an artery too. Whoever removed the arrow knew what they were doing. If they had tried to pull it out instead of pushing it on through, you would have died. I will rebandage it, give you some laudanum. It is an extract of opium in alcohol. I will leave enough of both for you. Laudanum is the most effective painkiller I have. However, it is quite addictive, so limit the amount you give him. If the area around the wound turns green or gray or starts to smell, you will need to get him to another doctor immediately."

"We will watch it very closely. How often should we change the bandage?" Sylvia asked.

"Use clean, sterile cloths and change it every evening until it scabs over. Once it scabs over, you will only need the bandages to keep it from tearing open the scabs. I will leave you a wad of clean, sterile wraps for you to use. Be sure to pour plenty of alcohol onto it whenever you change the bandage. That is about all I can help with." He climbed back onto his buggy and headed back into the settlement.

WOLVES

Mile after mile, the train continued to make its way west. They made about ten to fifteen miles per day. There were only a few settlements along the way, so whenever they came to a settlement, they stopped to stock up on essential supplies. Those that had resources shared everything with the other travelers. They found out early on that they had to work together and share everything they had if they were going to reach their destination alive.

The young couples worked hard and made friends. Whenever they stopped to make camp, both Ernest and Sylvia scurried around camp, helping with whatever they could. Sylvia and Margret helped cook over the open fire while Ernest helped with the animals. Some of the families complained, but the Walkers and Clarks were just grateful for being able to survive and found something good to say about everything. One evening, James talked to Ernest. "How would you like to go out with me before sunrise to help me hunt for camp meat? I will show you how to load, sight, and shoot that new rifle in your scabbard."

"I don't have much ammunition, so I have just practiced sighting without shooting . I don't believe I will have any trouble handlin' the firearm. It is light and feels natural when I lay it against my shoulder."

James and Joshua asked Ernest more often to go out and bring in the camp meat as they rolled along. He enjoyed hunting and not only brought in deer but occasionally brought in turkey. One day he spotted a very large shaggy brown animal with a large blunt head and little horns. He was not sure what it was, but it looked like it would feed the immigrants for several days. He shot and dragged in the big shaggy brute. The scout saw him riding in and rode up to him. "Hey, where did you find that beast?" Joshua called out admiring the animal.

"Well, I was scouting down below that ravine on the flats when I spotted this beast. I do not know what it is, but it looks like it would feed us for a while."

"That beast is called a bison. Some just call them buffalo. They were very prevalent a decade ago, but as travelers rode through this area, they slaughtered most of them just for their hides. The Indians have taken to the warpath over the hide hunters. They will kill the hunters on the spot if they find they are slaughtering the animals just to take their hides. The farther west we go, we might run into very large herds of these buffalo. At one time, they were so abundant that it would take days for them to run past us. I am glad you did not pass up the shot. They are very good eating. I am a little surprised though that you just saw one. Maybe it was a scout for a larger herd, or maybe it became lost and separated from the rest."

"I thought you would be back around this time," Sylvia said. "We have been hearing a few coyotes and wolves howling. I hope that they don't come into camp looking for food. They give me the shivers and sound very vicious. We did not have any wolves where we lived in Ireland, just a few coyotes."

"Don't worry about it," Joshua consoled. "They shouldn't come in as long as we keep our campfire going. Besides, they are afraid of human scent. They generally just follow a bison herd. Maybe that is why we are hearing them now. They probably found where Ernest dressed out the beast and are feasting on it. A herd of bison that ran through this area recently might have abandoned the one that Ernest shot. That bison stew sure smells good. I cannot wait to sink my teeth into it."

That night as they crawled under their sleeping blankets, Sylvia was still shivering. It was a little after midnight, and the howling started up again, only closer. Ernest had hobbled the horses and put them in the circle of the wagons. He heard them as they began to get nervous, whinnying and stomping their feet. "Red, I need to go out and check on the animals." Ernest told the frightened Sylvia. "Those wolves seem to be scaring the animals. I would sure hate for them to bolt through the wagons and get killed by that pack of canine hunters."

"Please be careful. I have a bad feeling about this. I have not slept all night worrying about them."

He crawled out from under the wagon and walked over to quiet the draft animals that were getting nervous. He spoke quietly to soothe their nerves and rubbed several of their necks. They had their ears raised and were looking toward the grove of trees they had spent the day in, but with the presence of Ernest, they quieted down.

Ernest walked back over to the fire and built it up. It cast eerie shadows around the wagons as it blew sparks in the mellow wind. When Ernest walked toward the Clarks' wagon, he heard a scream from the other side of the wagon. He grabbed a chunk of firewood that was handy and ran toward the commotion. As he approached, he saw a gray shadow pulling something out from under a wagon. Four other sets of bright-yellow eyes watched as Ernest approach. A wolf had grabbed Joseph's little booted foot and was trying to drag him out from the backside of their wagon. Ernest ran to where Joseph was being dragged and swung the club at the wolf. It saw him, let go of Joseph, slipped to its left, then squared off at Ernest, baring his teeth. Joseph scrambled back away from the vicious animal as Shirley was screaming for help.

Ernest wished he had grabbed his rifle, but his only weapon was a stick about three feet long. While he kept the wolf at bay, swinging the stick back and forth, four other gray shadows began to encircle him. He knew he was in trouble, but he would give them a fight. He reached down and pulled his long hunting knife out of his boot. When the large gray wolf that had attacked Joseph saw him bend down, he lunged at Ernest's throat, hitting him hard. He was just able to get the club up and kept the animal from tearing into his neck while he plunged his knife deep into its chest cavity. He felt the warm, sticky substance ooze from around his fingers as the beast clawed at him with his forefeet, trying to break free; all the while, the beast kept snapping with his teeth next to Ernest's ear. Ernest somehow had held the wolf's head away from his neck. He pulled the knife out and plunged it in again, then threw the dying beast off from him. The other four animals charged Ernest from behind to finish the kill. Three shots rang out, crippling two of the wolves, killing a third, and the fourth scrambled back into the trees. The two wounded animals yelped and began to limp away.

"Are you okay?" Sylvia cried as she ran to him holding a smoking pistol. "You are all bloody. Let me look you over. Where are you hurt?"

"I do not think I am. I don't feel any pain. I think all the blood is from the wolf, not me."

As Ernest brushed himself off, Sylvia inspected him. Lester and Joshua finished off the two wounded wolves. Only the one had escaped unscathed.

Joshua came over and reported to the gathering crowd. "Those gray devils must really be hungry to come in this close to our wagons. I should have posted more guards all around camp to keep us safe. I am sorry. I was lax on our security. It will not happen again. From now on, I will post guards every night to circle the perimeter of the wagons. Wolves generally don't come into a camp like this. In this country, they just follow along behind a herd of buffalo and pick up those who are sick or the old ones that cannot keep up. Was anyone hurt?"

"I do not think so," Sylvia responded. "Joseph had his foot dangling out from the wagon, and the wolf grabbed his boot, trying to pull him out. He was lucky that Ernest heard the commotion and stopped him. I think the wolves chewed on his boot a little, but he only has minor bite marks on his ankle. I will clean the chewed-up areas, disinfect them, put some salve on it, and wrap the ankle to keep it clean. I am sure he will be okay. The wolf scared him, and it will take some time for him to get over the shock of being attacked and dragged out of a deep sleep."

"Any of us would be scared to have something like that happen to them, Joseph. Just don't think that you are any less of a man for being scared." Ernest consoled the young shocked boy.

"I am sorry. I just did not know what was happening. That thing just grabbed me and started pulling me toward the trees. I was not sure why it was pulling me there until you all fought them off. Now, I am shivering and cannot stop crying just thinking about it."

"You were a brave man. It scared me to death myself." Ernest replied trying to comfort Joseph.

Throughout the rest of the night, since they could not sleep anyway, Lester, Ernest, and Joshua circled the wagons, watching for any more danger. Joshua skinned the four beasts and dragged their bodies away from camp. He stretched their hides out between two strong saplings for them to dry. Sylvia and Margret could not sleep either, so they kept the campfire going and brewed some coffee for the guards. The coyotes and wolves continued to howl until daylight but stayed away from camp.

"How are John and Joseph doing this morning?" Sylvia asked Shirley. "Your family has had a tough time lately with getting shot and almost eaten."

"They are doing very fine, thanks to you and Ernest. Joseph is still not sleeping well, and John's chest is still hurting. John wants to do his share of the work, but I have to hold him back. I think he is getting bored with not being able to do all the work he used to. He is getting stronger by the day, and I know he will soon be hitching and unhitching the team and insisting on driving. You cannot hold a good man down for long though."

"Well, there is plenty of work to be done. I think if he eases into it, he will heal a lot faster."

Buffalo Stampede

They continued to roll across the plains and stopped one evening on the flat prairie by a meandering creek. The women began to unload supplies and prepare their evening meal while the men started to unhitch the wagon teams. "Where is that thunder coming from?" Sylvia asked Margret. "I haven't seen any clouds in the sky all day or even smelled any moisture coming our way."

"I do not know, but the rumbling is getting louder."

Joshua came running up to the men unhitching the teams, hollering to them. "Get those wagons into the trees, and I mean now. We cannot afford to expose ourselves out here on the flat. Hurry, we don't have any time to waste."

That got things moving as their adrenaline rush hit. Even though no one knew exactly what was happening, everyone ran to their wagons, grabbed their reins, and slapped leather. The teams plunged into their harnesses, and soon the wagons were moving toward the tree line. Two teams had just been unhitched from their wagons, and the men were leading them away when they all heard the order. Ernest hurried in among the commotion to help. "What is it!" one wagon owner shouted.

"I do not know, but it isn't good. No time to explain, just get them hitched and the wagons moving." Ernest explained to one of the men. "You don't see Joshua excited like this unless it is some emergency." Without any wasted movement, he pushed, pulled, and shoved the nervous animals back to the wagons. When they had the teams rehitched, Ernest looked toward the rumbling end to his saddle horn, then pulled the hide right off the beast. "That is a lot of meat. We had better dry it out and just keep a few roasts for fresh meat."

The men cut the meat into long strips while others cut some green saplings to tie between some trees. They built a fire below the saplings and laid some of the long strips of juicy buffalo meat over the saplings to dry. Sylvia and Margret filled several kettles with water and set them to boil. Sylvia poured salt and spices into them. In one of the kettles, Shirley chopped up hot pepper and poured in several cupfuls. With the help of the other women, they soaked the strips of meat in the water and then hung them over the saplings. The boys kept the fire burning under the saplings and turned the drying meat throughout the evening. "That spiced jerky ought to get our juices flowing even when it is hot and dusty." John complimented and thanked his wife.

The rumble of the passing beasts continued the rest of the evening and into the next morning as the sun rose from the east. The rumble faded as the buffalo ran toward the rising sun. Throughout the next day, they continued drying the meat and storing it in the supply wagon. They roasted several humps of the buffalo from the young bulls and divided it up among the wagons.

"Watch the meat, and make sure that it does not turn bad on you. When I was aboard the ship, we had some meat that turned putrid, and many got sick. We do not want that to happen here."

"Aye Lassie, you should know, you delivered it to us poor sailors." Ernest teased, knowing he was stoking up the fire.

Sylvia's face turned beet red as she poked Ernest in the chest with her index finger and stuck her nose right in his face. "Listen, Laddie, I found the best rations that were available and passed them out. I could not help it if the ship did not store their poor supply of food properly. I talked to the captain several times about that poor process. I just gave up when he ordered me to stop or he would throw me overboard."

"You had better watch yourself." Lester smiled. "That gal will clean your clock, and you will find yourself sleeping in the woods. You can surely tell that she has some Irish blood running through her veins."

"Aye, that is one reason we get along so good. I love to see the fire in her eyes occasionally. Sometimes I have to stoke it up a little to see it, but it is never far from the surface."

"That fire is going to get you burned one of these days." Sylvia warned.

"Aye, but smothering out the flames is the best part." Ernest smiled with a sheepish grin.

A New Life

A couple of days later, after they had finished preparing the meat and the hides, they rolled on down the trail. Joshua approached James and Ernest and warned them, "For the next few days, we need to keep a sharp eye out for any wolves and Indians. They may be following the herd, looking for any stragglers. I will warn the folks to keep a sharp eye out and not to dangle any limbs out of their wagons. We cannot afford to have anyone else hurt."

James and Ernest rode on ahead to scout the trail. They wanted to make sure that the trail was clear and no obstacles would impede travel. They saw a few dark shadows scurrying through the brush, but they were after lagging buffalo that were either too old to keep up or sick or injured. The predators steered clear of the wagons. There were no sign of any Indians after the buffalo herd that they saw.

When they arrived back at camp, Ernest saw that Sylvia was holding her stomach and leaning over the side of the wagon. She looked a little peaked and had not been eating all day. He approached her and asked with concern what was ailing her. "Are you feeling ill again? You sure look like something is wrong."

"Ernest, I am sorry that I am so sick. It generally passes by midmorning. I do not know what is the matter with me. I cannot decide what herbs might help me. I think that it is best just to let whatever illness beseeches me run its course."

"Honey," Shirley, the woman in the lead wagon, having overheard the conversation, said, "I think you are pregnant."

"What? I cannot be. We are not ready for a family."

"Ha! Most times you never are. My husband John and I are on our fourth child, and never once was I ready for one. Nevertheless, Sylvia, they are a blessing. It is just a reminder of the love you share with your husband. John and I love each child more every day."

"This is so exciting!" Margret squealed. "I can tell that you are beginning to blossom. You will make a great mother."

"I am not blossoming. I am just sick."

Sylvia had been driving the wagon all day and was getting quite tired when they finally stopped for lunch. She crawled from the wagon seat and stood then leaned over and let everything out of her stomach.

Shirley helped prepare their noon meal to give Sylvia a break. Sylvia started to climb back onto the wagon seat when Shirley walked back with Mary. "Sylvia, do you mind Mary handling the team for you? She has been bored on my wagon and desperately needs a break from the other two. Edward and Joseph have been constantly giving her a bad time. She just needs to get away from them for a while. Otherwise, I will have to toss the two of them out of the wagon."

"Well, we cannot have that now, can we. You need not even ask. You know that she is most welcome to sit with me anytime. It is a little boring for me to drive this wagon by myself, so I really appreciate any company. I hope she does not mind me talking her leg off though. I have not had anyone to talk to all day. It gets lonely with Ernest helping James to scout. I would not ask him to do anything else though. He enjoys it so much. I think he is good at it too. Do you think you can handle this team of mules, Mary?"

"Oh, yes. I help Mom drive our wagon all the time. Harry even lets me drive the supply wagon occasionally. I enjoy it, but those two boys, Edward and Joseph, have been getting on my nerves today. It was bad enough with those two constantly squabbling, but when Harry joins in, it is just too much."

"Haha, brothers are like that, I hear. Unfortunately, I did not have any brothers so was not able to experience them. However, I will tell you, I would have loved to have one or two around. It is very lonely and frightening not to have any family around."

"You can have those three for all I care. I am getting tired of them poking fun at me all the time. If I do not get away from them, I am going to strangle out their life. If you don't mind me asking, how old are you anyway?"

"Now, you should not be asking a girl that, but since it is you, I just turned twenty-three. You should know that your brothers love you and think that you are wonderful. Otherwise, they would not give you such a hard time. Boys are like that. They love to tease those that they love just to get their attention."

"Well, they have certainly got my attention today. You are just a few years older than Harry and I. I hope you do not mind me asking you more personal questions, but how are you feeling?"

"Oh, I get tired quickly, but you and your family have helped me out a lot, lifting those heavy pots and carrying water and firewood. You and your brother have been wonderful the way you jump in to help. Edward and Joseph have helped Ernest with taking care of the livestock. I know that he dearly loves those two boys."

"My father, John, raised us in the upper New York region where he owned a hardware store. He and Mom worked very hard making a go of it. Harry and I had to jump in and help whenever needed. It seemed that the older we got, the more others need us. Dad initially ordered many of his products from England. When new manufacturing sprouted up around us, we would buy from them rather than have it shipped all the way across the ocean. Dad always had a hard time whenever he went to pick up his order from the docks. They seemed never to have received it, or it was coming on the next ship. It was getting so bad that he was losing more than he received and would have to reorder and pay for it twice. I think that they were just stealing it off the dock as soon as it arrived. He had much better luck when he found it locally and drove over to the manufacture facility to pick it up himself.

"People always wanted what we stocked, but they had trouble paying for it in cash. They always wanted to trade something that they had for it instead. We ended up with a whole barnyard full of chickens, cows, horses, and even pigs that needed constant attention. Even Freda and her husband picked up supplies from us and paid us in livestock. Dad did not mind the livestock, but unless we were able to sell them, we had trouble paying our own bills. Last year, Dad finally decided that he wanted to join a wagon train and head west. If he was going to raise livestock, he might just as well raise them out west instead of in the middle of a growing settlement."

Mary was a very capable girl. She handled the reins and popped the whip to the backside of the mules as good as any professional muleskinner could do. Sylvia was able to rest and really enjoyed talking with the young woman. It was not long before Harry wanted to trade with Mary. Sylvia enjoyed talking with both the twins. "Harry, what do you want to do when you grow up?" she asked.

"Well, ma'am, I thought I was grown up. I attended all the school that was available, unless I went to college. We did not have the money to do that. Besides, Dad and Mom needed my help around the hardware store. I delivered the heavy items wherever and whenever there was a need. I enjoyed the merchant business. Mary and Mom kept most of the books, but occasionally, I would have to help them. I like being outdoors the most. This trip has been hard on everyone, but even so, I have enjoyed it. I am glad that Ernest has let me help him hitch and unhitch the wagon teams. In addition, I am sure that Edward and Joseph idolize him. He plays with them and gives them the attention that they need."

"Well, Harry, you have helped me out a lot on this trip. I know that everyone else is pleased to have you on this trip. You never complain and are always willing to help anyone that asks."

Resupply

When the wagon train rolled in to Indianapolis, Indiana, it was mid-June. Joshua called a halt just before they reached the settlement. "Sylvia, check our supplies, and we will ride in and replenish them. We will be here for two days. If anyone needs anything, they had better ride in and get it. It will be a while before we reach another settlement."

"I will ride in with Red and see if there is a doctor there. She may be with child, and I want to make sure that nothing else is wrong." Ernest told Joshua.

"Lester and I will ride in with you. I would like to do a little shopping before we head out again, besides, I'd like to see what the doctor says to Sylvia and Lester." Margret told Ernest.

The two couples rode into the settlement, found the doctor's office, and went inside. The doctor checked over Sylvia. "Well, it does look like the young lady is with child, and she is several months along. She should be able to ride in the wagon, but be sure she does not lift over twenty pounds. In addition, it will be a good idea if she walks some and does not just sit on that wagon seat that continually bounces. If she starts bleeding, you need to stop and rest. Continual jarring in the wagon may do damage to both the baby and the mother."

He also looked at Lester's arm and told him that there was no infection and his arm was as good as new. "This morning, I also looked at the fellow that was shot through the chest with the arrow. I am impressed that you were able to extract it without causing further damage. You did the right thing by pushing it on through. If you had tried to pull it out as most people do, you would have caused severe trauma, and he would have died. Sylvia, if you ever decide to stay here, I could sure use your help here. You have a job with me anytime you want it."

"Thank ya, doctor, it was the first time I ever tried to remove an arrow and I was concerned about losing the arrowhead in his body. The procedure was quite trumatic on everyone, but I had a lot of good help. I appreciate the job offer, but as you can see, I'm going to have a big job myself for a few years." Sylvia responded as she patted her stomach. She then turned and left with the others. "I feel great. I would like to do a little shopping with Margret. Ernest, you and Lester can go over to the merchant and pick up the supplies we need for the supply wagon. Here is the list. Margret and I will meet you over at the merchant's when we are done."

"Don't spend it all in one place." Lester told the two girls as he and Ernest left to pick up the list of supplies.

The girls met Ernest and Lester back at the merchants, carrying a couple of bundles of personal effects. They boarded the wagon and headed back to camp before dark with their supplies. "We need to do this more often." The girls giggled. "We had such a good time."

"Where have you two been?" Ernest asked the two gigglers.

"We needed to have some girl time. We shopped for some undergarments, and I bought a few medical supplies. I found a long narrow curved knife I could use to pluck bullets and arrows out and a little booklet filled with a list of herbs and spices for cooking and healing. We got whistled at by a couple of soldiers in blue and had to tell them that we were already married."

"You were not molested, were you?"

"Oh no, they were gentlemen and just stood there leaning on posts holding up a building, whistling and tipping their hats. They were quite good-looking too."

"We had better get you two back to the wagon train. I think that you have had too much to drink."

"Nary a drop, but we are willing." They giggled.

The August heat found the wagon train in Independence, Missouri, which had gained a reputation as the perfect location for the gathering of wagons heading farther west. The city, founded on March 29, 1827, was east of the Kansas River. It joined with the Missouri River, which was as far west as paddleboats and other vessels could travel. Had peace been in America and if Ernest and Sylvia had more travel money, they could have traveled the waterways from the port at Boston to this location. Traveling by land was their only option from Independence west, though. Therefore, the wagon trains either passed through this stop or started their journey heading toward the setting sun.

Merchants had set up various shops in Independence. They offered an assortment of supplies, including wagons, draft animals, and guides for travelers. Sylvia found several travel booklets offered by the merchants. She purchased one that contained a map showing the mountains, streams, rivers, and settlements to the west.

Ernest found a blacksmith that reshod their animals and repacked the axles with grease. He had the spokes tightened and purchased a spare wheel for their wagon. He also purchased several boxes of ammunition for his rifle and pistol. With what little money they had left, he purchased some needed traveling supplies. They spent a week in Independence before they regrouped and continued their westward journey. It was a week well spent. They met many immigrants traveling the same direction and felt like they were embarking on a bigger adventure. While they rested, restocked, and regrouped, they saw two other wagon trains move out in their same direction.

While waiting for Joshua to move the wagons on west, Ernest and Sylvia sat on the tailgate of their wagon watching the beehive of activity of wagons, soldiers, and ex-soldiers coming and going.

It was quite entertaining. They had heard many tales from the men and women of the community explain how Independence had been a source of turmoil from its infancy. They had just endured a religious war and now the raging Civil War was tearing the settlement in different directions.

"Sylvia, this settlement seems at unrest. Both Union and Confederate soldiers are recruiting for the war and many merchants are becoming worried. It seems that battle lines are being formed and an armed conflict right here is imminent. I sure hope that Joshua does not wait to long to move out or we may be caught right in the middle of the conflict."

"Aye, while shopping, Margret and I talked to many and they were leaning to support the north rather than the south. They seemed sharply divided and several squabbles already broke out even among their employees."

Civil Unrest

In 1767, Charles Mason and Jeremiah Dixon drew an arbitrary line on a map to resolve a border dispute between British colonies. This line became known as the Mason-Dixon Line. A few years later, the Boston Tea Party started a sequence leading to the American Revolutionary War of Independence, keeping Britain from ruling the thirteen American colonies and gave America their independence.

In 1827, the Osage Indian settlement was named Independence and became a wild frontier town. Independence was the last stop steamboats and other cargo vessels could travel west. The river prior to the convergence of the Kansas River could no longer support their vessels. Trappers hauled their pelts to the fur traders from the many trails Lewis and Clark had previously mapped leading to the trade route.

In 1838, a sharp dispute arose between a religious group calling themselves, the Latter Day Saints, or Mormons, and the other inhabitants of Independence. The Mormons formed a secret society called the Danites to drive away those not conforming to their president. Hyrum Smith, Joseph Smith's brother their leader, signed the Danite Manifesto warning the dissenters to "depart or a more fatal calamity shall befall you." The ensuing Mormon War tore apart Independence and exchanged fighting with the Mormons in a bloody war. Governor Lilburn Boggs finally issued an "extermination order" to expel Smith's followers. The ousted Mormons fled to Illinois to a small settlement called

Commerce. In 1840, when the Mormons came to power, they renamed this settlement of Commerce to Nauvoo.

In 1861, right after Abraham Lincoln became the sixteenth president, eleven states seceded from the Union to declare themselves Confederate States of America. These Confederate states were South Carolina, Mississippi, Florida, Alabama, Georgia, Louisiana, Texas, Virginia, Arkansas, North Carolina, and Tennessee. These states dividing the nation were south of the Mason-Dixon Line.

On April 12 that same year, Confederate forces fired on Fort Sumter, South Carolina. President Lincoln quickly reacted and sent a volunteer army to recapture federal property. The president did not want to see the Union divided and decided to fight to keep the Union in tact. Escalation of the fighting started the Civil War. The Southern Confederates, or Rebels, called it the War of Northern Aggression. Even though there was never a Declaration of War issued by the presidential office, fighting commenced.

Ships docked in Independence loaded with armament, supplies, and blue-clad men of the Union Army. The new Union recruits swarmed around the settlement, boasting about how they were going to defeat the Rebels. Many of the old soldiers displayed the scars of war. Tensions grew as Confederate recruiters secretly swarmed around the wagon trains, trying to talk the men into joining their army. A few of the southern single men on the train succumbed to the recruiters' request to join up with them. The married men with unsettled families were not about to sign up.

Shirley and John sat on the back of their wagon, talking to his son Harry about the perils of war. "Harry, look at those old soldiers and their battle scars. They can tell you where and when they fought and how they got injured. I doubt that any of them can give you a good reason they fought. Mostly, they just succumbed to their peers' persuasion and the hype of protecting their own way of life. But before you go traipsing off, think of who you are wanting to kill and why. There is no glory in killing and maiming.

The rebel states are fighting against aggression of the northern states, while the Union states say that they are fighting to free the slaves. Both sides are fighting for the right of freedom, yet forcing their will on the other side. You are old enough to know that families have to settle differences without bloodshed. Would you kill or maim Mary because she wants something different from you? Can you see that the differences that you have argued about have faded with time? I expect that you have even come to appreciate some of the things that she argued for. It is the better man who can reason through conflicts than to stubbornly fight to the death over them."

"Is there ever a time that justifies fighting and killing?" Harry asked his father.

"That is a difficult question, but yes. You should defend yourself against any aggressor that attempts to kill or maim you or another without true and legal justification. Just remember that when you are in a war, you must kill. As a soldier, you just have to do what your superiors tell you. Once you enlist, you have surrendered your right to make any decision."

Within the circle of their wagons, Joshua gathered the men and women together, climbed up on the top of one of the wagon tailgates, and spoke loud to the pilgrims. "A civil war is tearing this country apart. If you men feel obligated to serve in either side of this conflict, let me know now. I will not take your wagon west if you elect to leave your families. I will not take wagons west that contain just women and children. They will have to stay here. I plan to stay quite north of the Mason-Dixon Line. Most of the fighting will occur south of that line. We may run into armies on both sides of this conflict. If you cannot stay neutral, then you had better depart now. I will not have you trying to pick a fight with either side. Since the armies will be concentrated on this conflict and the Unionists are pulling troops away from the forts, we may have more problems with the Indians and outlaws as we travel west. Stock up on ammunition. We may need it. If you have overloaded your wagon, your wagon will suffer and break down. We will ride away from any wagons not repairable. So unload the unneeded stuff now where you might sell it or give it to someone who can use it. My scout James has something more to say.

"There are four major trailheads here. The Oregon, California, Santa Fé, and the Lewis and Clark trails all converge here. We are going to follow the Santa Fé trail heading southwest. You could say that we are following what John O'Sullivan coined as the Manifest Destiny or the westward expansion. Most all of you that I have talked to are looking for new home. We pray that you will find what you are looking for. If we all work together and pool our resources, we might all find what we are looking for. If anyone continues to cause problems of any nature on this trail, we will ride away from you. This is a big train, and I am appointing Ernest Walker and Lester Clark as my lieutenants. If you cannot find me, their word is as good as mine or Joshua's. If you have any questions, see one of us. That is all."

"Wow! That was quite a speech." Sylvia told Margret. "I did not know that our husbands were going to be appointed lieutenants."

"I did not either. I am so proud of them. They both seem to have become quite the little leaders. I don't know where we are going, but am very glad we are."

When Ernest and Lester returned to their wagons, both Sylvia and Margret stood at attention and saluted their husbands. "Oh no, it looks like our wives have just heard." Lester told Ernest.

"At ease, women," Ernest said. "Now, you two privates need to prepare our meal. On the double now. We are hungry."

"Aye, aye, Lieutenant Walker. We will get right on it." Sylvia obediently replied, trotted over to the fire, dipped a ladle of stew into two bowls from the pot, and handed it to them.

On the morning of the eighth day in Independence, Missouri, six miles east of where the Kansas River joined the Missouri

River, Joshua Barker, their wagon master, held up his hand and then pointed southwest and shouted, "Wagons ho!" And all the wagons moved out in a straight line heading along the Santa Fé trail. They had picked up many more wagonloads of immigrants. These families had lived in America and decided to travel west to a more fertile ground. They headed west into Kansas following the Kansas River.

The wagon train camped west of the Lawrence settlement and had finished their evening meal and settled in for the evening. Joshua had posted guards around camp on a four-hour shift. Ernest, Lester, and John had the early morning shift just before they were to hitch up and head farther southwest. They were about halfway into their shift when they heard the first sounds of rifle fire to their east. Upon hearing the shooting, they awakened every passenger and looked to Joshua for direction. He stood up onto the tailgate of Ernest's wagon and spoke loud enough for everyone to hear. "This conflict is not ours, and we need to prepare to move out as soon as possible. We cannot stop and fight in this war. We would not know which side we should take. People who engage in battle must know that not everyone has to choose sides. I for one don't want to choose which Americans to kill. Let's move out and get to Oregon."

They did not know that they had entered into a hotbed of fighting between the two rivalries. A man and his family, fleeing from the slaughter, came riding in on a wagon and reported to Joshua. "Lawrence was the antislavery stronghold of Missouri and Quantrill planned his attack in retaliation for a raid by General James Lane's Jayhawkers in Osceola, Missouri, a couple of years earlier. The Quantrill Bushwhackers rode hard to reach Lawrence, and many even tied themselves onto their saddles to keep from falling off. Three columns converged and descended on the settlement in a fury of vengence. They pillaged and set fire to everything in their path. They looted the banks and stores and totally ravaged the settlement killing nearly every male in the attack, leaving women and children helpless. Quantrill and his raiders left behind the slaughtered and the ashes of the burning settlement. I lived on the outskirts of the town and heard the shooting. I rode into town to witness the killing and looting. The screams of the dieing and wounded still ring in my ears. A stench from the drifting smoke seared my nose and stung my eyes. There was nothing that I could do. I knew they would soon finish with the town and hit the outskirts of town. I rode hard back to my ranch, frantically loaded my family into this wagon, and just drove away before they came onto my place. I had to force myself to keep riding away to save my family. We had just driven into the trees out of view when my wife cried out. She was looking back seeing the smoke boil out from where our ranch once stood. I didn't stop but continued to race away. That didn't stop the sounds of them shooting my cattle and horses around my yard. We were lucky to get away. I will hide out today, then go back and try to recover."

They fed the fleeting family and gave them water and enough food to sustain them until they could get back to Lawrence and face the perilous times.

"I don't like to ride away from a fight where innocent men, women, and children are getting killed." James told Joshua.

"Neither do I, but like I said, this is not our war. If they attack this wagon train, we will fight and fight to win. Otherwise, we will ride away. Like I stated before, if you choose to fight, then get off this wagon train and go fight, but don't try to recruit any in this wagon train in your battles."

As they moved out, they could see the glow of many fires in the settlement. The shooting had stopped. "I just hate to ride away from where innocent people are getting killed and destroyed." Ernest told Lester. "However, I understand that if we were to ride back to Lawrence, we would be selecting sides and be right in the middle of this fight. As much as I hate to ride away, Joshua is right."

"I understand, as does everyone wheeling away. No one is happy about leaving, but on the other hand, no one wants to enter into this war."

"Ernest, if we were on our own, I would turn and ride into the settlement to try to stop this hatred, even though it would be an impossible task," Lester said.

"Aye, Lester, but you cannot go into a battle zone not knowing which side to take. If we rode in, our dilemma would only increase. No doubt, we would take the side of the underdog and then regret it for the rest of our lives. No, the best we can do for this country is to ride away and build up this great nation, not tear it down in fighting."

Battlefield

Two weeks later while James, Ernest, and Lester were scouting miles ahead of the wagon train, they heard the explosions of distant cannon and rifle fire. "Let's go look. I think the battle is over. The cannon firing has ceased, it is just scattered rifle fire now. Let's ride up over that next hill." Lester pointed.

The three scouts rode to the ridge in a grove of trees overlooking a field of battle. Two sides were pulling away from what was a major battle between the two civil war combatant armies. The wagon train scouts looked slack-jawed at the mass of bodies strung all over the battlefield. Thousands of soldiers died in the massive vicious battle. As the three scouts stared at the field of bodies sprawled out and staring through sightless eyes, the stench of the dust, carnage, and powder wrapped itself around their nostrils. Burial squads began moving their wagons into the field toward the dead. While one soldier drove the wagon, two walked behind it. One would grab the arms while the other would grab the feet of one of their dead and toss them onto the bed of the wagon. Arms and legs dangled off the bed, dripping in sweat and blood.

James shook his head, obviously disturbed. "There are no winners in a war like this one. One side may kill more than the other may, but in the end, they all lose. I will bet that if we ask any one of the soldiers who are alive and took part of this battle, neither would remember what they were fighting for, except hatred. If the politicians just took their disputes out behind the barn and duke it out until one hollers uncle, it would save this unnecessary killing. I hear brothers are fighting brothers on opposite sides, not knowing if their bullets are killing their own flesh and blood. What have they gained when the lead quits flying? Can they live with themselves better when they look back on this *victorious* scene? Can they go home to their families with stories of victory over killing their brother or father?"

"Oh my, look. There is a boy in gray struggling to get up. Oh no, that soldier in blue riding that horse just saw him struggling and turned his mount, charging at him. He is going to run him through with his sword. I cannot let that happen to that innocent boy. No!" Lester shouted as he started to raise his rifle and take aim.

"Don't do it." James commanded, then reached out and lowered Lester's rifle, fighting the bile that was building in his throat. "It is too late." They watched in horror as the Union officer swung his sword, decapitating the young boy.

"If we stay here any longer, we will be joining this fight. We cannot stop it. If we try, it will be the end of our families and us. We just have to walk away and turn a blind eye. This fight is not ours. We have to get back to our wagons and steer them around this scene. As much as I hate to admit it, Joshua was right." Ernest admitted.

"I should have pulled the trigger." Lester rebuffed himself as they descended from the tree grove back to where the wagon train was.

"By not pulling that trigger, you saved yourself, your family, and possibly the whole wagon train. We should fight battles that have meaning. If those men want to line up and shoot each other, brothers included, it is their choice, not ours. We cannot stop it or join it. Therefore, we just have to ride away from it, no matter how sick it makes us feel. Come on, let's get back to the living and report the battle to Joshua." Ernest told Lester.

"You two go back and report what we saw." James directed. "I want to do a little scouting to find a way around this mess. It looks like the Confederates are moving south, so they should not be a problem to avoid. However, the Unionists are working their way northeast. We have to move that wagon train, and I mean right now, to avoid them. I want to look at the back of the canyon that we saw. While I am scouting, get the wagons moving into it and cover our tracks. I will be back shortly."

On the way back to the wagons, Ernest and Lester were lost in thought of the scene they had just witnessed. Lester was still angry at having his rifle pulled away from him when he was trying to save the young rebel from losing his life. It pulled hard on his heartstrings not to help when he was able. He did understand though that if he had pulled that trigger, it would most likely have cost the lives of everyone on the wagon train. *Why were the issues of this war so important that they had to kill each other? Why were they not able to work out their issues through negotiations? Is humankind so stubborn that killing each other is the only way to solve a dispute?*

Ernest rode up to Joshua and reported the battle to him. "We are about ten miles away from that field of death. If we turn north, we can move into the canyon that we saw. James is scouting it to assure that there is a way out. I will start rubbing out our tracks if you get them moving into the canyon. We need to move out now and head away from that scene."

"Good. I don't want to get these wagons even close to that place. Furthermore, I do not want to run into either group of soldiers. I know how hard it was for you boys to ride away, but you did the right thing. If you would have engaged, we may all have perished. Now, we need to find a way to skirt around these armies. We don't want to skyline ourselves, or they will confiscate our wagons and horses, leaving us afoot. All right, let us move out quickly and quietly. I will tell the wagon drivers to tie down everything that makes noise. I don't want anyone to see or hear us until we get clear out of this area. We will head into this canyon and wait for James."

Ernest rode to the rear of the wagon train and began to brush out their tracks. He stopped to let Sylvia know what was going on and then worked his way backward for a mile, brushing out their tracks.

James rode ahead of the canyon to their northwest to assure that they could get through or back out, then he rode up to Joshua on his exhausted mount and reported, "We can make it through that canyon and out the other side. Start moving deep into it. It has a floor that is flat and will accommodate our wagons as long as it does not rain. I think that we can slip by them if we follow it. It leads north then back west. We can pull back out of it when it turns west and continue to follow the low ground. Ernest and Lester can ride the canyon rim and make sure that we don't run into any of the troops. Come on, boys, let's pick up some fresh mounts. We have some hard riding ahead."

Ernest rode north of the canyon rim while Lester rode the south rim, looking for any sign of the army or any other danger. James rode to the highest point, looking for the retreating armies. He wanted to make sure that the wagon train would not run into either group. It would be like threading a needle to sneak through them.

That evening, the scouts climbed to one of the tallest hills and looked in all directions. Off to the south, they spotted what looked like fireflies. "Look!" Lester pointed. "That looks like the Union Army campsite. If it is, they could still catch up to us."

"Aye, let's go back and talk to Joshua. If we scout close to the wagons, we should be able to travel all night and create some space between them and us. The farther we can get to the west of them, the safer we will be. I doubt that they will head west when the rebels and Yankee homes are east." Ernest advised.

They talked to Joshua, who stated, "If our horses will hold up, I don't see why we cannot keep going. I will have the wagon bringing up the rear drag some brush behind it to help rub out our tracks. Why don't you two go back to where we dropped down into this canyon and make sure we wiped out all of our tracks? Maybe it will save us from talking our way out of giving up our wagons and horses if they catch us."

Just before dawn, they reached the end of the canyon, and Joshua had to make a decision. "Do I go up and out of this canyon or camp here for the day?" Joshua asked James.

"We have water here and are hidden from view in these trees. We have exhausted our teams as well as our drivers. We need to camp quietly tonight and climb out at dusk. There is only a partial moon out tonight, and tomorrow we will have overcast skies. We should not be exposed if we stay quiet and move out again tomorrow night."

"Good." Joshua called the families together in their circle of wagons and explained, "We have water and feed for the livestock here. I don't want anyone to go outside this circle today. There will be no campfires. We have to remain hidden until we can move out tomorrow evening. Keep everything that will make noise secured. Remember, sound carries a long way, and both the Union and Confederate army will have scouts looking for supplies and renegades. We don't want to have a conflict with either side. We just want to slip on through undetected. Keep your talking to a minimum, and speak in low tones. Three men at a time will take shifts keeping our animals quiet. Another four men will be on guard around the wagons. Everyone must keep their children under control and be vigilant."

Confederate Soldiers

They remained huddled, talking in low tones and dozing throughout the day. Just as the sun slipped over the western horizon, Joshua gave the order to move out. Ernest and Lester had scouted ahead and found several ravines that would help hide the wagon trains as they headed west. Mary was again helping Sylvia drive her wagon and was handling the reins, riding drag.

Around midnight, two Confederate soldiers wearing gray popped out of the bush. They were carrying old musket rifles. They pointed them at Sylvia and Mary after they let all the other wagons pass. Mary let out a little squeal as Sylvia pulled up and asked, "What do you want?"

The soldier holding the other one up drawled. "I am sorry, ma'am, but we need you to hide my wounded friend in your wagon. He cannot travel any farther. He's wounded and totally exhausted."

"Sorry, we don't pick up vagrants and do not take sides in this war."

"Ma'am, this is not a request. You are taking us with you." He helped his friend hobble toward the wagon, dragging his left foot. The ankle had a dirty, bloody, soaked cloth wrapped around it. They climbed into the back of her wagon and pulled a blanket over themselves, hidden from anyone looking into the back.

Mary took the reins and cracked the whip close to the two mules, pulling her wagon to get them to catch up with the rest of the train. As she moved out, Sylvia asked, "What do you plan to do with us?"

"Ma'am, we need to just try to get away from the fighting for a while and find some help to tend my friend's wound. We would like stop fighting in this war, but we are no quitters. We thought we could make a difference and joined up to stop the northern aggression. It has not helped, and we can now see that it will make no difference whether we fight in this war or not. My friend needs to shed his gray uniform for a while and put on regular clothes. I see there is a box of men's clothes here, so I am going to help myself to an outfit for him."

"Those are my husband's, and I don't appreciate you stealing from us. He is out scouting, and when he returns, you had better not be anywhere close. He will run you down."

"Ma'am, if we get caught wearing this gray outfit, they will kill us and you two for harboring us. Please help me doctor my friend until he can walk again. I promise that I will not be a burden to either you or your husband."

Sylvia looked to the back of the wagon at the leg wound. "Mister, I see that he has a very nasty hole in his leg. You had better take this canteen and wash it off, then pour some alcohol on it and rewrap it with a clean cloth. You will find some alcohol in the upper shelf there. You had better not drink any of it, or I will take this bullwhip to you."

"No, ma'am, I will not drink any of it. By the way, my name is Louis Woods, and my wounded partner's name is Raymond Leigh. You can just call me Louis. I grew up on a hardscrabble farm in Texas near the Brazos River and plan on going to Montana to be with my brother Jack soon as this war is over. We lost our parents a few years back when a dozen young Comanche warriors raided our farm. They took our mustang horse herd that we had green broke and burned down our ranch. Jack and I ran them down and took our horses back. Our neighbors thought we were too young to be on our own, so we moved in with an older neighbor and started building a herd of Longhorn cattle. Charles Goodnight and some of his Texas Ranger friends talked to us about how the war needed many volunteers to join to repel the Union forces. I joined the fight while my brother spearheaded a trail drive to Montana. I told him that I would meet him there after the war.

"Ray here grew up in Arkansas on a little farm with his family. He joined up when the Unionists began running roughshod over them, telling them what they could and could not do. He wants to go back to his farm after the war. His farm is not too far from where we are now. If there was any way that I could have gotten him there by myself, I would have, but it was too far to travel in his condition. By the way, what can I do with his gray outfit?"

"Wrap it up tight, and when we pass that next bunch of bushes, throw it into the middle of it so that it cannot be spotted. We just cannot be caught with any of those clothes around."

"Thank you, ma'am. I do appreciate you being tolerant with us, but I had better hang on to it to replace your husband's clothes when Ray can walk again. I will just put his old gray clothes under your husband's wear. I will keep my gray outfit and will not bother your husband's for myself. If anyone shows up, I will hide in the bushes. However, I will trail along beside you just to make sure that my friend Ray gets the help he needs. Where are y'all heading anyway?"

"We are all going west looking for a new life free from all this suffering and war. I see he cannot even raise his foot. Let me crawl back there and help him. Mary, take the reins, and I will crawl back and have a look at that leg. It is really swollen. I do not see an exit wound, so the lead must still be in there. It has to come out, or he will get lead poisoning and lose his leg." Sylvia cleaned the leg with a clean cloth and water and then poured alcohol on it.

Ray let out a gasp and grabbed a hold of the side of the wagon, gritting his teeth. "That did hurt."

"Well, it is good to know that you can speak for yourself." Sylvia acknowledged and wrapped a clean cloth around the leg and told him, "This will have to be sufficient until we stop. It shouldn't be too much longer. The sky is turning gray, and we will find a hidden place to camp."

As dawn approached, the scouts found another good place to hold up the wagons during the day among the hardwoods. Lester and Ernest returned to their wagons exhausted. Joshua had some of the other men brush out the tracks that went into the trees. Ernest tied his horse to the back of his wagon and started to climb in. "Who are you two, and what are you doing in the back of my wagon wearing my clothes?" Ernest asked one of the men, holding a rifle pointed toward him.

"My name is Louis Woods, and I forced your wife and friend to hide us while we sought some medical help. I borrowed some of your clothes for my friend here, wrapped up his gray outfit, and stuffed it under your clothes. Please do not create a disturbance. We mean no one any harm. I am just trying to get some help for my friend's wound. The Yankees shot him in the leg in that last battle, and he could walk no farther. Your wife cleaned his wound and rewrapped it."

"You are holding a gun on me and telling me you mean us no harm? Put that gun down, and we will talk. Sylvia and Mary, are you two all right?"

"Aye, we are fine. I think that he is telling the truth. The one boy is wounded, and I need to work on his leg to see if we can save it." Sylvia told her husband.

Louis scooted to the end of the tailgate, holding up Ray's left foot. Sylvia lifted it, removed the bandages, and looked at it. "The bullet that is still in there has to come out now. It has to come out, or he will lose his foot. Ernest, start a smokeless fire and set some water on to boil. Louis, ya will have to trust us as we remove that bullet."

"We have no choice." Louis relented and lowered his rifle. "My rifle isn't loaded anyway. I ran out of ammunition and have no desire to fire it at anyone who is not wearing blue."

"I am not sure if we can help with that, but let us get that bullet out, then we will talk about what is going to happen next. Here, Ray, drink some of this laudanum. It will help numb the pain. Mary, tear off strips of that sheet to make bandages, and get me that long narrow knife out of my bag."

"Hey! What's going on?" Margret asked as she stepped around the corner of the wagon. "Who are these men? I thought something funny was going on back here when Ernest was building up a small fire, defying Joshua's strict orders. Are you taking in strangers, Sylvia?"

"Louis Woods, meet my best friend, Margret Clark. She just volunteered to help us remove this bullet out of Ray's leg. Here, take this knife and go heat it over the flames."

"I did? Ugh, that really looks bad. How long ago was he shot?"

"Please do not tell anyone, but we were in that ugly battle a few miles back. They wounded Ray late last evening." Louis told Margret.

"That bullet has been in you for too many hours already. Gangrene has probably already set in. Let us just hope that it has not started to fester. Lester, before we start, please let Joshua know of our stowaways. We cannot keep them hidden, and Joshua needs in on this too," Sylvia said.

Battle Scars

After Ray was numb from the laudanum, Sylvia told Ernest and Louis to hold him down while she worked the knife into the wound. Louis shoved a leather strap between Ray's teeth and told him to bite down on it and not scream. She ran the blade down the hole until it bumped against something solid. Ray let out a groan then passed out. She got the tip of the narrow knife under the bullet and worked it out. It was bleeding profusely as she showed them the musket ball.

"I don't think that we can stop the bleeding with just a piece of cloth. Ernest, put this knife back into the fire until it is glowing, and then bring it back to me. I will have to cauterize the wound to seal it. I know it will leave an ugly scar, but we have no other choice."

"What do you mean by cauterizing the wound?" Mary asked.

"You will see."

While the knife was heating, Sylvia poured alcohol onto a rag, rolled it around a small dowel, and then shoved the dowel with the rag into the hole back and forth several times to clean the hole from any infection.

When Ernest returned with the glowing knife, she placed the flat part on the opening of the hole until it quit sizzling and smoking. Then she placed the flat part on the exit hole.

"Whew!" Mary wrinkled her nose from the pungent smell. "That stinks. I am glad that Ray passed out before we branded him, or he would have brought the whole Union Army down on us with his screaming."

"Let's just hope that he did not lose too much blood and infection does not set in, or we will have to remove his leg." Sylvia explained.

"Oh, I don't think I could stomach that. I was barely able to help when you applied that hot knife to his leg." Mary cringed.

"What is the meaning of this?" Joshua asked as he approached the tailgate. "We cannot get involved in deserters on board this train. Do you know what will happen if the Confederates find them on our wagon train? They will shoot or imprison us for harboring deserters. Worse yet, if the Union Army finds him, they will kill him and take us in for treason. We must get them out of here, the sooner the better."

Louis stood up, walked up face-to-face to Joshua, and angrily glared at him. "Now you just hold on a minute, fella. I carried my friend here for help, and that is what he received. I will have a major issue if you try to abandon him now. I would like him to stay in your care 'til he is well enough to travel on his own. We don't want any harm to come to you or anyone on this wagon train. Now that you are caring for Ray, I will vanish into the brush, but Ray needs to stay here until he is well enough to travel. I hope I have made myself clear."

"It sounds like you are threatening us. Let me be clear to you: we will not tolerate anyone threatening us for any reason. I really do not care if you had to carry your friend clear across this continent. That is your problem. The wagon train and its welfare are mine. If I see you are a threat, one way or another, you will be gone."

"So, Joshua, you are saying that we just throw this wounded man off this wagon train in his condition? From what they have told us, I don't think they are deserters. They kept his gray outfit, and he indicated that he would put it back on after he is well. Who is to say that he is not a part of our family?" Sylvia argued.

"It will take several days for his fever to subside. Who knows, maybe he will die, and we will be rid of him. It is your choice, of course, but he cannot survive if we abandon him now. He will need constant care with good water and food to break his fever."

Lester thought back upon the battlefield that they had just witnessed. "I agree with Sylvia. We need to act as if he is a part of our wagon train until he can travel on his own. Joshua, if you would have seen that bloody killing field with thousands of blue and gray bodies, you would understand why we need to do this."

Ernest stepped in to face Joshua. "I will take the responsibility for him. He climbed aboard my wagon, and we have doctored him, so he is under my care. Anytime you think this situation is too dangerous for this wagon train, then we will depart ways. We will just follow along behind and try to catch up after he leaves our wagon."

"You put me in a tough predicament, Ernest. I will let him travel with you, but at the first opportunity, he must leave the train."

"Fair enough, and thanks," Ernest said.

"Since you do not have any bullet holes, you will have to leave." Joshua told Louis. Do you have a problem with that? We might be able to get by with one rebel, but two would surely get us all killed. I am sorry, but you will have to leave now."

"Oh, I understand. I know the risk you are taking. I appreciate it. As long as you do what you can to help my partner, Ray, I am very satisfied. I will take my leave now, and no one but us will have known I was here. I will be very close by though, just in case there are any problems. No one will see me, but I will not be very far away. When Ray is well enough to travel, I will be back to take him off your hands. Here, let me take his gray outfit with me so that no one will know he is a Confederate."

An hour after dark, Louis thanked the Walkers and took his leave. Joshua moved the wagons out again. Ray lay in the back of the Walkers' wagon, sweating profusely. Mary was obviously compassionate and concerned. "I will ride back with him and mop his face with the clean cool water we carry and try to keep him covered."

"Pour water from the barrel into a wooden cask, and then use the water from the cask. We do not want to contaminate the barrel of fresh water. Just as always, pour the water into a smaller container before you touch it. Never place any contaminates into the barrel, or it will contaminate it. That is what happened on the ship when we traveled from Ireland, and everyone on board got deathly sick."

"I understand that was a terrible trip. Mom told me that you lost many of the passengers."

"Aye. I will never forget the stench of the sick aboard. I had to serve them food that was so rotten, a hog would get sick on it. People were dying all around us. We could do nothing. I did speak to the captain several times. He almost threw me off the ship for speaking out. If Ernest had not been there, I am sure I would have been fish food."

Ray's foot continued to swell, and Sylvia was very worried that it might have to come off. When it looked like it might burst, Sylvia lacerated it and drained off the fluid. She was very worried that they had waited too long to extract the bullet.

Unionists

Ernest rode up to their wagon and told Sylvia, "A small detachment of Union soldiers are heading this way. Keep Ray hidden, and maybe they will ride on. If they ask, tell them that he is Mary's older brother, Ray Reynolds. I will tell the rest of the people the same story. If they ask what happened, just tell them we were hunting and I accidentally shot him."

Ernest rode from wagon to wagon, telling them what to say if questioned. He also told them to keep their rifles and shotguns loaded and ready to use. Louis had been traveling parallel to them and saw the blue bellies turn toward the wagons. He prepared to engage them if it was necessary.

Nine Unionists wearing blue came riding in hard. They asked, "Who is in charge of these wagons?"

Joshua stepped in front of the group. "I am. Who are you, and what can I do for you?"

"You can call me Sergeant Nettles. I am ordering you to stop and unload your wagons. We need them and any guns and ammunition you have. We also want to search to make sure that you are not harboring any rebels or deserters."

"Well, Sergeant, we are just peaceful civilians traveling west and are not going to do that. I can tell you that we are not harboring any rebels or Union deserters. You can just ride on and find someone else to harass."

"I was not asking. I am ordering you to unload every wagon right now. We will talk to every passenger you have and look through every piece of your belongings. Is that clear enough?"

James, Ernest, and Lester joined Joshua. "What's going on?" James asked.

"Men, draw your weapons." The sergeant ordered.

Before they could pull out their weapons, four fully loaded shotguns were pointing at them, and more were on their way. Joshua spoke. "I would not do that if I were you. We are peaceful but will not tolerate what you are ordering. Now you turn around and go back and report to your commanding officer. He is welcome to visit us, but he had better come in peace. We are not going to give any army our wagons and teams. You are welcome to talk to every passenger and assure none of them are rebels or deserters. I will even allow you to look into every wagon and assure that we are not harboring any armament. However, if you threaten these pilgrims in any way, we will not hesitate to blow you out of your saddles."

"We are federal troops, and you are obstructing this war."

"We are not obstructing any war. We are just traveling from New York to Oregon peacefully. You, sir, however, are obstructing our right to travel to the west."

The sergeant's face turned red as he yanked his horses around and rode back the way he had come without even looking into the wagons.

Joshua looked at the wagoners. "We had better keep moving. I do not think that we have heard the last of that hothead. I did not want to get involved with this war, but if they try to harm us in any way, we will fight either side to protect what are ours and our rights."

Around midnight after the men in blue left, a volley of shots sounded in the distance the direction they had gone. "I will bet that they found their rebels." James told Joshua.

"I never wanted to wish harm to anyone, but I sure wish they have met some rebels. We had better keep moving as long as these animals can put one foot in front of the other. I kept thinking what they would do if they found out that Ray was a Confederate. Have Sylvia continue to drag that brush behind her, blotting out our tracks."

Ernest rode up to Joshua. "I know. We would have had a tough decision to make. Kill or be killed. Neither choice is very appealing. Thank you for being tough, Joshua. I certainly am sorry to have put you and the members of this wagon train in that position."

"It is not your fault or Ray's. It is just the fault of hate versus love. You chose to love and are a better man for it. War is nothing but hatred and stubbornness in action."

They rolled down the trail again, moving from concealment to concealment that James found, always heading in a northwesterly direction. They did not travel any particular trail but made a trail of their own. The three scouts wore out their mounts looking for any sign of either army or barriers in the wagon train's path. Every family knew that they were a hair's breadth away from being plunged into the dreaded war. They also knew they were vulnerable to attack by Indians, outlaws, or renegades from either faction of the war. They all prayed that by traveling quietly at night, they would escape detection.

Mary sat with Ray, mopping his forehead and keeping him warm. She changed the bandage often as the wound drained out. "I am not sure whether he is getting better or worse." Mary told Sylvia. "I used Ernest's shaver to shave off his beard. He is quite good-looking now that you can see his face. With his big chest and those large arms, I will bet he is very strong."

"Keep pouring the laudanum down him as instructed. He needs to stay sedated and to sweat out his fever. The leg is still swollen, but it has not started to stink or turn gray yet, which is a good sign. Watch for any red lines around the leg going up it, which is a sign of blood poisoning." Sylvia instructed.

On the third morning after they had picked up Ray, as they made camp, Mary helped her mom make breakfast while Sylvia looked over Ray. She returned and told Mary, "Ray is awake. I think the fever broke last night. I told him he needed to rest today. Why don't you take him some coffee and a little breakfast? Do not give him any more laudanum. I think he is going to make it."

Mary was so excited and quickly poured him a cup and gathered a big breakfast for him to eat. She hurried to the wagon and tried to feed him his breakfast. He laughed. "Ma'am, I can feed myself. They shot my foot, not my hands. I am hungry, but you brought enough for ten people."

"I thought you were hungry. I am just trying to help. How old are you?" Mary asked.

"I think I turned eighteen last month. I want you to know I appreciate everything you and your family have done. I need to leave this wagon train before the Unionists find me. I sure don't want to put you or anyone else in harm's way."

"Ha, it is too late to be thinking of that. We have already had a run-in with the Unionists while you were sleeping. They wanted us to unload all the wagons so that they could take them and their teams. Dad and the other men ran them off. As soon as they left, they must have run into some of your rebel friends because we heard some shooting. They never came back."

Going Home

"What happened to Louis? Is he still around?"

"No, he left as soon as we removed the bullet from your leg. He said he would be close by if any bluecoats accost us." Mary told Ray.

"If I was a betting man, I'd bet that he had something to do with those shots you heard. He probably took after them as soon as they left and caught up to them when they camped."

"How could he think of fighting nine soldiers?"

"Ma'am, he is the toughest man I have ever met. He has no fear. He would take on a whole garrison to save a friend. Since the wagon train had befriended us, he would fight the complete Union Army if they saw this train as a threat. One time he and I traded our gray outfits for blue and slipped into one garrison at night. We blew up all their munitions without them knowing we were there and then did the same to two other garrisons that were merging toward our Confederate Army. We had to change back into our gray outfits to fight with our rebel friends. That was where I received this wound. He acted as my crutch as we made our way north, trying to reach my home. That is when we saw you coming toward us in that canyon."

Ray rested the rest of that day. The next evening, he slipped out of the back into the front seat and sat between Sylvia and Mary as they continued to travel during the night. He even took the reins a time or two.

"My farm is not too far from here." Ray told Ernest. "It is just west off Pine Bluff. The way we are traveling, you could drop me off at my front door. It is not much of a farm, just a house and a barn with some chicken coops."

"I will talk to Joshua and James. We will drop you off as close as we can. It seems that we are moving away from the main war activities."

Ernest talked to James about riding close to Pine Bluff. "We will probably be going right by it tomorrow. It will be a good place to drop him off."

"Is he strong enough to walk?"

"I don't think he can walk very far. Why don't I ride to his farm with him, leave him with his family, and then bring our horse back? I will be back before we break camp."

Ray thanked the Clarks, the Walkers, and the Reynoldses for their hospitality, hobbled around to the back of the wagon, and spoke to Mary. "I want to personally thank you for the time you spent tending my wound. I owe you and Sylvia my life. I will never forget you and will forever miss your gentleness. I wish that I could travel to Oregon with you and help you build your new home, but I have family waiting. I have not seen them for two years. I enlisted with the Confederates and rode away from the farm to the south, hoping against hope to quickly settle this conflict. My father, mother, and sister are waiting for me, and I know that Dad cannot handle our farm without help."

Mary was looking at her feet while Ray was talking. He reached over and took a hold of both her hands in his as he was talking. When he finished, she slowly looked up with tearful eyes, put her arms around his neck, and pulled him close. She could not stop her tears. She hugged him. "You had better take care of that leg. I will not be around to take care of it next time." Then she kissed him square on the mouth, ran up to her wagon, and crawled into its back.

Ray and Ernest rode north toward his farm. It was ten miles north of Pine Bluff near the Arkansas River. It took them several hours to skirt through the countryside. Ray looked at several homes that had burnt to the ground. He turned to Ernest. "These were good families that lived here. Quantrill must have stirred up a hornet's nest as he went through here on his way to Lawrence. That home belonged to the Lamberts. They were a good God-fearing family. Their two sons and I argued about the rivalry. They went north to join up with the Union Army while I went south. I just cannot believe that the war would have reached this far inland."

Ray was getting very spooked, nervous, and fidgety as they continued to travel north. All of a sudden, Ray raked his boots to the side of his horse and galloped on ahead. His horse skidded to a stop, and he crawled off near the remains of a cabin. He went limping through the ash field and then dropped to his knees, sobbing. His uncle's home, barn, and sheds were nothing but ash.

Ernest pulled his horse next to Ray's and tied them off. He walked around the yard and saw where a fresh pile of dirt covered human remains. He hollered at Ray and walked over to look down at two graves. Someone had put a marker on them, identifying his aunt and uncle that had died in the raid. Ray fell to his knees next to the graves, sobbing a prayer to them. It pulled on Ernest's heartstrings to see the boy so brokenhearted. After the prayers were over, they remounted and again headed toward his farm. Ray looked around at the devastation. "There is nothing left. That is the last of my relatives, except my mother, father, and sister. I should never have gone off to the war and left them alone. I should have been here with them. I just pray that my parents and sister are still alive."

"If you had stayed, I doubt it would have changed a thing. War is like that. There is absolutely nothing glorious to war. Come on, let's get to your family's ranch."

"Hey! Who is that coming this way?" Ray asked.

"It looks like the man in gray that brought you to our wagon."

Sure enough, Louis waved and rode up to them. "Howdy. Where are you going? I spotted you as you rode away from the wagons and thought it might be you. You still look a little peaked, Ray, but better than the last time I saw you."

"Where did you get the horses and supplies?" Ernest asked.

"Oh, some bluecoats did not need them anymore, and since they did not have many markings on them, I sort of relieved them of their burden. I thought you might want a mount of your own, Ray. Where're ya headed anyway?" Louis drawled.

"We are on our way to my farm. It is just another half a day's ride from here. Why don't you ride along with us? Several of the pioneers heard shots in the direction that the bluecoats went when they left. Is that where you picked up these horses?"

"They did not go very far before they made camp, and there were only nine of them. I did not want them to hassle the wagon train anymore and took care of it."

"You mean that you took on all nine of the Unionists?" Ernest questioned Louis.

"They were not very smart and were a little slow. They will not report back to their commanding officer in this lifetime."

"Well, it looks like you boys have things under control. If you don't mind, I will let you swap horses, Ray, and then I will head on back to the wagon train."

"Thank you for all you have done for me." Ray shook Ernest's hand. "I will pray for your safe journey. Tell Mary and Sylvia thanks for all their help."

"Just stay healthy from now on." Ernest told him as he headed back toward the wagons. When he arrived back, he explained what had happened and that Louis had rendezvoused with them.

"I doubt that we have seen or heard the last of those two. One never knows. Someday, they might just show up on our doorstep." Sylvia told the heartbroken Mary.

Mary looked sad. "I will miss him. He was the first man that I ever kissed, then for him to leave to go back into that war really makes me sad."

"Don't you fret any. You will find a young man who will sweep you off your feet. You never know, he might just jump out of the bushes when you are least expecting it, like Ray did, only he will carry you off." Sylvia told Mary.

Rocky Mountains

The wagon train rolled into Denver, Colorado, in mid-October. It was a beautiful time of the year. The leaves on the aspen were turning yellow and made the Rocky Mountains more majestic than ever. The mountain ash, hickory, cottonwood, poplar, maple, and oak trees were shedding their leaves, while the northern breeze was blowing the cotton off the cottonwood trees at the lower elevations. Many high mountain peaks had turned white with high-elevation snow. It made one shudder with chills just looking up at it. Areas in the mountains had a yellow tint from the turning of the aspen leaves.

"We are going to have to pick up the pace if we are going to get through the passes before they close." Joshua turned to the pilgrims when they stopped. "We will stop for one day and one evening here close to Denver so that we may pick up some winter clothing and a few supplies. We will soon be glad that we are bundled in warm clothes. When you pick out your winter clothes, remember it can get down to thirty degrees below zero. The hides that we have been collecting and tanning, we will need to finish making those made into winter clothes for facing the elements."

Everyone took Joshua seriously and wanted to purchase the items they needed with what was left of their cash reserves. They found the Denver area to be robust and emerging into a large settlement. They needed more boots and undergarments, so they rode into town to finish out their winter needs. Sylvia, Margret, and Shirley came out of a mercantile carrying a large bag of sewing supplies of needles, thread, scissors, and thimbles. Ernest and Lester looked around for a blacksmith while the women finished shopping. They wanted to make sure that their draft animals' shoes were in good shape. The blacksmith greased the wheels and checked for loose spokes. It was a short layover, so they did not waste any time. It was going to get cold.

Ernest was growing concerned over Sylvia's condition. She was getting bigger by the day and walking along the wagon more and more. It was just too hard for her to bounce on the wagon seat sixteen hours a day. He knew that he would have to leave the wagon train shortly to make a place for them to wait out the winter. Sylvia, Margret, and many of the other women in the train worked tirelessly on the hides to make themselves winter clothes. The ones they made were better than the store-bought clothes. They had not only made winter parkas, but also pants and hats to go with them. Their wives had also made sleeping blankets out of the hides that would keep the heat in. They would keep the cold out, but sometimes they would get too hot using them.

Margret approached Sylvia and told her, "I am getting sick every morning like you did several months ago. I think that I am also pregnant. I have not told Lester yet. I am so worried that he will be upset. We did not want to have any children until we were settled in our new home."

"That is what we wanted too, but we cannot have everything we want. I am so excited for you." They hugged. "Now you had better go right on over and tell that man of yours the good news. It will be wonderful. I am so happy for you and to know that I will not be the only pregnant woman on this wagon train."

Lester was elated. You could hear him let out a big whoop as he hollered and danced around the wagon with his wife. "I told you he would be excited." Sylvia told Margret.

The next morning, Joshua began moving the wagons north toward Cheyenne to where the wagons could cross over the Continental Divide at a lower elevation. While in Denver, Sylvia had picked up a newspaper, which talked about the Mormon movement. She read it one evening when they stopped and made camp. It read:

Mormons Populate Utah Territory

For centuries, Native American tribes built around the Utah Territory. The Pueblo Indians built large communities in southern Utah. The Ute Indian tribe, from which the territory takes its name, arrived after the Pueblo Tribe. Recently, Mormons moved in to Utah. Mormons are a religious group started by Joseph Smith in Illinois. Some said that Joseph Smith Jr. died as a horse thief, but that was a false rumor.

It all started when Joseph Smith's family squabbled for years over issues they heard every time they worshiped. No one seemed satisfied with the teachings received. Joseph at age fourteen claimed he saw the angel of God in a vision who told him to set things right by reinterpreting the Bible. Smith claimed Angel Moroni visited him many times. He called this new interpretation the Book of Mormon, after Angel Moroni. His ideas and influence began a movement that continued throughout his life until his death in mid-1844 by a mob. The late Mr. Smith was a mayor of Nauvoo, Illinois, and was running for president of the United States. He ordered a newspaper, the *Nauvoo Exposition*, to "cease and desist." The paper was discrediting Joseph and his movement by claiming that he was practicing polygamy and blasphemy of the Word of God. The newspaper owners claimed that Smith even tried to marry some of their wives. In addition, it claimed that many of Smith's other wives were also married to other men. Joseph and his brother, Hyrum, reportedly broke into the newspaper office, set it on fire, and destroyed one press and part of the building. That act further enraged the newspaper owners and its supporters. They surrendered themselves to the law, and their new home became the jail. While in jail, an armed mob of men broke into the jail seeking retribution. Joseph kept a small derringer hidden when he went behind bars. He shot a couple of the assailants with the gun. After Joseph started shooting, the assailants shot and killed Joseph and his brother Hyrum.

Following the death of Joseph, Brigham Young assumed the leadership of this new movement. They called themselves the Church of Jesus Christ of Latter-Day Saints, LDS. As instructed by Moroni, they modified and updated the Book of Mormon. This became their "Latter Day" prophecy. They left Illinois to find a new place to settle. The first wave of immigrants crossed Iowa and wintered in Nebraska. This was an advance party, so they only brought with them a few women and a couple of children. They sent out advanced scouts and headed for the Salt Lake Valley, just across the Rocky Mountains in Utah Territory.

The new land contained plenty of fresh water with good rich soil. Since it was late in the growing season, they immediately sunk plows into the earth, tilling its soil, and planted their potatoes, carrots, onions, corn, grain, and other seeds that they had brought. Others began clearing building sites to build shelters for themselves and the families to come. There was a shortage of trees for logs in the immediate area, but along the mountain ridges, they found plenty of stone. They cut granite blocks from nearby quarries to build their houses and places of worship.

In their first year, a late frost brought a plague of crickets that practically consumed their entire harvest. Their neighbors called these crickets Mormon crickets. Having tried everything they could think of to fight the swarm that was devastating all they had worked for, they feared the large hungry bugs would ruin their winter supply to feed themselves and their Indian neighbors. After much prayer, flocks of seagulls flew into the community to consume enough of the crickets to save them from starvation. This same year, Mexico signed a treaty with the United States declaring the Utah Territory a part of the United States. The Mormons claimed that the seagulls were a miracle they received in response to their prayers.

Young told his followers that it was cheaper to feed the Indians than to fight them. As long as they could produce an abundance of produce, they would feed them. Yet as the Mormon settlement expanded north and south along the front range, conflict increased with Indians. The Indians, with their loss of hunting grounds and foraging areas, became more dependent on the handouts from the Mormons.

The California gold rush brought many immigrants through the Great Salt Lake City area as they raced to the California gold fields. Many of these immigrants settled around the community. Trade with these sojourners brought the valley a good measure of prosperity, although agriculture continued as their mainstay. Hundreds of copper, silver, gold, and lead mines opened in the nearby canyons. Gigantic smelters built to refine metal-bearing minerals dotted their mountainsides.

In the fall of 1857, the Baker-Fancher wagon train of immigrant families traveling from Arkansas through Utah Territory to California were found killed. Most of the immigrants perished at the Mountain Meadows in southern Utah as well as some Paiute Indians. Mormons took the surviving children back to their settlement to adopt. Blame was given to Mormon militiamen disguised as Native Americans. Further investigations on this matter are on hold due to the Civil War raging in this nation. Soldiers are camping near the city during this Civil War time.

The settlement around the Salt Lake is ripe for farming and raising a family where the Indians are still friendly. The community expects that refugees from the war will be flocking to this safe haven to escape the wrath of retaliation.

After reading the article, Sylvia showed it to Ernest. "Look at this article. This might be a good place for the wagon train to conclude the trip for the winter. It is still a long way away, but by the time we arrive, winter will be set in. Let's talk to Joshua and the Clarks to see what they think."

Joshua looked at them, after Ernest discussed the possibility of everyone in the wagon train stopping over in Utah. "Let's just wait and see when we get closer. It is something to think about if the storms stall us on our route to Oregon."

Elk Mountain

Northern winds whipped across the prairie and brought with it a biting cold. They kept the high Rocky Mountains to their south as they rode west through the prairie of scattered sage. There were a few deer to augment the food supply and a few streams to fill their water barrels. It was a barren land to the north of the high mountain range.

"Ireland was cold in the winter, but this is almost unbearable." Sylvia shivered with Margret as they bundled together around the campfire.

There was little protection from the wind as the wagon train turned west before they reached Cheyenne. Joshua was anxious to move the wagons across the eastern slope of the Rocky Mountains before the winter showed its ugly face. "This cold and wind is nothing compared to the way it will be another month from now. We have to cross this desolate land while we are able. It is either cross it now or hunker down and wait out the winter, which will last for at least three months in this part of the country next to the Rocky Mountains. If we can make it far beyond the western slope of the Rockies, the winter will be much milder and easier for us to survive." Joshua explained to the wagoners.

The travel was hard, and the days and nights were long with boredom. The men would go out during the evening and try to bring down the elusive antelope. One evening, James led Ernest and Lester out into the plains to try to bring in some camp meat. "Let me show you how an old mountain man, Jim Bridger, taught me to lure these animals in." James explained when they had spotted a dozen antelope about half a mile away in the flats. James took a white rag, tied it to the end of the barrel of his gun, and waved it in the air. When an antelope raised its head and spotted the object, he lowered it. "Antelope are a very curious animal and hopefully will investigate."

As he spoke, the group of American pronghorns started angling toward the two hunters. James continued to taunt the animals by raising the flag and waving it into the air to keep up their curiosity. It was cold lying out in the flat just under the crest of a little rise, waiting for the animals to get closer. When they were within a hundred yards, James lowered the flag. "Ernest, you take the animals on the right of that leader, and I will take those on the left. I will raise the flag one more time. When they stop moving forward this time and look away, let us take our shots. When they run, shoot quickly. We need to bring down as many as we can. They are very fast, so don't waste any time." When he lowered the flag for the last time, James removed the white cloth from the end of his gun and slowly leveled it at the group's leader. "Shoot at my count of three." At three, they fired their rifles then quickly reloaded and fired again. The animals took off and were out of range after their third shot.

"That was good shooting." James told Ernest. "We've shot five good animals, and that is a lot better than I expected."

James went right to work dressing them out while Ernest walked a mile back to an arroyo where they had staked their mounts and pack animals. They loaded the game animals up on their pack animals and headed back to camp. They were very cold when they reached the circle of wagons and welcomed the cup of coffee Sylvia handed to them.

Joshua met them as they got into camp. "It looks like you had some good luck this time."

"Aye," Ernest answered. "I keep learning new tricks of hunting from James. When I think I know what to do, he shows me some new trick."

"He is a good man and has been around the mountain a few times. You are becoming a very good scout and hunter yourself. You sure are a different man than when I first saw you. You were as green as grass. You and Sylvia have been a big help on this trip."

As they continued west, they came close to the tall mountains to the south. The teams were tired, and Joshua called a halt. "We will rest here for three days before we move out again. That will give each of you time to repair harnesses, wagons, and rest your teams."

James told Ernest and Lester, "I would like for you two to take a ride with me. Pack enough rations to last three days. Our rations are running short, and I think we can get some game animals in those mountains, but it will take a few days. I doubt either one of you has ever seen elk, but they are abundant in that tall mountain to our south. Some mountain men have named it Elk Mountain. It will be a rugged trip, so take some warm clothes along. Have your wives pack us something to hold us over. That ole buffalo jerky that we have should help, but we will need some other substance. We will need some coffee and beans to go along. I want to leave early tomorrow morning, long before sunrise. The wagon train should not have any problems while we are gone. This time of the year, neither Indians nor outlaws like this weather any better than we do."

John walked over to James. "I hear that you are heading to that high mountain. Harry has bugged me to ask you to take him along on this hunting expedition. He has practiced his shooting skills with Ernest and has become quite adept. I don't think that he would be a burden to you. He has idolized Ernest and wants to grow up just like him."

"He seems to be quite grown up now. I will talk to him and let him know what he is getting into. It is going to be very cold and hard traveling. Those mountains look quite inviting down here, but when you are in them, they can be as deadly as an ole grizzly."

"Harry, your dad said that you would like to go with us on this hunt. You ought to know a few things before we start hunting. First, hunting elk is tedious work. You will be colder and probably more exhausted than you have ever been before. In final analysis, it will be rewarding, but you probably will not realize it until a few days after we get back. On a hunting trip like this, you have to be tough mentally and physically. You will have to pull your weight and not complain about any burden asked of you. I know that you are excited to be going, and we are excited to have you. Dress warm and listen to those of us who have faced perilous situations like this before. Get a good night's sleep, and be ready to head out about three hours before daylight. That's about it. We will see you in the morning, if you are still of the mind to go."

"I will be ready to go when you are. You will not have to wait on me, Mr. Lenny. Just let me know what to do, and I will do it. If I am doing anything wrong, just tell me."

"Be very careful." Sylvia and Margret instructed their husbands as they stuffed their saddlebags with some final provisions.

It was frosty that morning as the four men headed toward the towering peaks, leading a string of pack animals. James led them directly to a game trail, and they began their climb. It took them all day to climb that rugged mountain. The animals were weary as they crossed over the top of the mountain and down to a stream. The sun dropped quickly in the mountains as did the temperature.

"What is that whistling I keep hearing?" Harry asked James.

"That, my young friend, is coming from the two front teeth of the animals we are looking for. The bull elk will whistle or bugle to give signals to his herd. They create the whistle by blowing air through their front teeth to communicate to their herd. Sometimes it is a challenge to the young bulls that circle his herd to breed with the cows. He has to fight the young bulls to secure his position as leader. Sometimes, his whistle is a warning for the herd to get moving. Hearing the whistle gives me confidence that we are in the right place. I have only brought a few of the big animals down in my lifetime. I killed one a few years back that had a six-foot antler spread. Man, that bull was a big animal. It was bigger than my horse, and it took me three trips to pack it out. We will camp here tonight." James instructed. "I have never hunted this area before but have talked to some ole mountain men that have been all through here. These elk run in herds of ten to a hundred in a herd. The old bulls are always watchful. They will move their herd away from any sound that is abnormal. I expect a nice little valley over that next mountain is where all the bugling is coming from. Therefore, in the morning, we will ride up there and stake out our positions and wait for daybreak. We need to be positioned before daybreak so that they cannot see us moving around. If we are very quiet as we move and do not step on any twigs, they may not notice us. We will leave our pack animals here. After we make our kill, we will return and bring the pack animals back to where we killed them."

Long before sunrise, the four rode to the crest of the next mountain and overlooked a nice sparsely wooded valley. James had them tie their horses up in a shelter of some trees below the ridge. He kept a ridge between them and the valley to keep their movement from being seen. "Harry, I would like you to tag along with Ernest. Maybe you can show him how to bring down that big bull." James whispered.

"Yeah, I would like to do that."

James smiled. "Be sure to walk very carefully. A snapped twig can be heard a long ways off, especially by the keen senses of those big watchful bulls."

He located each of them about a third of the way around the little valley so that they had it covered. They waited and waited past first light. The sun peered over the mountain peak to the east and began to burn the morning dew off the leaves that had turned yellow from the sap running back into the ground. As the glow from the sun rose over the peak, the moisture from the dew filtered up through the aspen and pine in the morning fog. There was a little breeze, but it was nothing too strong and blowing away from the valley. Their scent would not drift down to the elks' sensitive nostrils.

As they waited, they each heard the trees creak as the branches rubbed against other branches and the leaves rustled in the wind. The morning birds came out to sing and tweet, and some rabbits scurried for their holes. As the men dug into their spot to wait and watch their section of the valley, the sun burned off the morning dew. It was beginning to warm up rapidly. The men held their place, watching intently down into the valley. James could see what looked like a small game trail that led through the valley and wondered where it originated. Ernest poked Harry in the ribs and pointed out a nice buck mule deer meandering along just below their rim overlook. Harry pointed to his rifle, but Ernest shook his head as they debated about shooting it even though James told them not to shoot anything but elk. James told them only shoot the elk when they spotted the herd, so the others could be a part of the action too.

It was hard to wait when game presented itself as that buck did. Several more hours passed. As the sun bore down on them, the men quietly pulled out the meal that their wives and mother had fixed them. They were all thankful for the nourishment for it had been a long morning. They ate quietly for James had warned them that the elk could hear and smell abnormalities of any kind from long distances. Anything out of the ordinary will alert them to potential danger and further sharpen their senses toward that area.

Camp Meat

After they ate and became a little drowsy, the valley below them started coming to life. They heard the bugle of the bull elk and saw him as he wandered out into the opening, summoning his herd. Then moments later, several cows started emerging from the brushy thickets surrounding the creek that meandered its way through the valley. They were too far away for a good shot, so they waited as the elk began to feed in the meadow. A large young spike bull moved out of the woods broadside in front of James. It was too big a temptation, and he leveled his sights and shot him right behind the front shoulders. The big animal made one long leap and then toppled over as James jacketed another round into his rifle. The herd began to move away from where they had heard the shot, but right into the path of Lester.

Lester peered over a big rock. He waited until a large cow came busting through the trees right in front of him, took aim, and brought her down with a neck shot. The herd scattered and headed toward Ernest and Harry, who had repositioned themselves to lean over a deadfall. Ernest had positioned Harry to his right with a good field of fire. Ernest took the left side and had a good field to watch away from Harry.

As they heard the other men open up with their rifles, Harry began fidgeting and was getting anxious for a shot. He aimed his rifle toward a little clearing just fifty yards in front of him and anxiously waited for the elk to emerge. The big buck that had gone into the valley suddenly emerged right in front of Ernest.

He could wait no longer and took the shot. He knew he should have waited for an elk, but the ball was already open. He did not want to leave empty-handed. While he jacketed another shell into the magazine, a large bull came running through the trees through his area, then right in front of Harry. Harry quickly took aim and squeezed the trigger. The bull went down but staggered back up. He again took aim and downed the animal with his second shot. The bull fell and did not move. A yearling calf came charging through Ernest's area. He downed him with a head shot. Again, they heard James shooting, and then all was quiet.

The elk herd had drifted into the trees and vanished out of range. They could not believe that so many big animals could just disappear so quickly and quietly. Ernest walked over to the big buck and quickly dressed him out then tackled the calf that weighed at least two hundred pounds more than the buck. The big bull that Harry shot was another matter. He was big and impossible to move by himself. Ernest helped Harry, and they finally managed to dress him out. They took the hearts and liver from their kill and placed them into a canvas bag Ernest had brought. Harry was very excited as he joked with Ernest about just killing a little deer and calf as they walked back to where they had left their mounts. Lester, already there, had untied his horse and was mounting as Ernest and Harry walked up.

"That was fun," Lester commented. "I killed a big cow. I cannot believe how big she was. How did you two do? I heard several shots in your direction."

"Well, I killed a nice-sized buck, and then this big monster bull came barreling through the trees next to me while I was reloading. He ran right into Harry's area. He shot him and knocked him down, but that big beast got right back up, and so he had to shoot him again. I could not believe how big he was. He was bigger than my horse. I sure hope we don't have more meat than we can pack out of here."

"Wait a minute." Lester laughed. "Let me get this right: you shot a deer while young Harry here shot the bull?"

"Aye, that is about the size of it. I should have just said that I passed up my shot to let Harry have the big one."

"Oh, but you did shoot a little calf along with that mule deer." Harry chuckled.

"While you wait for James, I will go back to camp and bring in the pack horses."

About that time, James came around the tree line. "Hold up. I have two elk down myself. We need to string these animals up high enough so that predators don't ruin them. It is going to get dark on us before we can finish tying them up. After we tie them up to drain, we should take what we can back to camp. Then in the morning, we can bring the pack animals back and load them."

Since James's position was the closest, they rode over to where he had made his kill. He had shot one large spike bull and one good-sized cow. Lester cut down a small tree about three inches in diameter and tied it between two large tree branches. Then they threw their rope around the tree and onto the back legs of the big cow and pulled her up using their saddle horses. It was more than Ernest's horse could pull, so Lester tied another rope to its back legs, and both Ernest and Lester pulled the beast up to the three-inch crossbar. Harry stood on the back of his horse and tied the big cow to the crossbar.

"That ought to hold her there. I don't think that tree will hold the other one, so we had better find another crossbar to hold the spike." James stated.

After they pulled the other elk up about four feet off the ground, they rode over to where Ernest and Harry had made their kill.

"That is one big bull you shot there." James told Harry. "I don't see how we can pull it up off the ground. It has to weigh more than our horses."

"Maybe if we were to cut it in two, we could pull half of it up." Harry suggested excitedly.

"That is a good idea, but it is going to take us all night to cut it in two with our knives." Ernest predicted.

"It so happens I brought along a saw and an ax. We can cut that monster's head off and then cut through the backstrap to expose its backbone. If you tie your ropes onto its front legs and pull in the opposite direction, I will cut through the backbone." James explained to the hunters.

They stripped the hide off the bull and cut off the backstrap. Then James and Harry set to work and sawed through the length of the backbone from its neck to its tail. Once they had it cut in half, they pulled each half up and tied it to a crossbar like the one they had done with James's cow. It was growing dark when they finished.

"We need to carry this big buck and calf over to where Lester made his kill and finish this up while we can still see to get back to camp. Harry and I will carry the backstrap. One of the pack animals can haul the buck, and the other can haul the calf." They cut the buck in two so that both Lester and Ernest could carry some of the load. They followed Lester over to where he had shot his cow.

"Wow, that cow is almost as big as Harry's bull." James helped them cut the cow in half as they had done with the big bull. It was fully dark by the time they had the cow tied off on its crossbar. "We had better just haul this buck and calf back to camp. I will lead the way while you three follow behind with your loads," James said.

Bringing It Home

It was well past midnight when they reached camp. They tied the buck and calf up off the ground. Lester started up the campfire and cooked up a meal from the heart and liver they had removed from the buck. Harry helped Ernest unsaddle their horses and lead them off to drink and then hobbled them next to the pack animals to graze. James retrieved a pot of water from the creek and set it on to boil. "I know our wives are great cooks, but a hunting camp meal like this is about the best I have ever eaten," Lester said.

After the men had eaten their fill and loaded up with coffee, they laid their heads against their saddles, pulled a blanket over themselves, and fell immediately off to sleep.

Morning came too quickly as they awoke to the aroma of coffee and steak cooking over the campfire by James. The trees wore a frost coat, and it looked like they had a dusting of snow. James looked a little concerned. "You had better get up and begin packing our meat off this mountain before a blizzard locks us here all winter. I am not sure our pack animals can carry all our meat down to the wagons. We might have to leave some of it behind."

Lester shook his head. "I'd sure hate to do that. I would have soon not shot anything if we had to leave it behind."

"Since it is almost all downhill, maybe we could just drag it down." Harry suggested.

"That's not a bad idea, but we would ruin the meat to bounce it over the rocks," Ernest stated.

James considered the problem and scratched his head. "Wait a minute, Harry has a good idea. We can build a travois like the ones I have seen built by Indians. They haul some heavy objects on these. I think that we could bring out all our meat on travoises tied to the back of our horses. Yep, I think it will work."

"It sure will not hurt to try," Ernest stated.

They led the pack animals over to where James had killed his two animals and lowered the first one down onto the pack animal. The bull was more than a pack animal could carry, so James said, "Harry, ride over to that grove of trees and cut down several saplings eight to ten feet long, at least three inches in diameter. Cut several other strong ones at least three feet long."

James looked around his kill site. "It looks like the predators were busy last night and cleaned up the mess we left for them when we dressed out the animals. I see where they even tried to reach the animals that we tied up off the ground. It was good that we raised them off the ground as high as we did, or otherwise they would have dragged them down."

When Harry returned, they tied one of the long poles on each side of one of the pack animals and tied the three-foot crossbars between the two poles with strips of hide they took from the elk. Next, they pulled it under the young bull and lowered it onto the travois. James secured the bull to the travois. The pack animals did not appear to be too overloaded. They led the pack animals over to the cow elk and tied the loaded pack animals off while they dropped half of James's cow onto each of two travoises and led them back to Lester's kill site.

The remaining pack horse could not carry Lester's cow, so he made another travois to haul the big elk down. They went over to Harry's big bull and loaded it on two travoises. Fully loaded now, they worked their way back to their campsite. It was slow going, but by noon, they pulled in to their evening camp. They quickly loaded half the buck on Ernest's horse and the other half on Lester's. James took the lead, trailing one of the pack animals toting the travois.

Harry looked at the sun as it slowly began sinking low in the west. "We are not going to make it down before dark. Should we look for another camp?"

James considered the alternatives. "No. We had better just keep moving no matter how long it takes. We need to get back to our wagons. Stopping and unloading then reloading will be as much work as if we just keep on moving on down the hill."

They rested the horses often, and James led them directly back down to the wagon camp. They arrived at midnight. Their families were very worried about them and waited up with coffee brewing until they arrived. Sylvia and Margret ran into the weary arms of their husbands.

"We were so worried that one of you might have gotten hurt," Sylvia said. "And Shirley was very worried about Harry. Even Mary showed her concern over her twin."

"Shirley shouldn't have worried over Harry. He brought down the biggest bull I have ever seen. He has not stopped bragging about it since he shot it. No doubt, he will fill everyone in on every detail. He could not stop talking about it all the way down the mountain. He reminds me of myself when I brought in my first deer." Ernest teased.

The men unloaded their burden. Ernest and Harry led their horses to water and let them graze. The men crawled into their blankets and slept until dawn.

The men of the camp had already begun the process of cutting up the meat the hunters had brought in. They had a fire going under the meat that they cut into strips. Joshua made a decision. "We had better stay over one more day to dry the rest of this meat and work on the hides. We were running low, and this will see us through for quite a while. Since the ladies have roasted the backstrap, we ought to have a good celebration today on the return of our hunters."

When James, Lester, Harry, and Ernest arose, they walked over to where John was directing the drying process. "Hey, guys, it looks like they don't need us to help them make jerky. I think they have the hang of it." James smiled.

John looked over at the pile of meat. "Whenever someone brings in the meat, we can do our part and dry it for you. You boys have done enough, so enjoy your families this day and take the rest of the day off. We owe you that much for all you've done."

"Son." John told Harry, "I would have told you last night, but you just grunted and dragged yourself into the back of our wagon and went right to sleep. Your mother and I are very proud of you. Your sister cannot stop talking about that big bull you brought in. She just cannot wait until you tell us all about your hunting trip."

"Oh no, do not get him started. You will not be able to stop that boy once he gets to running his lips." Ernest teased.

Harry walked right over and told Mary and his mom an exaggerated version of how he had killed the big elk. After the long-drawn-out story, Mary said with a smirk, "Now that is a lot of bull."

"Mary!" her mother reprimanded.

"I am sorry." Mary said with a giggle. "I just could not help myself."

"Thank you for cutting up the meat." James came around the tree line munching on a big chunk of backstrap. "We will take you up on your recommendation and take the rest of the day off. I believe that we have enough meat to last for a long time, especially after it is salted, seasoned, and dried."

The next morning, the fully loaded wagon train moved out again toward the west. The mountains loomed higher on their left, and rolling hills sprouted on their right. Joshua routed the train between the two mountain ranges. James, Ernest, and Lester rode ahead, scouting for any sign of danger. "The Blackfeet roam through this area." James told the other two scouts. "Be on the lookout for any sign of unshod hoofprints or any sign of recent

Indian campsites. The Blackfeet are a vicious warring band of Indians that love to lift scalps from any white eyes they find."

Lester ran his fingers through his hair. "I for one am rather attached to my hair. I sure don't want to lose it before it naturally falls out like ole James here. Ernest, Sylvia would be some upset to see that flaming red hair of yours sticking on the rod of some spear."

"I'd be rather upset of that happening myself. I will ride a few miles to the north and look over the valley in that direction," Ernest said.

"While in Denver, I spoke to some mountain men. They said that a few years ago, the president commissioned Lewis and Clark to take an expedition through this area. They mapped out good trade routes to the west. I am not sure how far they have traveled, but from what I heard, they planned to travel all the way to the Pacific Ocean, close to where we are heading. They met a Shoshone woman called Sacagawea that agreed to guide them. I would sure like to meet up with them and look over the maps that they are producing," James said.

"I read that she died back in 1812," Ernest said. "As a young maiden, she was bought by that French trapper, Toussaint Charbonneau. She apparently became his wife and had two children by him. One boy by the name of Jean-Baptiste and gave birth to a girl by the name of Lizette. I heard a lot of different tales as to what happened to her. Some said that she died just a few years after giving birth to Lizette, while others said she lived to be quite old. Apparently, William Clark took the boy with him to give him a white man's education in Missouri. The boy even went to Europe and learned many languages, then returned to travel throughout the west as a frontiersman."

An hour later after Lester left to return to the wagons, Ernest tied his horse to a sapling and, as was his practice, cautiously approached the valley and peered over the crest overlooking the valley. He stood motionless as he surveyed the area, knowing that any movement was the first sign an observer would detect. He scanned the area himself for any sign of movement and listened intently for any unnatural sound. There was a little cool breeze blowing from the west. The breeze would keep his scent from by any animal, either four- or two-legged. He watched for half an hour before retrieving his mount and riding through the tree line around the valley to its north.

The valley contained scrub oak and sage. The pinion pine trees that lined the valley were windblown and showed evidence of their struggle with nature to survive. They could tell a story themselves of the hardship they had faced in their lifetime. Ernest wished they could speak and would love to hear the tales of their survival. Some areas showed signs of a recent fire; other areas showed how high winds had toppled them over. He had heard of high straight line winds knocking down hundreds of acres of forest but had never experienced it himself. Many small trails meandered through the area and showed various prints of animals. He did not see any unshod hoofprints of Indians but was not deceived into thinking that there was none in the area. He let his mind wander a bit and wondered what his future held. *Would he live to enjoy a peaceful time with his children tagging along with him to experience the beauty of nature? Would Sylvia and their children ever enjoy the smell of fresh-turned soil and witness the life-giving seedlings springing from the earth that they had planted? Would they enjoy peaceful Indian neighbors, or have a continual fight to survive the harsh land?*

Tomcat

While he was reminiscing, the ears of his horse suddenly sprung up, and it looked off to his right. Ernest brought the horse to a stop, pulled his rifle from its scabbard, and laid it across his lap as his horse stood trembling. A loud yowl brought his eyes to the top of a branch just overhead. A golden-tan mountain lion flung itself toward them as his mount lunged to its left in trying to spring out of its way. Ernest lifted his rifle and fired it by instinct as he felt the impact of the beast dislodge him from the saddle and felt its claws ripping through his coat. He flew from the saddle and hit the ground hard, knocking the air from his lungs. He had managed to hang on to the rifle and automatically chambered in another round while he looked around for the large cat. It had landed ten feet from him and was squirreling around in a circle.

Ernest, gasping for a breath and ignoring his pain, leaned over and shot the beast again. It reared up on its hind legs, glaring viciously at him with its evil-looking eyes, let out another ear-piercing scream, fell over backward quivering, then lay still. Having regained his breath, Ernest sat up and surveyed the damage to himself and his horse. His horse was still running and kicking down into the valley with the stirrups flying in the breeze, bumping into its sides. Ernest hoped his horse would calm down shortly and let him track him down. He felt a sticky substance oozing from his shoulder and looked down to find the claws had penetrated his heavy coat and pierced his right arm just below the shoulder. The mountain lion that had attacked him looked to weigh over 250 pounds. He thought of Sylvia and wished that she were there to attend his wounds. After watching her tend the wounds of many others, he knew what she would have him do. He first had to tend to his own wounds, and then search for his horse.

He took off the heavy buffalo coat that had saved his life and began to wipe away the blood. After he cleaned it the best he could with his shirttail, he ripped the sleeve off his left arm and used it to bandage his right arm. He was sore but felt very lucky to be alive. Had his first shot gone astray, the cat would have killed him instantly. He trudged back into his coat, walked over, and kicked the lion. He had heard the ole mountain men brag about how sweet the meat of a big cat tasted. Therefore, he dressed out the cat and wedged it into a tree to drain then went looking for his horse. His bay had been a good riding companion and should not have run to far off.

It took two hours to track down the bay that stood grazing in a little meadow. Ernest talked softly so as not to spook her. As gently as possible, he reached up and took a hold of her bridle. She was still nervous as he checked her over to see that she was not hurt, then he mounted and rode back to where he had killed the lion. His bay did not want to get anywhere close to the big cat, but with gentle persuasion, he succeeded in tying her nearby. It was getting late, and he had not brought much to eat, so he built a little fire and cooked a little of the cat. The old mountain men knew what they were talking about, so he decided to carry it back to the wagon train with him. His bay did not like the idea of carrying that cat but succumbed to his will.

It was well after dark when Ernest rode into the circle of the wagons. They were all worried about him, and Sylvia came running up to him and saw the blood-soaked coat he was wearing and the big cat he had draped over the back of the bay.

"What happened?" Sylvia asked. "Lester came back a long time ago and was forming a group to go out to look for you. Are you all right? Why did you bring in that?"

"I am fine. I just had a little dance with this ole tomcat. He tried to jump into my lap while I was scoping out a little valley. I was lucky and had already drawn my rifle. He did not fair so well though. As he knocked me off my horse, he ran his claws through my coat and clawed me a little."

"Well, get down and take your coat off while I go get my medicine bag and some clean cloth. Cats' claws are laden with rotten meat, and when something gets clawed by one, infection sets in rather quickly." Sylvia hurried off to their wagon and grabbed her medicine bag. They already had hot water boiling on the campfire preparing for coffee, and she poured some out into a pan and started cleaning the wound.

James and Lester hurried over from their wagons, and they looked very concerned. "We got a little worried when you hadn't shown up. We thought that you had run into some Indian trouble since you were late getting in. I see that you still have most of your hair, so you must not have had any problems with them. Whoa now, that is a fine-looking scar. It will make a nice little story to tell your grandkids." Lester looked at what Ernest brought in. "Just what do you want us to do with that big ole tom?"

"I ate a little of his hind quarter, and he tasted pretty good. I heard that the old mountain men can make some good stew with them."

"I am not touching that thing." Sylvia pointed to the big cat.

Shirley came over, an old hand at cooking whatever was available, and said, "That's all right. While you doctor up Ernest's shoulder, I will begin cooking that ole boy up. If it tastes decent, we can share it with the rest of the camp. I am glad that you brought it in with its coat on. It will make your wife a beautiful coat. I am sure she will be glad to wear it when I finish tanning and sewing it."

"I do not know. It will just remind me how close we came to losing you."

"Ouch!" Ernest exclaimed. "What are you doing?"

"I am just pouring on a little whiskey onto your wound to disinfect it."

"Why don't you just rub a little salt into it while you are at it?"

"You keep it up, I just might. The wound is pretty deep, so I will need to put some stitches in it to close it up."

"I had a feeling that you would want to do something like that. You had better let me have a little drink before you start poking needles in me."

"I am not going to let you have any whiskey. You can have some laudanum instead."

"Here, I thought you would be a fun-loving wife."

"Oh, I am fun and loving, yes. However, I cannot be that way when you are wounded and drunk. Now bite down on this leather strap and show me how big a man you are."

"Yeeow! You need to let that laudanum work before you start poking me."

"You big baby, just bite down a little harder on that strap. I will be done before you know it."

"That really smells good." John sniffed as he came into camp from his guard duty. "Whatcha got cookin', darlin'?" he asked Shirley and grabbed her around the waist, hugging her.

"Here, taste it, and let me know what ya think." Shirley handed him a ladle filled with tomcat stew.

"Hmm... That does taste good. I sure would like a couple bowls of that. What is in it?"

"Well, I added some vegetables and wild onions to this tomcat stew I made. Do you think it is good enough to share with the rest of the camp?"

"I don't care if it is groundhog. It tastes really good. By all means, it is good enough to share with the King of England."

"See, Red, I told you it was worth bringing back to camp," Ernest said.

"It may taste good to you, but in my condition, I don't think I could hold a bit of it down."

Mary came over to Sylvia and put her arms around her. "I am sorry you are not feeling well. I am sure that it will all be worth it though. I just cannot wait to see little redheaded Johnny or a little Susie running around, tugging at your skirt."

"Thank you, that makes this sick feeling seem so miniscule. Someday, you will have your knight in shining armor and children of your own. I don't think it will be too far from now either. You are blossoming into a beautiful woman. I can't wait to see who you will find and what he will look like."

"I was kind of wishing that Ray would stick around and I could get to know him better, but I expect I will never see him or Louis again. At night, I dream about the battles they are in and shudder. I pray that they will not be harmed and make it out of the war unharmed."

"Honey, you need to start looking ahead, not behind to what could have been. God saw fit to send them on their way. You have to start living your own life and not fret about those two. I know that you miss him. I would never ask you not to pray for anyone's well-being. I learned a long time ago that to help someone, you should not get too emotionally involved with your patient. You have to learn to give them care without letting them pull at your heartstrings. That is the hardest thing to do when you help someone, to show them care without caring too much for them."

"I don't know if I could ever do that. When I care for a hurt animal, I start to love it, and it tears me up to send it on its way after it heals up."

"That is what makes you such a good caregiver. You care. Just don't care so much that it breaks your heart every time. Remember, love is a complex emotion. You can give care with love, but always reserve your special love for something that will love you back. Be very sure before you give that special love for your one and only. You only have one chance to give that special love, so you must be absolutely sure before you give it away."

"Thank you, Sylvia. You are a wonderful friend."

Utah Territory

It was December when the wagon train reached a mining settlement in the Utah Territory. Ernest looked at Sylvia. "Did you know it has been over nine months since we had left Ireland? I do not know about you, but I am ready to settle down to a quieter life. This is beautiful country. Why don't we tell Joshua, our wagon master, that we will leave here and find us a place to live out the winter?"

"I am ready. I am getting as big as a barn. I remember that newspaper article we received in Denver. It read, 'Throughout the Utah Territory, soldiers are in place during this Civil War time. The settlement around the Salt Lake is ripe for farming, mining, and raising a family where the Indians are still friendly.' I know it is full of egotistical Mormons, but there are others as well as friendly Indians. Mormons are religious people who generally treat others right. All anyone can ask is fair treatment. I just don't want to give birth to our baby aboard a wagon train that is in continual motion. We will want some quiet time with it and with each other. Besides, I never thought I would be starting our family before I had a roof over my head."

"You will not be. I promise, we will find a spot and erect a cabin before the baby comes. Maybe we can even find that little garden spot overlooking a little stream with the mountains in the background that you dreamed about."

That evening when they stopped just north of a mountain range, Sylvia spoke to Margret and Shirley. "Margret, Ernest and

I are leaving the wagon train and are planning to cross over these mountains to the south into the Utah Valley and build a cabin to winter there. From everything I have read, it is a beautiful valley, and we should be happy there. I hate to leave the wagon train and all our wonderful friends here without completing the journey, but I have to think about giving birth shortly."

"Well, I need to talk to Lester and get him to agree to stop here too. I do not want you to have your baby alone. I have grown too close to you both. We want to live beside you. Besides, as the old saying goes, two hands are better than one. We need each other, and if that is as rich a valley as we have heard, how can we go wrong? I see no reason to continue farther west."

Shirley looked at Sylvia with tears in her eyes. "John does not want to stop until we reach Oregon. We set out with Oregon in mind, and we have given up everything to reach it. I tried to convince him that we should stop here and build our place alongside of yours and Lester's, but John's heart is set on reaching Oregon before we stop. I am sorry, but we are going to continue on to Oregon. My heart and love go out to you. We will miss you and will pray for your safety. Please, if you ever get to Oregon, stop and look us up."

Sylvia hugged Mary and Shirley and said their good-byes. Mary cried as she hugged Sylvia. "I want to go with you so bad and watch your family grow. However, I think you are right, that I must make some choices myself. My heart hurts, but I know you are making the right decision for your family. If Mom and Dad's heart was not so set on Oregon and the free homestead land there, I might have been able to change their minds. I tried, but they are determined to make it to the West Coast before winter. I love you and will miss you so much."

Ernest and Lester shook Joshua's and John's hands and thanked them for everything they had done. Ernest shook Harry's hand and told him to keep his powder dry and that he might have to scout for Joshua as they traveled on into Oregon. Edward and

Joseph also shook Ernest's and Lester's hands and hugged Sylvia and Margret. "We are going to miss you all," they said, teary-eyed, as the two couples went down the line shaking and hugging everyone on the train, saying their good-byes.

Ernest ruffled up Joseph's hair. "You never know, we just might see each other again one day. We know where you are headed in Oregon, and if we ever get a chance, we will look ya up."

Early the next morning as the wagon train prepared to leave, the Walkers and Clarks pulled their wagons out of the circle and headed south over the mountain pass while the wagon train continued west. They had made many friends, but no matter how painful, they had to make some choices of their own.

It took another three days of hard travel to cross over the mountain and down into the salty valley, but their excitement was building. Both families looked forward to a new beginning and sinking roots into what had become their childhood dreams. Looking down into the valley from the top of the mountain, they saw a busy community. Smoke rose from the settlement and its smelting plants that were scattered in the hills.

"Let's continue west away from the hustle and bustle of those communities where the farm ground has not been broken up yet."

Ernest found a beautiful little stream at the edge of a mountain. "The mountains will protect us from the wind, and it has a beautiful overlook view. This is where we are going to live." Ernest told Sylvia. "I am going to build us your cabin right here. The ground is fertile, and there are plenty of timber and rock for us to use. What do you think of this, Lester?"

"I think we should park our wagons and start building our cabins."

"In the morning, Lester and I will ride into the settlement and find out what the process is for calling this land ours. While we are gone, you two women can start a campfire and get us settled. Also, you might want to look around and see where you might want us to build our cabins. Keep up a vigil watching for Indians. We do not know this area yet, who or what is lingering about."

Early the next morning while the dew was still on the tall grass and fog rose from the great salty lake, Ernest and Lester rode into the settlement. The pioneers that had laid out this town showed forethought and strict governing. The streets ran north, south, east, and west in even blocks. Houses were not adjacent to the business district. The settlement was waking up as the two men rode down the street, looking at the names of the businesses. They tied their mounts to the rail in front of a building that toted the sign of Land Office and walked in. There were maps strung around the office on its walls with circles drawn on them. Ernest located the area where they had made camp while Lester spoke to the agent. "We came on a wagon train all the way from New York and want to settle in this valley. Two of us split off from the wagon train that is on its way to Oregon, but we decided to build our farms here. Ernest can show you on the map where we are currently camped. We would like to know what we need to do to file a claim on that property."

"Well now, let me take a look and see where you are camped." The agent scanned the map where Ernest pointed. "I am sorry, but that whole area you are looking at is part of the Ute Indian nation that we have reserved for them. They don't do much with it except ride their horses over it and shoot a few deer. I cannot assist you there. If your heart is set on that land, you will have to get permission from the Ute nation. They have a camp just north of where you pointed and don't take kindly to any squatters setting on their land."

"Well, can you show us where land is available for us to settle on?" Ernest asked with a little discust.

He traced his finger around on a red line that marked where the valley was. "Unless you are Mormon and have permission from the bishop, you cannot settle anyplace within this area. The area outside this region is a reservation for the Indians that were here when we arrived. You will have to deal with them if you are wanting to squat on their land. Sometimes they make exception and allow farms to raise produce. However, they do require a large portion of whatever you produce to feed their tribes."

The answer was not what they wanted to hear. "Where is this bishop at that we have to get permission from?" Ernest asked.

"Well, he lives in that large stone structure that is in the center of the settlement. You cannot miss it. If he gives you permission to settle within the church's valley, he will let you know our requirements. You won't be able to own the land, but you can live on it and grow produce for yourselves and the church."

As Ernest and Lester left the land office, Ernest told Lester, "I thought that we could make a claim on that property. I am very disappointed. I don't know about you, but I do not want to be controlled by their church. Besides, I know what my Irish wife would say to me if I told her she would have to become a Mormon to live here."

"I am with you. Maybe it is best we head back over the mountains and catch up with the wagon train and head to Oregon."

"If Red was not so far along, I would agree with you. Let's go over and talk to the Utes and see if we can negotiate with them."

UTE LAND

It was getting late in the day when they rode up to the Ute Indian camp. The Ute children were running through the camp playing games when they saw the two white men ride in. They ran around the two men talking rapidly in a language that neither could understand. The boys had a hold of their horses' reins and led them to a teepee in the center of their village. A broad-shouldered Indian opened the teepee's flap and stood before the two riders with his arms crossed across his chest, staring at the two.

Ernest spoke. "My name is Ernest Walker, and this is Lester Clark. We have traveled a long way looking for a place to settle. Our two wagons are about five miles south of here. We thought we could get claim on the land by talking to the land agent in the settlement southeast of here. They explained that we would have to get permission from you to settle there."

"Hmmp, you belong to that religion?" The chieftain spoke in perfect broken English.

"No. When we rode into Denver, we read a newspaper article that described their religion. My wife and I are from Ireland and are not part of their religious movement, nor do we plan to be converted. We were traveling to Oregon and would have continued, but our wives became pregnant, and we are both expecting our first child. We were worried about them and thought we could build our lives here in this beautiful valley. We want to till the land, grow crops, and maybe raise some sheep. We are peaceful and do not want any trouble."

"You keep on moving. Oregon west of here. You find good dirt there to sink plows into."

"Our wives cannot travel that far in their condition. We have to make a shelter here for them or they will perish, and we could not stand for that to happen. We will do everything we can to be good neighbors to you. We know that this is land you use and will be honored if you will let us share it with you," Ernest stated.

"That is what Mormon invaders said. Now, they enslave our young people and demand we work in their fields. Additionally, they demand we believe as they do. We will not. What you want from us?"

Ernest looked at Lester and told the chieftain. "Only that you accept our hospitality and let us work a few acres of land for our own needs. We would like to be good neighbors to you and will share anything we have that we do not need. We only want to use this land to build and grow our family. We do have needs, but they are few. We will need to use some timber to build our cabins and will need to trade with you for livestock that we may grow. We don't expect anything free but will trade honestly for anything we get. We are honest, hardworking, peaceful families. We would never take anything from you without your approval. I believe that we could help each other out. We offer our strong backs and will be peaceful neighbors to you. If we are ever a burden to you, tell us what we can do to correct the situation. If we cannot, we will move on. That is the best that we can do."

"What will you do when those religious people want to take the land you are on or want to take one of your family members?"

"They will not. It is not our land. We are just using it. We would fight anyone who would try enslaving or harming any of our family members. We came from a country where people enslaved others, and we will fight for that not to happen to us here. If it comes to that, we will fight or move and search out a more peaceful settlement." Ernest spoke his convictions.

"You may stay as long as you do what you say. If you break your word, steal anything, or cause us any harm, my people will kill you, burn down your cabins, and take your livestock. We are a peaceful people, until someone tries to take advantage. When that happens, we can be a very vicious neighbor."

"Thank you. You will not regret having us as your neighbor," Lester said.

With that, they turned their mounts and headed back to their wagons. They had camped alongside a clear little creek that flowed from the nearby mountain. They were on a gentle slope that overlooked the beautiful flowered green valley. It was a beautiful spot and would make a good ranch. Their horses plodded among the tall grass as they made their way back to their wagon camp. "I think that we will be happy here," Ernest spoke to Lester. "We have traveled very far, and this is the most beautiful spot we have seen. I am sure there are other areas that would be a good place to live, but I think that we were lucky to find this area with peaceful neighbors."

Sylvia looked off to the north. "Here they come. I am a bit surprised that they are coming back from that direction when the settlement is to our east. I wonder where they've been and am anxious to hear all about it."

When they pulled up, Margret and Sylvia were all questions. It was getting dark, so they sat around the fire while Ernest explained to them that they were on the Ute land and only granted permission to use their land. "We do not have claim on this land but have just been granted permission to stay as long as we are good neighbors. I gave them our word that we would. They seem to be upset with the Mormon community and want nothing to do with them. Apparently, the Mormons have been ruling over the Indians since they arrived. These Native Americans have inhabited this land for many generations, and now they have to share it with outsiders, strange people with strange customs. They are having trouble accepting this change. I think that if we will just be friendly and good neighbors, not trying to change their way of life, that we will be welcome here. I just don't know about those Mormons and their strange customs. I am worried that when they outgrow their community, they will push to inhabit this land and run the Utes farther off their land. However, that should be several years away. We just have to keep in mind that we may have to leave here when they begin to push this way."

"Margret and I have staked out our cabins. We put them close together for security, but far enough away that we will not get in each other's way. You can see in the morning where we would like them to be built. Now all you two boys have to do is build us cabins that we can live in and call home. We know that it may be temporary, but so is this life. We are here in this life God gave us for a short time, and we need to live it the best we can." Sylvia excitedly explained to their husbands.

"It has been a hard day. Let's turn in and see what you wo women have decided in the morning," Lester said.

Early the next morning, Ernest and Lester surveyed where their wives had staked out their cabins. "It looks like they had given a lot of thought into where they wanted these cabins built. I guess we had better get started if we are going to get them up before the snow flies. I will hitch up Ole Blue and start clearing a space for our foundation," Lester said.

"It looks like you have a good plan. While you are doing that, I will hitch up the wagon and haul in those large flat rocks from the creek to set the cabin on," Ernest said.

While they were working, two families of the Utes came over to Lester, who was leveling out the runway for the foundation. "We help you."

"Well, we don't have much we can give you for your help right now. We are just getting started."

"We not asked for anything. We just help with work."

"I don't know what to say except thank you. We just do not want to take advantage of you or your family."

"You are not. They just sitting around being lazy. You helping us by letting us help you. My name Bear Claw, this my squaw Blue Sky, and my young brave Running Dog."

Another family went over to help Ernest load the rocks onto the wagon. "We here to help you build shelter. My name Sees Far. This my squaw Mare-ah and my daughter, Perl. Mare-ah and I help load rock. Perl drive your wagon."

Ernest did not know what to say, so he just said, "Thank you. Your help is appreciated."

The squaw grabbed a rock, grunted, and placed it on the wagon while the young Ute maiden climbed aboard the wagon and moved it forward. It did not take long before the wagon was loaded and back to the cabin site, unloading the rock. Ernest was very grateful for their help. "I cannot believe that you would just come over to help us, but thank you very much."

"We glad to help. We rather help you than the Mormons. They expect it and quite demanding. We work for food, if you have something decent to eat."

"Lunch is ready!" Sylvia hollered. "I saw we had some guests and prepared an extra portion for them."

Bear Claw sniffed the air. "It smells good enough to eat. We hope you don't mind us sitting down and eating with you. We usually sit on blanket to eat. Mormons laugh at us for our practices. They try get us sit on chairs and at their table. They try get us not eat with our fingers. What fingers for, if not use them put food into our mouths? We don't mind that too much, but they constantly demand we conform to their ways. We Utes have our own ways that we are used to and comfortable with. We are resistant to conforming to the ways of others. We think our ways are as good as theirs."

"Hi, my name is Sylvia, and this is my friend Margret," Sylvia said to the squaw that had been helping Lester. "Bear Claw has said that you are resistant to change. Are not we all. I grew up in Ireland and lived out of a wagon for most of my life. I believe that I now want to live in something that is not constantly moving."

Black Bear

The squaw turned to Sylvia. "My English name Mare-ah. I see you full in stomach, and your friend filling up too. When your time here, my friend Blue Sky and I help. We've much experience giving life."

"Aye." Sylvia laughed. "We are both pregnant. I am due to give birth shortly, and Margret is a few months away. Please join us for lunch, and thank you for helping construct our cabins. I am glad that you speak English. That way we can communicate easily. I speak a few languages. Maybe you can teach me to speak yours."

"Yes, I love teach you our tongue and even our sign language."

After lunch, Ernest brought over several more loads of rock, thanks to the help of the Ute family. "I think I will take one of the draft animals and look over the timber we need for our cabin. Maybe I can bring back a log or two for the foundation to set the cabin on before it gets too dark."

He found the logs he was looking for. It was not a thick forest but did contain a good selection of solid large trees. As he started to dismount, he saw a little movement in the trees. He pulled his rifle out of its scabbard and watched intently among the trees. A large buck stepped into a clearing, investigating the animals that Ernest had rode in on. It was his fatal mistake. Ernest brought up his rifle and downed the deer. He dressed out the deer and then cut down the log he spotted. He loaded the deer onto his mount, hooked the draft animal up to the log, and brought them both back to the wagons.

"I thought I heard a shot." Lester said and helped Ernest lower the buck. You brought us a mighty fine-looking buck. Why don't we share half of it with our Ute friends?"

"Good idea. I was hoping that we could find something to give back to them to show them our goodwill."

Ernest split the deer down the middle and hauled half the carcass over to the Ute families who had helped them with the cabin. They were pleased and nodded their approval as Blue Sky and Mare-ah began unloading the gift. "Thank you for your help and for the land to use. You are welcome to come by and visit us anytime."

The next morning, the two Ute families returned to help. They all worked hard. One family helped Lester to finish placing the rocks and notch the logs. Lester used the plow and dragged a log over the ground to level it off for the second cabin site. They placed the log that Ernest had brought in on top of a pile of rocks on one side for the first cabin. Lester told him, "We are going to need a lot more of logs about this same size you brought in. I think that we have enough rocks for a while, so why don't you use Sees Far and his family, Mare-ah and Perl, to help you."

Ernest helped Perl and Mare-ah up on two of the large draft animals while Sees Far crawled on another. Perl laughed. "It feels like I can touch sky from way up here. This a very big animal, the biggest I ever been on."

"Well, you be careful up there, and don't fall off. It is a long ways to the ground from the top of Ole Blue. He is one of our biggest animals, but he is as gentle as a kitten."

"I do not see how I fall off this wide platform." She giggled. "It feels like I am doing splits."

Sylvia and Margret watched as Ernest led the procession north toward the work site.

The Ute, Bear Claw, who was helping Lester, told him, "My boy and I build the fireplace for you. I helped Mormons and learned know how to construct it." Running Dog searched the creek and found a spot that contained generous portions of clay. He gathered the clay mud from the creek and dumped it into a bucket. Blue Sky mixed the mud with hair from the hide off the buck and handed the muck to Bear Claw to form the fireplace. They worked hard for the next three days. When they finished, it was not just a fireplace but contained an oven as well. Lester was very impressed as he watched Bear Claw and his family construct the structure.

Ernest was busy chopping down trees while Sees Far handled the draft horses. Mare-ah and Perl trimmed the branches off the fallen trees. Sees Far tied the ropes to the fallen logs and brought them down for the cabin walls. Whenever a log arrived, Bear Claw and Sees Far helped Lester to lift the log on top of another to begin to form the walls. Then Sees Far rode back to where Ernest was working to rope another log. While Sees Far was gone, Mare-ah and Perl searched through the brush and spotted a hillside of blueberry bushes. It was late in the year, but there were still some loaded with berries. They picked the berries and placed them in a scarf they had brought. It was not long before they had several bunches of berries.

Ernest fell another tree as he saw the two approaching. "I wondered where you two went. I see you have been very busy."

Perl handed her basket to Ernest. "Here, try one."

"Mmm, those are very sweet and juicy. Are there any left?"

Mare-ah smiled. "Oh, yes. We only picked a few of them. There is whole hillside of them."

When they finished for the day, Ernest brought a handful of the berries back to the wagon and showed Sylvia and Margret. They were quite excited and begged to go with him the next morning to pick the blueberries.

Early the next morning, Ernest hitched up the wagon, handed Margret the reins, and helped Sylvia aboard.

"You know, I can still ride a horse."

"I shouldn't even let you ride in the wagon. It looks like you are very close to delivery. I told you that you should just stay here at the wagons and stay off your feet."

"I may be as big as a barn, but I am not crippled. I am looking forward to picking the berries. I need some exercise too. If I get too tired, I will just stop and rest."

While Ernest and Sees Far's family worked on the logs, Sylvia and Margret picked blueberries. It was midafternoon when he heard Sylvia scream. He grabbed his rifle and ran to where they were picking the berries. They were backing away from the berry patch, and a large black bear was feasting on the berries they had already gathered in their basket. It was looking at the screaming women with what seemed like a smile that was dripping with berry juice. Ernest would have laughed at their antics, but he was worried about the women. At any moment, the bear might take a notion to charge the frightened screamers before him. If he shot and wounded the bear, it would attack his wife and friend. He took careful aim and shot.

The bear let out a loud roar, reeled backward, took two steps, then dropped dead. He quivered and kicked once, then lay still. Sylvia looked back at Ernest and then sat down shaking. Margret put her arm around her and told her that they needed to get back to their wagon camp. "I was worried that it would harm our unborn child more than I was about myself. When I rose up from dropping a handful of berries in the basket, he was staring right at me within a foot from my face. I was so shocked that I was surprised I did not have our baby right there on the spot."

Margret said, "When I looked over to see what you were screaming at, all I could see was something big and black. The brush was hiding you because I could not see you at all. It took me a moment to see what was happening."

Nancy Walker

Ernest brought the wagon over and loaded their berries and the big black bear onto the back of it. "That is the last of your berry picking this year, darlin'. I don't want to lose either you or our baby. I think that you have had enough excitement and exercise to last a while."

"I am sorry. I just wanted to have something special to cook for Christmas."

"I know." He hugged her. "I love you, but we have to watch your health for your sake as well as the baby's. We will have a special Christmas no matter what we eat. You have picked enough for us anyway. Now you need to go back and learn to stay off your feet."

John had given Lester some tools that he had brought from the hardware store he used to manage. Lester was proficient with the tools John had graciously given him. Among the tools he had been given by John and Shirley were an ax, a bit and auger, saw, shovel, and plow. Lester told Bear Claw when he asked about the tools, "We were fortunate to have befriended a family that used to own a hardware store in New York. He brought many tools with him when they left. When we departed from the wagon train, he gave me these to help us with our construction. I sure miss them and hope that they made it to Oregon. Someday, maybe we can meet up with them, and I can repay them for everything they gave us. The other tools we have are ones that Ernest inherited when given a wagon already loaded with supplies. Delaware Indians killed the previous owners of his wagon when they raided us. Our wagon master, Joshua, gave the wagon and all its content to Ernest and Sylvia since they did not have one."

"Hmph." Bear Claw grunted. "Heard about that tribe. Thought they peaceful, but any tribe become hostile when pushed into corner and get feathers ruffled."

"Well, you are right about that. Trappers and settlers taking all their hunting ground had overrun them. Then one of the trappers assulted the sister of the chief. He was seeking revenge and saw us as an easy target as we lumbered across the plains. We were very lucky to have only lost one couple that owned that wagon the Walkers now own. It was quick thinking by our wagon master that saved the rest of us."

The friendly Utes helped them, and within a week, they had the foundations laid and fireplaces made from the rocks in the nearby creek. Three weeks later, just as the first flurries of snow began to fly, they finished roofing their cabins. The women had already moved their belongings from the wagons into their cabin and were cooking over the wood stoves that Ernest had swapped a draft animal for at the Mormon settlement. Before they finished the interior of their cabins, they built a corral and barn where the horses could get out of the weather that was just around the corner. As the winter set in, they used the barn to begin fashioning furniture for the cabin. Lester was a master builder and built a table with chairs and a crib for the baby. One morning, Ernest slipped away, cut down a couple of small fir trees, and brought them into the cabins.

"What is that for?" Sylvia asked.

"Haven't you heard next week is Christmas? Having a Christmas tree is a tradition in this new land we live in. We are going to be having many Christmases here, so we had just as well start. I thought you might want to help decorate it with something to brighten our cabin."

"I had no idea we were that close to Christmas." Sylvia told Margret. "This will be the best Christmas of our new life. I have my husband, cabin, and—oh no! My baby!" Sylvia rose up as her water broke.

"I had better run and fetch Mare-ah and Blue Sky." Ernest ran out the door. Ernest hollered at Lester and then ran to their Ute friends that had helped him build the cabin and told them that Sylvia's water broke, and he needed their help right away. "We're having a baby!" he shouted.

They ran back to the cabin and began preparing to make the delivery. Margret had already poured a bucket of water into a kettle to boil and gathered some clean cloths. "You need to leave now and let us handle the rest." Margret told Ernest. "Blue Sky, Mare-ah, and I have a lot of work to do and you will just get in the way."

The women continually came out of the closed-off room to get more hot water. In one bucket of hot water, they boiled blood-soaked cloths. "You better bring in another bucket of water." Blue Sky told Ernest. "We about out."

An hour later, Ernest stopped his pacing along the front of the cabin when the Ute midwife, Mare-ah, emerged carrying a bundle. "You have baby girl." The midwife handed Ernest a pink baby wrapped in a blanket. "And your wife had normal delivery."

"What a Christmas this will be. I cannot think of a better gift than having a baby girl. I am so excited that I want to shout and sing."

"Go ahead. I am very happy for you as well. Sylvia doing great. She just resting and will awake shortly to feed her," Blue Sky said.

Ernest held the baby up high and danced around the yard singing praises. Lester laughed at his charades.

Margret cut some twigs off a red-berry bush and started decorating the tree. She made a colorful rope with some colored yarn she had and wrapped it around the tree multiple times in a spiral fashion.

Blue Sky pointed out, "Those berries poisonous. It okay to use now, but don't let baby have any of them. They kill her."

Ernest and Lester traded another one of their draft horses to the Utes for a small flock of sheep, a few chickens, a cow, and a sheepdog. They thought they would need the milk from the cow to strengthen Sylvia and the new girl. They named the baby girl Nancy, after Sylvia's mother. The young Great Pyrenean Mountain sheepdog they named Ole Shep.

Sylvia was excited about having the big sheepdog. She explained. "Ernest, this breed has been used for hundred of years by the Basque. It will grow to a large white nocturnal guard dog and is very aggressive at night whenever a predator threatens its flock. It will keep the wolves away from our sheep and help protect our children."

"When do we expect these sheep to give birth to their lambs?" Lester asked Bear Claw.

"Takes around four moons from time ram mates with ewe. They much faster than people. Me think. Ewes will give birth when robins return in spring."

"I was just wondering since we will need to build a shelter for them to keep them from freezing."

Lester kept busy building pens for the cow, sheep, and the chickens. They did not have much but shared everything with each other. Lester loved working the ranch, which gave Ernest time to go hunting. They needed the meat that he brought in to survive the winter. Whenever they had more than they needed, they shared it with their Ute neighbors.

While gathering firewood from the deadfall in the nearby forest, Ernest discovered the presence of turkey droppings and feathers beneath the trees. For the next two hours, he searched the ground and peered into the trees to try to spot any additional roost trees. When he returned to the cabin with firewood, he went to the barn where Lester was working on a special Christmas project and told Lester that he had found where a flock of turkey had been roosting. "Lester, remember when I went hunting with James and brought back a couple of turkeys? James said that he had used several methods to create loud noises, creating a response from turkey. The mature male turkey would respond to these noises with what he called a *shock gobble*. They respond at loud noises such as an owl's hoot, a hawk's scream, a crow's call, or even thunder from a lightning strike. It forces a tom turkey to gobble, thus giving away their location. Once you hear where they are located, it becomes a matter of stealth to find their roost and make your kill. I was thinking that you could make us a couple of types of these noise makers with your wood craftsman skill."

"I will give it a try." Lester pulled out a couple of pieces of hardwood. An hour later, he had a couple of models that they both tried out. They had to practice several times before they achieved the desired results.

"Let's give it a try in the morning. I think it would be a real treat to have several turkeys ready for our Christmas."

First Christmas

Ernest and Lester went hunting before sunrise the next morning, the day before Christmas. It was very dark and chilly as they rode up to the forest where a couple of inches of snow had fallen. When they neared the site where Ernest had found the turkey droppings and feathers under the trees, they used the calls that Lester had fashioned. They tried an owl hoot, made by blowing a short burst of air through a hole Lester had bored in a branch of hardwood. The mimic of an owl's hoot surprisingly produced an immediate turkey gobble response just ahead of them in the trees. They quietly separated and slowly approached the trees. Lester was at the left and Ernest to the right. They waited quietly while the sun began to rise in the east enough for them to see the large dark blobs sitting on tree branches high above them. The two hunters raised their shotguns and took aim. With a signal from Ernest, they both squeezed the trigger. Two of the largest bundle of feathers fell from the trees. They both quickly chambered another round in and fired again as the turkeys flew in every direction from the trees. Two more birds fell. One of Lester's birds started running toward some underbrush, and he ran and made a running dive on it before it hid.

"Look out!" Ernest yelled as he ran to assist Lester, who was wrestling with the wild bird, striking him with its sharp feet. Ernest was able to step on its head and break its neck before it did too much damage to Lester.

"Thank you. That bird was just about to claw out my eyes. It sure ought to make quite a feast. Margret will be excited to cook something besides venison."

Margret was excited to receive the big birds. She had Ernest and Lester clean and pluck all of the feathers off the big birds. After they had plucked all the feathers off, they used a flaming stick and singed all of the rest of the down feathers off the skin of the turkey. She boiled the liver, heart, neck, and gizzard with seasoning that Sylvia kept with her spices. Next, she thinly sliced all of the meat off the neck and mixed it with the other sliced meat. She mixed the meat, pine nuts, and seasoning with some bread she had made and stuffed the turkey. Then she slowly roasted two of them in the oven near their fireplace that the Utes had made. Ernest took the two big birds over to the Ute camp, gave one to Blue Sky and the other to Mare-ah, and wished them a Merry Christmas. They were very excited with the gift they received.

A winter storm dropped two feet of heavy snow on them. Early Christmas morning, Ernest plowed a path from their cabin to Lester's and to the barn. Lester went to the barn and milked the cow they called Daisy while Margret fired up her oven and placed the other two stuffed turkeys inside. Sylvia nursed and changed the cooing Nancy then prepared a special breakfast of hot coffee, fried eggs, pancakes, and hot maple syrup. Before she was finished, Ernest and Lester sat at her table drinking the hot coffee, soaking in the aroma of the breakfast, and telling their wives about how they fooled the turkeys into thinking they were an owl. Margret arrived shortly and helped her finish setting breakfast onto the table. Ernest gave a thoughtful prayer of thanks, and they tore into their makings.

Sylvia beamed. "This is the best Christmas ever. Having this bundle of joy straight from God and such wonderful friends is such a blessing. When I left Ireland, I did not know whether I would survive another day. But this"—she motioned with her arms—"is far more than I ever believed was possible. I thank God every morning and evening for all the blessings he has poured on us. I especially thank him for my big ole burly husband, our baby, and our true friends."

Ernest was holding and teasing Nancy. "Well, I think I was the one that was blessed the most. When I left Ireland, I was not sure what was in store for me in this new land. When I accidentally ran into this fiery redhead, she turned my life upside down. I thought I would become a sailor, and then a farmer, then a wagon train master, then it did not matter as long as I could take care of my beautiful wife. When we met this young couple on the wagon train, they became more like our brother and sister that we never had. Lester, you and Margret have been such a blessing to us that has exceeded anything we could have ever dreamed. When this beautiful bundle of joy came along, I realized that nothing else mattered in this world as long as I could keep my wife and child happy. I could live anywhere and do anything. This is living with family and friends."

"Ernest, you and Sylvia have been best thing that has ever happened to Lester and I. I had been praying for someone to befriend, and when I first saw you and Ernest, I knew in my heart that we had found a couple that we would want to spend the rest of our life with as friends. Now you have a child, and I am sprouting one myself. I pray every day that it will be healthy and grow up loving your family as much as we love you."

"I guess it is my turn. I thought I had things together when I married the love of my life. I thought Margret was all that I would ever need, and we were heading for a wonderful life. Well, I was partially right. I have found that life is a continuum of struggles, learning, and growing. I keep thinking that what I have completes me, but then something happens that changes everything. Seeing you two and baby has taught me that nothing completes a family like having an offspring that culminates the love of life. I have to thank God for my wife, you two, and even our Ute neighbors who have kept at peace with us. If it were not for the Mormons, this would be a perfect place to spend the rest of our life. I am concerned about their aggression and whether we will be able to survive their constant taunting us and our Ute neighbors."

"Speaking of Ute neighbors," Sylvia said. "They have arrived to wish us a Merry Christmas." Sylvia rose to greet them at the door. Blue Sky, Mare-ah, and Perl immediately came over to hold Nancy. She cooed, smiled, and laughed at them as they tickled and touched her nose and ears. Mare-ah motioned to Perl to go out and fetch the bundle wrapped up on the back of her horse. She returned and handed the bundle to Sylvia. She was excited as she looked at her gift. It was an Indian blanket for Nancy made from soft doeskin. Inside the blanket was multicolored; it had a couple of handmade baby rattles tied on its edge. Sylvia hugged and thanked them for the beautiful gift.

A few minutes later, Lester returned from his trip to the barn and brought in several packages. He had handmade a wooden baby cradle that rocked. Margret had sewn a couple blankets together and stuffed them with wool to make a soft mattress and pillow for the cradle. They laid Nancy onto the mattress, and she wiggled and cooed, seemingly enjoying her new bed. Having a full stomach and a dry bottom, Nancy soon fell asleep with the constant rocking motion.

Lester handed Running Dog a long package. He opened it to find a precurved bow made of laminated maple wood and half a dozen arrows with turkey feather fletching and stone tips. He handed Bear Claw and Sees Far a bundle of turkey feathers and tanned deer hides. Margret handed Perl a silver comb and a mirror. "I have been carrying these since we left New York. I think that you and Mare-ah can put them to good use. I don't want Blue Sky to be too jealous, so here is a set for her also."

Margret invited them to stay for dinner. "I have roasted a turkey with stuffing, cranberry sauce, mashed potato and gravy, and vegetables. Sylvia made us a special blueberry pie as well. She calls it her blue bearberry pie." She laughed.

"Thank you, but have to return to camp and eat turkey you brought us with rest of tribe."

Ernest held up his hand. "Wait! Before you go, I have one more package that I would like to give you. I cannot just hand it to you. I will have to haul it over to your camp on the wagon. I have a buffalo and a bear hide that has been looking for a good home. I hope that you might find some purpose for it."

"Well, if you cannot eat with us, you can take some of Red's blue bearberry preserves she made." Margret handed them four jars of preserves.

They thanked the Walkers and Clarks for their hospitality and gifts then left to return home.

"Wow, Margret, that was the best meal I think I have ever eaten. I think I had better go out to the barn and milk the cow. Otherwise, I may never get up." Lester told his wife patting his stomach.

"Well, hurry up and milk Daisy. We will have a special dessert and some hot coffee when you return."

When he returned, he had large slices of Sylvia's blue bearberry pie. "Now that was the best dessert I have ever tasted. Uh-oh, sorry, honey, but it was very good, and you do make the best dessert, dear."

"I know. I had a piece of it myself, and it was very good."

They made it through the winter in their cabins with the warmth of their fireplaces. They had a large stack of wood from the leftovers from their building. Ernest had brought down several wagonloads of wood from where they had trimmed the trees. They were sure thankful that their Ute neighbors had helped them. They sure knew how to build a fireplace.

Daniel Clark

When the robins returned singing their melodies in the spring, Bear Claw told Lester that the sheep needed shearing. He had a set of shears and would bring them to him and show him how to use them.

"Don't we have to shear them after they give birth to the new lambs?"

"No, sheepherders think need shear 'em just before lamb. Some, however, think it best wait 'til after lamb. I think former best as long as don't upset ewes. Now, 'fore we start, need washed. Best if wash 'em in warm water, so need make fire and boil water."

Ernest stacked up the wood and started the fire while Running Dog and Perl filled a pot with water from the creek. When the water was warm, they poured the warm water over the backs of the sheep and brushed the dirt and grease off them. Perl and Sylvia laughed at Ernest as he slipped in the mud, and a sheep ran over the top of him.

"Ya know, that reminds me of the time I first met Ernest." Sylvia reminisced laughing. "We were aboard the same ship that sailed from Ireland, and I brought food out on large trays to feed the passengers. When I turned the corner, this big burly boy knocked the tray out of my hands, then slipped and knocked me off my feet as well. When he tried to get up, he slipped on the spilled food, slid around, and fell again. I just could not help it. I just busted out laughing at this big clumsy galoot. I guess you could say he made a big impact on me when we first met."

"All right, Red, come on over and show me how you do this."

"Oh, I would, but I hear Nancy calling for me. Sorry."

Ernest and Lester watched as Bear Claw grabbed one of the washed ewes, gently laid her on her back between his legs, and clipped all of the wool off its underside and then clipped off the wool from her side and back. He handed Ernest the shears. "Think your turn now."

"Ah, go ahead, Lester. I want to watch you first."

Lester grabbed the ewe and gently laid her over on her other side and began clipping off the wool. The shears bound with wool would not cut it. "What am I doing wrong?" the frustrated Lester asked Bear Claw.

Bear Claw stood laughing. "Keep blades of shear together as you clip 'em. If you not keep blades of shear together, they not cut and bind."

"All right, I will try again. Now that works better."

Bear Claw grimaced. "Yes, but you stab her and cut hide, causing her bleed. You keep point from jabbing and keep blades even with body."

"That is harder than I thought it would be. Now, it is your time, Mr. Walker. Here are the shears."

Ernest grabbed another sheep and laid her gently on her back between his legs. He started clipping off the belly wool. He stabbed her in the belly, and Bear Claw cautioned him, "Don't want dress her out like deer, just clip wool off. Those shear blades sharp and can gut animal if you not careful."

Gritting his teeth, Ernest proceeded to clip off the wool, trying to mimic what Bear Claw had done. When he finished clipping the whole animal, Lester called out to Sylvia to bring her medicine bag. "You will need to put salve on those knife wounds on the sheep." Lester told her.

Bear Claw laughed at their antics. "You get better with more practice. When done your flock, we have flock needs shearing as well."

Both Ernest and Lester looked at each other and groaned.

"What do we do with all this wool?" Ernest asked Bear Claw.

"You either trade to Mormons or some Indian tribe or weave on loom to make cloth. We have our own looms that squaws use. We show your squaws how make cloth."

Ernest looked over at Sylvia. "That is a good idea. Hey, Red, when we are done with all this shearing, Mare-ah and Blue Sky will show you how to weave all this wool into cloth. Lester and I need some new clothes."

"If Lester will make me a loom, I will be glad to weave it whenever I have some spare time. It is not as if I have not used a loom before. We used to make our own clothes when I traveled with my family in Ireland."

Margret tried to help Sylvia in the garden but was unable to do too much.

"You had better stop trying to work the garden." Sylvia warned. "You are getting too big to bend over. I remember how much trouble I had bending over picking those blueberries. I think that you are almost due to have the baby. I pray every day that you will deliver a fine, healthy infant."

"I just hope it is very healthy. I don't know what I would do if he or she was not."

"Stop worrying. God has been good to both our families. We have a nice roof over our heads and are no longer bouncing on the seat of the wagon. We are so lucky to have found each other. We work together so well. I don't know what we would have done had we not met. Lester and Ernest are very hardworking, loving men, and we have some very good Indian neighbors that are not trying to scalp us."

In less than a week later, Margret gave birth to a strapping boy with blond curly hair like his dad. It was a good birth, and they both were doing well. The Ute midwives that had helped Sylvia deliver also helped Margret. They named the baby Daniel. Margret said that she just heard many stories when she was growing up about a boy by that name that was in a lion's den, and God intervened.

As time passed, they built up their flock of sheep on their little ranch. The Walkers and Clarks prospered, and their flock of sheep grew, as did Sylvia and Margret's garden that they had planted with the seed they had traded for some wool to the Mormons. The Mormons tried to convert both the Walkers and the Clarks every time they went into their settlement. They even sent out missionaries to their cabins to try to convince them that they needed their religion.

Ernest went into the Mormon settlement and picked up some supplies. While he was there, he picked up a newly printed newspaper. There was an article titled "Civil War Ends." It read:

> In January 31, 1865, the House of Representatives passed the Thirteenth Amendment to the Constitution to abolish slavery. However, both Unionists and Confederates continued to seek victory through war. The bloodiest engagements occurred over the next three months. Finally, on April 9, 1965, the Unionists received word that Robert E. Lee surrendered to Ulysses S. Grant, which meant the end of the Civil War. The Unionists sent word to the Confederates to let them know the war was over. They were free to go home, but only if they signed an oath not to use further aggression against the North and surrender their arms. If they failed to sign the oath or relinquish their arms, they would stand before a firing squad. Five days after the end of the war, John Wilkes Booth shot President Abraham Lincoln in Ford's Theater, who died the next morning leaving the nation in turmoil.

When he returned, he showed the paper to Sylvia and Lester. Lester ran over and showed it to Margret. "Look, Margret, the war has ended. I sure hope Louis and Ray are safe and not injured. I wonder if Louis has gone to Montana and whether Ray's family is okay up in Arkansas."

"Well, we may never know, but I know our prayers have been given daily to watch over them. I am sure glad that we came here to the Utah Territory where that war does not seem to have too much effect. Look at this other article. It says that even though the war was lost by the Southerners and has ended, the Yankee fighters continue to burn, loot, assult, and murder in the south as they plunder the settlements after the war. I am sure glad that we slipped through before we saw any of that, or we would have gotten involved for sure."

Sylvia and Margret with their children would go into the mountains and search for food. They would take their Ute neighbors with them and one or two men with rifles or bows for protection. In the spring, they would dig cactus, various barks and seeds, roots, and tubers. In the summer and fall, they would search and gather berries, wild onions, and asparagus. Many of these plants and seeds were dried, placed in baskets, and stored in pits dug in the ground and then covered, as a squirrel would do. The wild strawberries, boysenberries, raspberries, and blueberries that they picked they would make preserves, and some they would dry. Many of the wild plants they would plant in their garden, trying to domesticate them. Sometimes they would just prepare the seeds to plant the next spring. Other seeds that they wanted, they would trade with the Mormons. Their gardens grew in size and flourished with a lot of variety of substance.

Ernest, Lester, and their two Ute brothers went to hunt often. They brought in their meat to dry for storing. Many of the choice cuts they would cook and eat immediately, joined by the other tribe members. The hides normally went to the tribe. Sometimes, though, they would trade them with the Mormons for produce. They tried to domesticate the wild turkey and partridge and were somewhat successful; however, they remained wild and a bit stringy.

Lester built a large brooder, and their chicken hatched and produced a large flock that gave them plenty of sustainable meat and enough eggs to trade with the Mormons. The sheep produced many lambs, and their flock grew rapidly. They found a market within the Mormon settlement that they could trade with for other items needed. Overall, they became very productive and independent.

Springtime

Nancy and Daniel grew while their families traded produce, wool, and mutton with their Ute Indian friends and the Mormons for their needs. During one trip of trading with the Mormon settlement, Ernest returned with two young mules. He gave one to the Clarks and kept one for their own needs. The Indians traded work with their two neighbors and treated both families with respect. Whenever Ernest went hunting, he would always take them along or bring them a share of what he had shot. A small mission provided them with some seed they needed for their garden and ranch. Ernest and Lester, having grown up on a farm, had tilled several acres and planted corn and wheat. Since their acreage was below the creek, they had little trouble watering their crops. They would keep about 10 percent of the crop back for the next spring seeding and store the rest in sacks in the barn. Whenever the Indians needed some corn or wheat, they would fill their baskets from the sacks. They were a happy little community and worked well together.

Nancy and Daniel grew up fast and played outdoors together with Ole Shep and their Indian friends. Sylvia taught Nancy how to cook, sew, and garden. Sometimes Nancy and Daniel would even go out hunting with their dads. They loved the outdoors and roamed freely throughout the community.

Late one afternoon, Nancy came running into their cabin and exclaimed, "Mommy, Daddy, we are getting new neighbors."

A long line of wagons flowed over the mountain into the valley. Mile after mile, the wagons rolled in. They were a strange lot with several women and children riding in each wagon, with one man handling the reins. Over seventy wagons loaded rolled over the pass along with their herds of livestock. A man on a large black horse led the group. Ernest rode out of the field he was planting to greet the man. "My name is Ernest Walker. Welcome to this valley."

"Good to meet you. I have been leading these worn-out souls here following Christ. He has led me to this valley of paradise following our Apostle Brigham Young that established this settlement. It has been a long journey, and we are anxious to begin our new lives in this valley."

"Really, well, it will be good to have some more neighbors here. We have lived here several years now, and my families have lived in peace with the Indians in the area and the Mormons. I hope that you are a peaceful group and will live in harmony with the natives. Where did you start this journey from?"

"Since God brought us here, I am confident that we will find peace with the Indians, just as you did. We will bring honor and religion to this area. As I rode over the mountain, I saw exactly where God has been leading us. We are going to camp over near our brothers. I have brought over seventy wagonloads of saints here with livestock, and there will be more to follow. We started out in Missouri, traveled along the Platte River through Nebraska, and then across Wyoming to here, just like Brigham Young did several years ago."

Ernest left the group to settle in and went back to his cabin. "Red, the new arrivals are a little strange. They plan to establish another colony of religious order here. I am a little concerned that they think they own everything around them. They brought herds of livestock with them. They plan to establish a community of their own. I think that this group is a little different than the one that was initially established when we got here. This group seems to have a different air about them."

"Well, it is good to have a little religion here in this valley, unless of course they try to jam it down our throats."

"They look worn out and are a ragged group of travelers. What they told us confused me a little. The leader said his wives have had a very hard time on this trip. I am not sure why he said *wives* instead of *wife*, unless of course he has more than one wife."

"You are probably right. I heard that Joseph Smith had several wives that he shared with other husbands. This group might be of that culture. I sure hope that they don't try to push us off this Ute land."

"We will just have to wait and see. We will try to be good neighbors, but I will not conform to their beliefs."

"Why, don't you want another woman?"

"Are you kidding? You are more woman than I can handle." He smiled.

Mormons

It did not take long for the Walkers to find out that many of the Mormon men did indeed have multiple wives. They began building their cabins close to the Walkers and Clarks without even talking to the Utes. At first, they tried to assist them in cutting down trees and help them build their cabins. They built their cabins with many rooms to house the wives and children of the owner. They had a master builder that was very demanding. Soon, Ernest and Lester found that they no longer had the desire to assist them in their construction. They not only used the help of a few Indians, but also demanded the help of the whole tribe.

Lester looked worried. "Ernest, they have upset the Utes. I just got back from talking to Bear Claw, and he seems ready to push this last group of Mormons out of the valley. He told me that they were not like the first group that arrived. They are demanding that they conform and work for them or leave. Some of that new bunch that arrived is building on the Ute land without getting permission from them. They have also taken the Utes' young women as their wives. The chief is livid. I don't think that he will control his anger or the anger of the rest of his band before blood starts flowing. The Utes have been here a long time and are not ready to conform or leave. I am afraid that there will be an armed conflict shortly."

"They are a proud people and have been very friendly to us. I would hate to see them try to drive out the Mormons. The Mormons are well armed and have increased in number. I expect there are far more Mormons here than Utes. The Utes have a long heritage in this area. While talking to Sees Far, he said they have hunted in this area for hundreds of years. Their families died, and they buried them here. If those Mormon settlers don't stop taking their land, there will be a war, and we will be right in the middle of the fighting. I think I will go and talk to Bear Claw and see if there is anything that we can do to help."

Ernest rode over to the Ute camp. There was a lot of activity. Bear Claw came out of his teepee and greeted Ernest. "Chief, I would like to talk to you about the problem you are having with those Mormons. I know that they have trespassed on your land, the land of your fathers and their fathers. They have taken your hunting ground and are claiming it as their own. You have been very generous and a very good neighbor to us. We owe you a lot. Can we help you settle this conflict in any way?"

"No. You good neighbors, but those new Mormons have different ideas than first group. Could stand first group, but this new wave of zealots irrational and no longer welcome. If they reform and become decent like those first arrived, we not be in conflict. They will not. In fact, they try to convert first group into their thinking. We been reasonable with them, but they not returned favor. They no longer provide those in south with beef promised. They insult us everyday and think us dirt under feet. They take our young maidens as wives, even though already have more than one wife, and demand we work in their fields without compensation."

Additionally, the new lot of radical Mormons expected Ernest and Lester to provide them with sustained substance. However, it did not take long for them to run out of food. They were not about to dig into the seed they had set aside for the next year's planting. The Mormons would borrow their tools but forget to return them. It was always late in the planting season when the Mormons broke ground. After they planted, they constantly watered. This took the water from the creek that Ernest and Lester were using for their garden and fields.

Ernest went to talk to their leader. "I don't mind sharing the water with you, but you have dammed the creek up and are taking all of our water for your fields."

"The Lord's work must come first. We have to feed his flock before you heathens. Now do not worry. If you get hungry, the Lord will provide. You need to join our Order so that we can work together in our family."

"We were here first," Ernest responded. "You are stealing our water, and I demand that you tear down your dams and share the water with us."

"Sorry, we take orders from our Lord, and he has given us this land. That is my final answer. Now leave us alone."

This fanatical group had invaded their valley and had taken up root. They claimed that God had directed them to that salty valley and proceeded to take ownership. The men had many wives and children. They took God at his word when he said go forth, multiply, and inherit the earth. Little by little, they elbowed their way in. They converted what Indians they could and banished the others. Those that did not accept their doctrine were heathens and shunned. They tolerated little and rode roughshod over the entire region. Unfortunately, the Walkers, Clarks, and Utes lived in their valley. They would not listen to their decrees and doctrine. The Mormons set out to rid the valley of the likes of them.

Lester was mad clear through and ready to take up arms against the new religious fanatics. "Let's go talk to the Ute chief and run these troublemakers out of here."

"Lester, if we try to run them off, they will unite with the other Mormons to the east, and we will not have a chance. Even with our Ute friends, we would be unable to win. We have to think of our families. I don't want to lose any of our family for the sake of this land."

Black Hawk War

It had been a long winter, and the southern Utes were starving. Ernest and Lester had given their Ute neighbors all they had to spare. However, the Mormons, who had plenty, would not share any more with the ones in the south. A small group of starving Utes of the south rustled some of the Mormon cattle to feed their starving families. When the Mormon militia confronted the family, one of their leaders lost his temper and violently jerked a young chieftain from his horse. The Indian was insulted, and a young Ute named Antonga Black Hawk promised retaliation. Over the next few days, Black Hawk and his followers raided the ranches of the Mormon cattle and fled into the mountains to feed their families. Black Hawk did not have the support of all the Indians of Utah, but he succeeded in uniting factions of the Ute, Paiute, and Navajo tribes. The Mormon militiamen chased the Indians throughout the wilderness but were unable to take revenge on their illusive adversaries.

Bear Claw and Sees Far sat in a council and told Ernest and Lester, Mormon militia been pushing us farther and farther off our land and land to south. They refused to help us with feeding our families. I am taking my tribe south where we might help Paiute and Navajo allies in conflict with Mormons who try to hunt down followers of Black Hawk. Unfortunately, our once-friendly nation turned vicious as Mormon militia push us farther and farther off our land."

Ernest looked disappointed. "I am sorry to hear that. Tell your family, Blue Sky, Running Dog, Mare-ah, and Perl that we will miss them. We may not be here when you return. The Mormons are striving to push us out as well. We will be unable to defend ourselves when they decide to drive us out."

The next morning, Ernest and Sylvia awoke from the pounding at their front door. Ernest jumped up, threw on his trousers, and ran to the front door to find Perl crying. "Militiamen came shooting and shouting throughout camp around midnight. They claimed we been rustling herds and stealing horses. They killed Running Dog and Sees Far. Bear Claw grabbed bow and went after seeking revenge while I came here seeking help."

"Red, grab your medical bag, and I will run over and get the Clarks. We may be gone for a while, so I will take Nancy over to have Margret care for her while we are gone." Ernest left running. He awoke the Clarks and told them of the raid on the Utes.

"Margret, I want you to take care of Nancy while we are gone, and Lester, grab your rifle and hitch up your team. I will hitch up mine and meet you back here in ten minutes."

"Margret and I are going with you," Nancy said. "We can help out also."

"Well, all right. Sometimes, I think that you are your mother's child."

"I am."

"You two can come in the other wagon after we have gone. We cannot wait for you. We have to go now."

Ernest hitched up his team to their wagon and returned to find Sylvia dressed and ready to travel. He helped her onto the wagon seat as Lester brought his team to a halt in front of their cabin. "Perl, why don't you ride with Lester and leave your horse in the corral."

When they reached the Indian camp, they saw that many of the young braves had gathered and were heading out toward the Mormon settlement.

Ernest stepped down from the wagon and asked Blue Sky, "How can Red and I help?"

Blue Sky showed Sylvia where several of the wounded were lying on blankets, being prayed over. She went to work helping the wounded and comforting the forlorn. She dug several bullets out of the wounded. One girl in her early teens broke her heart as she died just as Sylvia arrived to render aid. She was Perl's best friend and had run out into the hail of bullets. Ernest and Lester helped carry the wounded to the blankets and kept the fire going to boil water. They did all they could as the Ute camp packed up to head south where their main camps were located.

It was late in the evening when some of the young braves returned with their wounded and dead, telling their stories of revenge carried out against the Mormons. Bear Claw was furious and shot in the arm. Sylvia quickly began working on him to remove the bullet lodged against his bone. They expected retaliation back from them as the war commenced. Hurriedly, they began to finish tearing down their teepees and loading their belongings onto the back of their horses and wagons to move them south. It was heartbreaking to see their Ute neighbors wounded and moving away from their home. It left a big void in their hearts and exposed them more to the Mormon militia.

"We leave now." Bear Claw told his tribe. "Mormon militiamen who have superior weapons outnumber us. Thank you, Sylvia, for help. Ernest and Lester, thank you for being good neighbors, unlike Mormons. We leave to protect our families and would recommend you prepare to leave area as well. I see nothing but heartache now. Good luck to you and your families."

Eviction Notice

A week later, while Ernest and Lester were up in the hills hunting, an armed group of Mormon militia rode into the Walkers' yard. Margret and Daniel were visiting with Sylvia and Nancy. A man with a long black beard sat on his horse wearing a black frock coat. "I am giving you a final warning, ma'am. You and your men have given aid to the Utes that attacked us. Thus, you and your men are fighting against us, and we must consider you as enemies. Since you helped the Utes after they attacked us, refuse to honor our Order, and your sheep are trespassing and ruining the valley's grassland, your men must leave. We will not tolerate their presence any longer. This is your last notice. Your men had better leave by this time tomorrow, or we will tie them up and throw them into our hog pens. They get hungry right after they farrow, and your men will make them a good meal. You two women and even your brood can stay here with us if you want, but your husbands must leave and never return."

Sylvia, angered, replied, "You are the ones that have invaded this land and stolen our water. You claim to be religious, but you are on the side of the devil, not God's side. You need to take a good long look at yourselves to see how you are violating God's law. God would never have authorized you to kill the innocent and let those that have labored in your fields to starve. What gives you the right to change his laws and decrees?"

"Oh, we believe the Bible as far as it is translated correctly. Ma'am, we have every right to correct the errors of man. God has authorized us to make whatever changes necessary to correct the translations. He visited Joseph Smith and told him what changes to make to give support to His Latter-Day Saints through our apostles and prophets. Ma'am, you and your friends must learn obedience to this new Order." As they turned to leave, they laughed as they rode their horses over her garden, stomping and tearing it up.

Sylvia turned to Margret and said, "They are in for a rude awakening when they enter the pearly gates."

Sylvia and Margret met Ernest and Lester as they rode into the yard. They were mad and upset, as were Nancy and Daniel. "We have to leave." Sylvia told Ernest. "The Mormon militia have given us twenty-four hours to pack up and move out. They said that they would be back tomorrow by noon with force."

Ernest shook his head. "Aye, we had better start packing up to leave. They have attacked, killed, and run off our Ute friends. They took over their camp and killed many of their number. I think that we are next on their list of cleansing if we don't leave. We came here with a wagon and promises. We can leave with the same. I would rather leave now than to have any one of us to suffer from the likes of them. We always said that this might be just a stopping place until we could travel on west. Now, it is time to hitch up our wagons and continue our westward journey."

"I think you are right, Ernest. If it were just me, I would fight. I have to think about my family. Margret, Daniel, and I will start packing tonight and be ready to move out with you in the morning."

"Get Nancy and let's get out of here, Red. Those Mormons will be back this way if we don't move out immediately. I cannot understand why they think that our sheep are ruining the valley's grassland. I am sure that is only an excuse. They want our land and our cabins for their own. I have loaded the wagon with everything that we brought into this valley and many bags of seeds, nuts, and dried fruit. I cannot stuff any more on it. What is left, I think we should just burn to keep it out of their hands. I would hate to leave them anything for running us off."

"Ernest, you know it isn't just the sheep. That is just an excuse. Those Mormon men just don't cotton to Basque women and Irish men and their beliefs."

"From what I've heard, Red, Mormon men don't much care where their women come from as long as they have a flock of them unto themselves."

"Well, this is one ewe they ain't a-goin' to shepherd."

Sylvia and her young daughter, Nancy, mounted the wagon and took up the reins. Ernest drove their little band of sheep behind the wagon with Ole Shep rounding up the strays and directing the drive.

Lester, Margret, and Daniel were already packed and ready to travel by dawn. They had worked all night, sorting and packing for their departure. They tied Daisy, their cow, behind their wagon and stuck a pen of chickens in the back of their wagon. While Margret and Daniel handled the wagon, Lester rode beside them, armed for protection.

Sylvia and Margret pointed their wagons west, out of the salty valley they had come to love. As more and more Mormons had streamed into the valley, the more they took over everything around them. They were a ruthless lot and had little tolerance of anyone outside their Order. It was a simple threat the Walkers and Clarks had been given at noon the day before: "Move out or die wrapped up in a wire package."

Ernest and Lester both elected to move out to save their family. "I'm sorry, Red. I thought we could live at peace in this valley. They just could not see that we were not a threat to them."

Leaving Home

"Don't worry about it, Ernest. The Basque have been wandering this world without a nation long before any Mormons were born."

"Aye, and that's why we are going to find a settlement where we are accepted. I hear over in the Boise Basin, the Basque and immigrants have settled in. They have met some resistance, but their numbers have increased where they can protect themselves now. Therefore, that is where we are going to go. The Clarks and we will find a decent place to build where there are no Mormon bigots."

As Ernest rode from their home, he spoke to Lester. "Lester, we should ride back and burn our cabins and barns. I hate to see those bigots prosper from what we built. The land belongs to the Ute, but we built the cabins and barns. Now that the ladies cannot see their cabins going up in smoke, I think that we should torch them."

"I sure hate to see all our work go up in smoke, Ernest, but seeing or hearing that those fanatics have prospered from our hands would make me sicker. I am with you. Let's get the job done before we change our minds."

They rode back to their cabins. While Lester torched his cabin and barns, Ernest set fire to his place. Both men were somber as they rode west to catch up with their wagons.

"What's all that black smoke?" Daniel asked Margret as he looked back. She looked over at Sylvia and Nancy.

Sylvia responded to the unasked question, "That, dear Daniel, is our hope and dreams of the salty valley going up in smoke."

Their travel was slow with the band of sheep and cow following behind their wagons. At noon the next day, the Mormons caught up to them as they left the valley.

"So, Irishman, you've decided to accept our request, tuck tail, and move out. We had plans for your cabins and barns. Why would you burn down what took you years to build? We ought to teach you never to enter our land again. What do you say, brethren?"

As the leader of the mob started to grab for his pistol, Sylvia pulled up the Greener shotgun that she had set under the springboard seat. "Mister, if you bring that pistol up one more inch and don't turn yourselves around this instant, I'll fill you and your sacred brethren so full of holes that even we'll call you holy. Now get moving if you don't want me to send you exactly where you belong."

"Now, lady, don't get excited. We were just funnin' with ya."

"I've seen enough of your funnin'. Now move out or die."

"You heard the lady." Margret and Lester responded, leveling their shotguns at the roughriders.

Their exit from the salty valley went without further incident from the Mormons. They just simply wanted to leave.

It was lonely traveling out in the open prairie with just two wagons. At night with the smell of sheep, the coyotes would howl and begin to circle their camp. Ole Shep was very busy keeping the sheep bunched and nipping at the fleeting varmints that attacked the defenseless sheep. A few would get too close and meet his iron jaws. Ernest would fire his thunder buster a few times at night to let them know they were not welcome.

Their travel was very slow. A flock of sheep and cow would only move so fast. Ernest knew the general direction to travel, but the wind was constantly blowing, and with the heat, their water supply soon ran out. The sheep began to die from the heat and wind exhaustion draining out their lives. The cow, walking behind the Clarks' wagon, began to stumble.

Ernest said to Sylvia, "Stop the wagon. We cannot make it this way. We have to throw out everything we don't absolutely need for survival."

"I understand. I never had much anyway. All I care about is for you, Nancy, and the Clarks. Nothing else matters."

"I'm the luckiest man in the world and the richest with two beautiful women at my side."

Ernest, with the help of Lester and Daniel, caught seven of the strongest ewes and two rams, then tied their feet together and placed them into the back of his wagon. He climbed aboard and took the reins from Sylvia. With tears in their eyes, they moved forward, leaving the remaining flock of dying sheep to the coyotes. He had to drag Ole Shep aboard to keep him with them. Maybe with a little luck, they could find water before they all perished.

At dusk the seventh day out, Ernest's tired lead mule's ears picked up, as did her pace. They gave their mule, Sissy, her head, and she turned to the right and headed toward a little draw lined with some green shrubs and a little pond of brackish water.

Ernest and Lester let the animals drink a little but then pulled them away while Sylvia and Margret filled their barrels with the water before it became too muddy from the animals.

They made camp there for the evening to rest. The little water helped, but their rejoice was limited. They still had a long way to go. Even Nancy's tears had ceased. After several more grueling days, they topped a little rise and saw a most beautiful line of trees with a clear river running in between.

They were parched, and Daisy had been staggering the last few miles. Now, they had new hope and new life.

Sylvia and Margret were having a problem holding their mules, Sissy and Hank.

Idaho Territory

The flowing water was cool and clear. Ernest led the animals away after a small drink as he did not want them to founder. The sheep were almost dead too. Daniel and Nancy worked their little hearts out, forcing water down them and cooling them down slowly. They camped that night and stayed another three days at the water's edge while they gained back some of their strength.

Following the river west, they passed a lava flow from ancient times. A small trail led them through. It would be a disaster to the hooves of the mules and the wheels of the wagons to get off the trail. The river they were following dipped down into a tremendously deep canyon, but they stayed on the trail above.

They kept the sheep tied in the back of the wagon and would only let them out whenever they camped. Ole Shep would gather and protect them.

At the lava flow, Nancy and Daniel wandered off and found a little cave that turned into a cavern as they explored. The deeper they went, the cooler it became until they found where the water dripped to make large icicles. Nancy was so excited about her find. She broke several pieces off and ran back to show her mom and dad.

"Nancy, how can you walk out in the heat of the day into a lava bed and come back with ice? You are a great wonder," her mother said.

They all went back to see the ice cave. Even Ole Shep enjoyed its coolness.

"Aye, this is great, but we cannot take it with us. We must keep movin' on and find us another place we can call our own before another winter sets in." Ernest directed the party.

"Aw, a little coolness helps though, Ernest. We are so lucky to have such a wonderful daughter."

"Aye, and she is pretty too."

"Okay, I'm ready to go now. You're embarrassing me," Nancy said.

A few days later, they began to meet other travelers on the trail. Most of them were just seeking a better life. Some were looking to leave their own problems and past behind.

"We need to look to the future and not concern ourselves with what could have been but what will be," Ernest philosophized.

"Ernest, I can't keep any food down, and even the water makes me nauseous."

"We had a rough go of it across that hot, windy prairie, Red. I'm sure you just overdid it or drank too much of that brackish water."

"That's probably it all right, but it kind of feels a bit more serious."

"You know, we don't have time for you to be sick like that now. So you have just got to get over it."

"I'll try."

They came upon an encampment of families traveling the same direction and stopped to join them.

"Hey! Ya know what trail this is?" Ernest asked.

Oregon Trail

"Yes, sir. This here is the Oregon Trail you are on, and we plan to take it all the way to the Boise Settlement where there is a lot of homestead property. We plan to settle there. From what we have heard, the area is growing rapidly along the Boise River with an influx of merchants, farmers, miners, and loggers."

"You folks want a little company?" Sylvia asked.

"Sure, if you don't mind sheep that is. Many of us have a little flock just over that rise. They are getting a little water and feed. My name is Julio Martinez, and we are a Basque family."

"I'm a Basque too," Sylvia said. "We just got booted out of our ranch by a bunch of Mormon bigots. I was hoping that I might find someone else that could speak Shelta."

"Oh, we can speak Shelta quite fluently. Lillian my wife and I speak it to each other, especially when we are alone. Sometimes we mix English with Shelta just to keep things interesting."

"If it's okay, then we will take our few sheep over there as well."

"Sure, Ernest. Just tell the little shepherd boy which ones are yours, and he will watch them for you. The boy's name is Jeremiah, and he is our son. You may leave that fine-looking Great Pyrenean Mountain sheepdog with him too, if you'd like."

"Thanks. His name is Ole Shep, and he has protected what's left of our flock for a long time. He lives with them. Sometimes, I think, he thinks he is one of them."

"The Great Pyrenees is a very old breed of sheepdog that has been used for hundreds of years to herd and protect our sheep from predators by our Basque families who inhabit the region around the Pyrenees Mountains near northern Spain. Daniel, why don't you and Nancy take the sheep and your Ole Shep over to where Jeremiah is herding. I am sure that Jeremiah will be glad to have some human company."

"Great. He and our boy will get along fine."

"Your wife does not look like she is feeling too well."

"No, Red has been sick for the past few days, especially in the morning and at meals. Our daughter, Nancy, has been doing her mom's work."

"You have a fine-looking family. If you ask me, I would think you were about to increase the lot. I'll have my wife Lillian look in on her if it's okay with you."

"By George, that's what we've been thinking too. I was hoping that wasn't the case, but I guess the increase comes when God wills."

"It kind of feels like that time several years ago when I thought I had the influenza," Sylvia remarked.

"Aye, you were sick all right for nine months. Nancy came out a-hollering," Margret said.

That evening as they sat around the campfire, they told each other their stories. Each one had a unique story. They were the same in that they each were survivors of conflict. While their children played, Sylvia, Lillian, and Margret fixed their evening meal. They had roasted lamb, vegetables, biscuits, and good hot coffee. Sylvia told them of her adventure from Ireland and her meeting Ernest. Margret told of her marriage to Lester in New York. Additionally, she told them how they hooked up with the wagon train. Lillian spoke of her and Julio's marriage. She told how she looked forward to getting together in a community where the Basques were not discriminated. She said, "I sure can understand how some of the black folks of the south feel. People shunned and excluded us from normal necessities and lifestyle because we were from a different race. We did not have to fight a war to become accepted. We just have to find a community where we can band together when needed for support. Julio and I have heard that we can find such a place near the settlement of Boise."

"Well, I hope you are right," Sylvia said, "because that is such a place we would like to end up as well. I don't mean to say that every one of our neighbors have to be Basque, but as you said, as long as we are not discriminated against and have a chance of an honest, decent life."

Ernest, Lester, and Julio talked of what they wanted as far as farm and ranch land. "It seems that our goals are very similar. I just want to make sure that where we settle, fanatical bigots don't overrun us. I do not mean that all Mormons are fanatical. The first group was honest and decent. However, the last group that came in were impossible to work with," Ernest said. "I enjoy hunting and fishing and scouting probably more than I do farmwork. I think that I would love to go hunting for some wild mustangs when we get settled."

Lester told them, "I like to work with my hands. I do enjoy farm and ranch work almost as much as woodwork. However, to be honest, I think that I enjoy working with wood a little more than I do with the land. With wood, I can see immediate progress. It takes longer to see your work materialize with the land."

Julio stated, "My joy has always been with tilling the land and watching the plants grow. I enjoy tending sheep and other farm animals as well. Smelling fresh-turned soil just brings great enjoyment to me."

Homesteading

Ernest's and Lester's families traveled with the caravan until they reached the Boise Basin area. Sylvia and Margret became good friends with Lillian while Nancy and Daniel tagged after Jeremiah, helping him with the sheep. Sylvia and Lillian tried teaching Margret the Shelta language but did not have much luck. Nancy and Jeremiah even chatted in Shelta a little when they were by themselves but just spoke English whenever Daniel was around. Some of the travelers began spinning away as they headed off toward their own destiny. Some went to work in the logging camps, some mining, but Julio, Ernest, and Lester stopped at the land office at the Boise settlement and found the secluded homesteads they were looking for. The homesteads were located in a little valley surrounded by mountain ranges around fifty miles north of Boise. It had a unique setting with the main entrance next to the Payette River. They were the first homesteads assigned in that area. The agent did caution them that some Indians did roam through that area but, for the most part, were peaceful, unless someone riled them up.

"Well, we sure wouldn't want to do that," Ernest said. "We lived next to a Ute tribe in the Utah Territory. We got along well with them and even traded work back and forth. We even went hunting together occasionally. They were peaceful until a group of Mormons started pushing them around. Maybe you heard of Black Hawk and the war he is waging on them right now. That is one reason we left our homes and moved out, not because of the

Utes, but because of the Mormons. I sure hope you do not have any religious fanatics in this area."

"Not yet we don't," the agent said. "There are some Mormons in the area, but they are not troublesome. There are enough immigrants moving in this area that have enough of bark on to expel any fanatics that start to cause trouble of that nature."

"That is good to hear because we will take up arms before we vacate another home like we had to in Utah."

"The main trouble we have here is with the loggers and the miners letting off steam. You might want to be careful around the Horseshoe Bend area at night. That seems to be where they head to have their fun. That is, if you call drinking, gambling, and fighting fun."

"Thanks, we will keep that in mind."

They made their way along the Boise River and then dropped down to the Payette River. They rode through the small settlement of Horseshoe Bend. Ernest commented, "This doesn't look like much of a settlement. There is the sawmill area the agent told us about. We might be able to get some planks there for our cabins."

"It looks like there is one mercantile here for every five saloons," Lillian commented.

The scene along the Payette River was breathtaking. The white water rapids ran south, and then it made an acute bend and headed west. At the bend, loggers were busy pulling logs from the water that had floated on the river to them from somewhere upriver. It was quite a sight to watch the loggers walking the logs while they floated. They held long spears with hooks to maneuver the logs into a pond. The logs, removed from the pond, made lumber. They called the settlement Horseshoe Bend after the bend the river made.

Sylvia and Margret drove their wagons into the little valley just east of the Payette River and north of Horseshoe Bend following

Lillian's wagon. They looked at the hand-drawn map that the land agent had sketched. Julio, Lillian, and Jeremiah stopped and pointed to the south side of the little creek and told Ernest that was their homestead. He pointed farther east and told Ernest and Lester, "It looks like your homesteads are north of the creek and east of mine. We are all within sight of each other, so we should be more secure this way. I am on the southern slope while you two are on the northern slope. There is enough flatland next to the creek for planting. I think we will be happy here."

"This is it, Red. I believe that we've found our new home," Ernest said.

"Yup, an' if any fanatical Mormons come a-calling, Ernest, I will personally fill their backside with buckshot. I am not a-movin' again, nor will I be run off from this home."

"Looks like you will have your hands full looking after two young ones, Red."

"There's a lot of work to do before this one's ready to hatch. We need to build us a cabin, a corral, and a barn before winter sets in. It looks like there is plenty of timber over that ridge. Nancy, you will need to do the cooking for us. I'm going to have to depend on you a lot for the next few years."

"Yes, Mama. I'll cook, fetch water, and care for the baby while you and Papa get the ranch going."

"Ole Shep, get those sheep fed and watered." Ernest directed as he whistled and pointed to the water. Ole Shep took the cue and circled the little flock and moved them over to the water.

Surveying

"Lester, it looks like we need to build us a few more cabins. Unfortunately, we will not have our Ute friends to help us with the building. We both learned a lot from them when we built our last cabins."

"The Martinez family will be a big help. Why don't we start with your cabin, Ernest, since your wife needs to get in out of the weather as soon as possible?"

"I can build a fireplace with the rocks from the creek bottom," Julio said. "My father was a master mason and passed along his skill to me."

"Before we get started on the cabins," Ernest said, "I would like to ride around the area to see the lay of the land. Why don't you and Julio ride along with me so we can get the lay of the land before we start any building? I am sure that our three families are tired and can use the time to stretch their legs and look over our property for our building sites."

They parked the wagons next to each other and, with the help of the hand-drawn map, marked off the corners of their homestead with rocks they piled on top of each other. "It sure is nice that our homesteads border each other. That way, no one will be able to build between us. There is a lot of graze land behind our homesteads for our livestock. I doubt anyone can file on it since there is no access except through our property. We should be able to utilize that land for many generations."

That night as they slept under the wagons, Sylvia snuggled next to Ernest as she heard the howling of the wolves. It sent chills up her spine, and she was worried about their livestock. "Don't worry, Red," Ernest said. "If they get anywhere close, Ole Shep will let us know."

Early the next morning, the men saddled their mounts and rode up the creek to the east. The area surrounding their valley was nice rolling foothills that extended right up to the base of the tall Rocky Mountains to the east. The mountains surrounded their valley and should protect them from any major storm that rolled through. The mountains to the east were loaded with tall pines that would be perfect for building. The tall pines were a ways from their cabin sites, and it would take a while to drag down the big logs.

The men rode to the top of the first mountain ridge and saw where loggers were devastating the forestland. They were stripping the land of the big pines and sliding them down the mountain. They loaded the logs onto wagons and headed to the mill. The logging left behind their piles of branches and brush that would die and create a fire hazard. Their skid trails would cause erosion and mudslides during heavy rains.

"I am sure glad that there are a few mountains between us and the logging activity." Ernest told the other two men. "I sure hope they don't try to harvest the trees on this side of the mountain, or we might have some problem with fire or heavy rain."

"When I talked to the agent," Julio said, "he stated that they were only granted permission to log east of the mountain they were currently logging. We should be safe from their activity for a while at least. They have plenty of timber east of where they are to keep them busy for years. He further stated that the main mining activity was east of where they were logging."

"Well, it looks like we are safe from their activity for a few years at least," Ernest said.

As they rode along the ridge of the mountain to the north, Lester commented, "It is sure chilly up here. I don't know how high we are, but we can see our entire valley from these peaks. It looks like the Payette flows from the north and joined by another river branch. One branch flows into it from the east and another from the north."

"As I recall," Julio added, "the branch from the east is called the South Fork of the Payette. The tributaries from the north just merge into one larger river. The Payette River runs into the Snake River west of us and eventually runs into the Columbia River. The Columbia River runs into the Pacific Ocean to the west."

"I will bet that is where our old wagon train headed. I think that Oregon lies in that direction," Ernest said. "I wonder how far it is from where we are to Oregon. Someday, I would like to ride over that direction and visit our old travel companions. We became quite close to many of those immigrants. We had to separate from the wagon train just before winter set in. Sylvia was expecting our first child, Nancy, and it was getting hard for her to travel farther. Lester and Margret separated from the train with us, and we built cabins on Ute property just before the first snow. It sure was nice to have neighbors like the Utes. I sure do miss them."

"Well, I think that we are less than a hundred miles from Oregon. You can go there after we get settled. Oregon is a big territory, and unless you know where your friends have settled, you might have a hard time finding them. I know that the main land office is in a settlement called Ontario. You might want to check with them since that office issues the homesteads. It is only about seventy miles from us, and they should have records showing where they settled."

"Lester, what do you think?" Ernest asked. "How would you like to take a trip over to Ontario with me next year and check out where the Reynolds settled? I wish I had thought to ask the land agent when we were in Boise. They may have settled here in the Idaho Territory instead of traveling all the way to Oregon."

"Well, I expect that once we settle here that we will be making a few trips back to Boise to resupply. We can certainly stop in and ask the agent. I think that land offices communicate to each other. Therefore, they may be able to find out about the Reynolds as well."

The three men rode the mountain ridge, which turned south toward the Payette River. Ernest spotted a large doe, shot, and dressed it out. He loaded half of it on his mount and the other half on Lester's mount. They rode along the Payette River on a well-used trail then reentered their valley and back to where the wagons were parked. It was turning dusk, and they were glad to see that their families had coffee boiling. They unloaded the buck and finished cutting it up.

Nez Percé

"It is about time you three arrived back." Sylvia teased. "I just knew that if we cooked a pot of stew and started some coffee brewing that you would show up. For a while, we thought we might be in trouble as five Indians rode up and looked us over. Ole Shep growled and showed them his teeth. They kept a wary eye on him and did not dismount until I spoke sharply to the dog. They only dismounted after Shep retreated and I invited them too. Two men wore buckskin shirts, breechcloths, leather leggings, and moccasins. The two squaws wore fringed leather dresses decorated with beadwork, shells, and some paintings. One boy riding a pinto dressed like the men. We were able to communicate to them. They spoke in broken English but were understandable. I tried to speak to them in the Ute language, but they could not comprehend it any better than they could English. I was able to communicate to them in the universal sign language that the Utes taught me."

"Did they identify what tribe they were from?" Ernest asked.

"The Indians were from a peaceable Nez Percé tribe that lived across the river where they fished and hunted. They did not paint themselves for war but were just curious about what we were doing. I told them that we planned on building our cabins and living right here. They did not seem upset. One man saw my red scarf and wanted it. I gave it to him, and he handed it to one of the squaws as a gift. She must have been either his wife or girlfriend. When I gave it to him, he seemed very pleased.

They seemed friendly and even invited you menfolk and us for a visit. They wandered through our camp looking at everything, especially my personal items. I think they were just curious. They were heading up into the mountain slope to hunt for food. In the mountains, they said that they dig up wild carrots, potato, blue camas bulbs, bitterroot, and gather comfrey leaves. I don't know what all of that is, but it seems to sustain them throughout the winter."

"It sounds like they have a lot in common with the Utes," Ernest said.

"One of the squaws said that they pick berries, similar to what we did in Utah. They also look for pine nuts and other nuts and seeds. One buck did mention that in the spring, they form hunting parties and capture wild horses. They saw our stack of hides and pelts and asked if the wolf pelts were new. I told them that our sheepdog had fought and killed a couple last night. He growled at them and seemed vicious, but I told them that he protects us. I explained that he is a Pyrenean Mountain sheepdog, a very special breed that lives with the sheep and protects them. I told him that he also protects us when any strangers approach. He was very curious to know if the wolves had attacked our sheep."

"I am glad to hear that they were friendly. I would hate to have seen your red hair hanging from a wickiup somewhere. We did see some smoke drifting from some campfires across the river, but we never saw any Indians. Maybe we can go visit them after we get our cabins up," Ernest said.

"I would like that. I would like to make friends with them like we did with the Utes. Maybe they will even take time to teach me their language. It would make it a lot easier for us to communicate to them."

Ernest explained what they saw on their roundabout ride. He spoke of his concern about the hardcore loggers and miners that were just over the mountain. "I would like to take a trip to Horseshoe Bend and pick us up some lumber to help with the building," Ernest remarked. "It would also give me a chance to size them up and see what they are like as neighbors. I would also like to see what law enforcement is in the region in case they get out of hand. I am concerned that they might have an argument with the Indians the way they are destroying their hunting ground and disrupting their fishing by running logs through the river."

"I understand what you are saying. That would disturb me also. I think it is a good idea to visit Horseshoe Bend. However, you might want to wait until we have the walls up. We shouldn't need the cut lumber until then," Julio said.

Cabin Building

The next morning, Julio set right to work. Jeremiah drove the wagon with Lillian's help while Julio sorted through the rocks from the bottom of the creek. Julio picked out the best rocks and stacked them in the back of the wagon. When loaded, Jeremiah slapped the reins to the back of their mules and returned the load to the cabin site. As Lester began to unload the rocks, he commented, "Hey, these rocks have a little shiny luster to them. It looks like they have little gold flakes running through them. They will sure make a pretty rock fireplace. It's too bad that I cannot pick the gold out of that granite. We would be rich."

Julio concentrated working on the rocks for the foundation and the fireplace. He found a large reservoir of mud that, when hardened, would hold the rocks in place. He scooped out several bucketfuls and loaded them onto the back of his wagon.

Lester dug out the footer and laid large rocks down for a good solid foundation. He set the first log onto the foundation he had laid. He notched the log and tied it into another log that he placed perpendicular to the first one, making a solid corner for the cabin. He drilled a hole through the notch and drove a wooden dowel through it for strength.

During Julio's walk along the creek, he found a source of flat rock. He dug them out, loaded them onto his wagon, and told Lillian that they would make an excellent floor. He had to haul some sand to lay onto the ground for a base to level the rock for the floor. When he completed muddying in the cracks, the floor was even. It would keep the cabin far cleaner than a dirt floor. When he completed the floor, he began laying the rock for the fireplace and even fashioned an oven into it.

"Wow!" Sylvia exclaimed. "That is even better than the fireplace we had in our last cabin. Julio, you sure know how to make a girl smile."

"Well, practice makes perfect. We learned a lot when we built our last cabins, just as your family did in Utah. I would have loved to watch the Utes build the fireplace that Lester described. They must have been masters at that craft."

Ernest worked hard cutting and dragging down the timber with Sissy while Lester fashioned the logs to making them a four-room log cabin. Lester, with the help of little Daniel and Jeremiah, formed the logs and set them in place at the cabin site.

"Why are we building such a large cabin?" Daniel asked Lester.

"Well, they need one room for parents to sleep in, one for Nancy, one for the baby, and one to live in—that makes four. Three of the rooms are small with just a bed and a place to hang their own clothes, and then the main room is where they will cook, eat, and sit to read and tell stories."

"Couldn't they just all sleep in the same room?"

"Yes, they could, but when Ernest snores, it would keep the others awake."

"So are all of us going to get four rooms in our cabins?"

"I think that we will try to build them all alike. That way no family gets more or less than the other. Even though two of us have only one child apiece, you never know when another will come along."

"You mean that I might have a baby brother or sister too?"

"Yes, it could happen anytime. If someone comes to visit you, wouldn't it be nice if they had their own room to stay in?"

"Yes, I see what you mean. Four rooms are about all we can build anyway, until the snow flies. As time goes on, we can always add another room if needed."

It was hard physical work to build cabins. The three families worked in concert with each other. They had their own areas of work but did not hesitate in stopping to help the other when needed. While the men worked hard to construct the cabin, the wives took time to till up a garden spot and plant some of the seeds they had brought with them.

"I love the smell of fresh turned soil." Margret commented as she used the shovel to turn the soil over. "This ground must have some sand as well as rich clay in it. It is not that hard to turn over. Of course, that last shower we had helped loosen it. I am glad we found this spot just below the creek for our garden. Otherwise, we may have to carry water to it. I think that with the little help of our men, we can easily water it."

Sylvia tried very hard to help where she could, but the more she worked, the sicker she became. Nancy was a little trooper. She cooked their meals and ran errands. Daniel and Nancy helped Lillian and Margret with the garden while Sylvia kept off her feet.

Horseshoe Bend Sawmill

Lester cut an opening for a door and another for a window and told Ernest, "I think that now is a good time for you to pick up some lumber for our cabins. We will need it for the door, window, and some furniture."

"Good. I will head out first thing in the morning."

When Ernest drove their wagon into Horseshoe Bend, he saw a beehive of activity around a building that looked to be their mill. He stopped and asked the supervisor, "I am looking to pick up a load of dry cut lumber for our cabin door, windows, and some furniture."

The supervisor showed him where the office was and told him that he could place his order there. Once he had paid for it and had a receipt, he could bring his wagon to the backyard where they would load it up for him. Ernest went into the office where an older man met him. "What can I do for you?"

Ernest told him what he wanted, and the older man wrote out his order. After he paid for the lumber, he talked to the clerk. "I see many hardworking men in the area with many saloons. We are building our homes just north of here, and we would like to know what the area is like. What kind problems do you have?"

"Well, the men like to let off steam once in a while, usually at night after their shift. There are some bar fights, mainly between the loggers and the miners. They seem to get into it often. So far, the fights have been relatively minor. We have just started this mill up and are just barely meeting the building demands. Several settlements are growing rapidly and utilizing all we can produce. By the way, if are you looking for a good job, I can fix you up."

"No thank you, but thanks for asking. I think that I will stick to farming. What kind of law enforcement is in the area?"

"We only have local law enforcement at this time. There is a new US Marshal by the name of Tye Parker that roams around the area. He is a good man, a little too young if you ask me though. He has a lot of territory to cover. We seldom see him here unless he has to solve a murder. His office resides in the courthouse in Boise. Whenever we have need of him, we have to send a runner over to fetch him. It may take him a few days to get here since he is usually out running around somewhere."

"Well, thanks for the advice. I think I will go over to the mercantile before I load the lumber."

Ernest drove over to the mercantile and picked up some needed items. While he was there, he asked the owner if they had any trouble with the Indians.

"No sir, the Indians have been quite peaceful so far. They don't come in here very often, but once in a while, they will darken my door. They like to trade hides and animal pelts with me for what they want. Generally, they are quite reasonable. Occasionally, they will get the best of me though. The superintendents of the loggers and miners have warned their workers to treat them with respect. With more loggers and miners coming into the area, I worry that they could spark a conflict at anytime though. The barkeepers in the saloons know they are not to serve them any alcohol. When this settlement grows a little more, we might be able to afford a local peacekeeper, but right now we do not have the funds."

Ernest brought the lumber he wanted back to the cabin site. Lester and Julio helped him unload it. Lester went right to work to make a large rectangular door and, with the help of Julio and Ernest, hung the door using leather hinges. Margret made a curtain for the window from material that Ernest bought from the mercantile.

When they finished the first cabin, Sylvia and Nancy moved what belongings they had left into it. Ernest rolled the water barrels into the cabin and laid the wagon's tailgate on top of it for a makeshift table. He brought in some stumps that were left over from cutting of the logs for chairs. Sylvia, Margret, and Lillian made a housewarming dinner celebration for the completion of their first cabin. It had taken them two months to complete the building.

Sylvia played her guitar and sang some old Irish songs. Soon they all joined in the singing and dancing over their accomplishments. Ernest gave a prayer of thankfulness that all were healthy and for the solid foundation the cabin was sitting on and especially for the camaraderie of the three families.

"If we can keep working like we did on this cabin, we will all have a roof over our heads in four more months. The garden that our wives planted is starting to sprout, and we should be able to have fresh vegetables to eat before long. The potatoes, onions, and carrots are sure taking root. I think that the corn and wheat that Lester planted, along with our vegetable garden, should sustain us throughout the winter. We should be complete with the cabins by the time we have our second child. I am so thankful for everything everyone has done," Ernest said.

They took the weekend off from building cabins to do a few things they had neglected. Ernest went hunting. He killed and brought in a large buck. Lester and Julio surveyed the area and planned where he would like to make a shed for their growing flock of sheep and livestock. "Initially, I think that we should build one barn away from the cabin sites." Lester told Julio. "Then as our livestock increase, we should build a barn for each of us."

"I agree. I think we should construct the first one on your homestead, far enough away to allow for growth but close enough that you can keep an eye on it from your cabin. Next, we should build one next to Ernest and my cabin. They should all be close enough that we all can see them. With the wolves, coyotes, and other predators roaming the area, we need to keep a close watch on the barns and livestock. We found this beautiful little valley. It sits right between two mountain ranges. The mountain to the east has a lot of timber, and just over the mountain to the west has the Payette River. Someday, I would like to explore the area upriver from where we entered the valley."

The wolves began to descend closer and became braver. They would try to sneak in and grab a lamb, but Ole Shep would keep them at bay. As they began to get smarter, one would make noise at one end of the flock while others would wreak havoc at the other end. Since Ole Shep could not be in two places at a time, they began to succeed in grabbing the lambs.

Julio was frustrated and decided to pen them up every night close to the barn. He would sleep in the loft next to the pen, and whenever he heard Ole Shep fighting with the wolves, he would unlimber his Greener and take a shot at them. His success was limited. He began to pen all the animals up tightly at night. That meant that their barn was full and needed expansion.

Ernest theorized that the logging activity was driving the wolves out of their natural feeding ground in the mountains; therefore, they looked elsewhere for food. He cautioned Nancy, Daniel, and Jeremiah not to venture outside at night without an adult carrying a rifle. He also began to teach them how to shoot.

Nez Percé Camp

"Since we are taking a little time off, I think that I will take a load of wolf pelts and deer hides over to our Nez Percé friends across the river and see what they have that they would like to trade for. If they have nothing to trade, I will just give them the hides as a gesture of good faith. Maybe they are as friendly as the Utes were in Utah," Ernest said.

Ernest rode west to the river and looked for a place to cross over to the other side. The river was not easy to cross, but he found a relatively calm place to ford. Ernest took off his clothes, placed them in a watertight bag, and led his horse into the cold water. His horse struggled to swim across the swift-running water, even without Ernest in the saddle. He did hang on to its tail though to have him pull him across the water. They finally reached the other side and found solid footing. Ernest was soaked to the bone and built a fire to dry off. He rubbed his horse down then put on his dry clothes, remounted, and rode up over the bank of the river.

The ground on the west side of the river was flat and fertile until it reached the base of the mountains. On the flat, he found the Nez Percé camp. They were moving around their camp when they noticed his approach. He introduced himself to the warrior that greeted him and told him that they had just built a cabin across the river in the little valley. The warrior's wife emerged from her wigwam and wore Sylvia's scarf around her neck. Ernest immediately recognized it, pointed to it, and said that it used to belong to his wife. The Indian nodded his head and remembered greeting Sylvia. "You have big white dog." The big Indian commented. "My name Gray Elk, and this my wife Babbling Brook. We visited your wagons, and your squaw gave us this scarf. You are welcome to our camp."

"Thank you. My name is Ernest Walker. We would like to be good neighbors to you. We have built one cabin and are in the process of building two more. How long have you lived near this river?"

"We been here three generations. Moved here from west near where this river joins with what they call Snake River. Our people have large camp there."

"You speak good English. Where did you learn to speak it so well?"

"There was expedition through here several years ago. They guided by Sacagawea, a member of Shoshone Nation. Her brother was chief of Shoshones. She named many rivers and tributaries along their trail. We fed Lewis and Clark's expedition salmon from river. They friendly and stayed with us for a spell. His followers taught us this language. Since they left, people speaking that language are overrunning this area. We learned to accept them. However, we very disturbed what those loggers do to forest. We hope they clean up mess they make on mountains. Unless they control mess they make, deer will have no place to live. We already see wolves scurrying away from area and hunting down next to our camps. Same loggers use river to float logs down and tangle nets we use to catch fish. We have complained to chiefs, but they don't know whom to counsel. They have talked to Indian agent, but he cannot hear."

"Maybe I can find someone you may give your complaints to the next time I go to Boise settlement. I make no promises though. The loggers are a headstrong group, and there is a big demand for wood products."

"Those nice-looking wolf pelts and deer hides on horse. What you planning to do with those?"

"Well, I brought them over to see if you could use them. Since we are no longer traveling in a wagon, we have little use for so many."

"We use them," Gray Elk spoke. "They protect us against cold when snow falls. Our squaws know how make them soft and pliable. They sew beautiful ornaments on them. What can I give in return for such gift?"

"The pelts are a neighborly gift, and we ask nothing in return. I am sure there are trading posts around that I could use if I wanted to make a trade."

"Oh yes. Upriver where this one joins another, there is new trading post there. It not much and just getting started, but has potential. They seem honest. They trade most anything with you. A decent man named Parks owns it. He has good supply of food and clothes he gets from Boise."

Gray Elk showed Ernest around their camp. He saw a pen of wild mustangs and watched as some of the braves were trying to gentle them. "I see you have some wild mustangs penned up. Maybe you will take me with you when you go mustanging or fishing and show me how to trap them."

"We captured and traded many horses to US Army. They call mustangs, feral horses. They wild, that for sure. It hard work to trap mustangs and takes several weeks. They run wild in hills southwest of us and are wilder than elk. They run in herds, cover vast territory, and constantly on move. They stay healthy and fit from exercise of running and foraging. Our brothers west sometimes go with us. We found several box canyons that we use to trap them. It depends how many there are as how we hunt. If we have large number of hunters, we circle large area and run herd into one box canyon then close barricade on them. When only a few hunters, we use more skill and tactics."

"That sounds like a lot of fun," Ernest replied.

"The real fun begins when we try to gentle down wild ones. It takes a lot of patience, and we receive many bruises. Those wild animals are fighters. We use ones that we break to trade for needs. It seems that ranchers in high meadows to north have constant need, as do immigrants coming from east. There is high demand for horseflesh. Civil War created big need, and Union Army would stop by to trade for them. I am somewhat glad to hear that war is over but don't look forward to new migration coming west. As long as those in east were fighting each other, they left us alone. Now fighting is over, they turn their attention to driving us off our land again. Next spring, we planning big hunt with brothers to west and be glad to take you along."

"Thanks. Well, I have to be getting back. It has been good to finally get to meet you. You are welcome to come by and visit us anytime you want and bring your family."

"Thank you for gift. We use pelts. Ride safe."

Ernest returned to his cabin and told Lester and Julio of the frustration that the Nez Percé were having with the loggers.

"I am afraid that we are all going to have to get used to the mess they are creating until some federal organization can make laws to control them with enough law enforcement in the area to enforce the law. I like the products they are making, but that doesn't mean they shouldn't clean up their mess," Lester said.

They completed the cabins with time to spare before winter set in. Lester had even found time to harvest the field of corn and wheat. It was not a lot, but it would sustain them through the winter. Ernest went hunting to keep them in stock with fresh meat. Julio watched over the sheep and livestock. He would milk the cows every morning and evening and make cheese and butter with what fresh milk they were able to use. He would also gather eggs from the chickens every morning. When they had leftover food and wool, they would trade with the Nez Percé for fish, both fresh and dried.

CLAYMORE WALKER

One day, Nancy came running up to Ernest, who was tilling the ground out in a meadow with Sissy. "Daddy, Mama's real sick. I think it's more than just the baby."

"I'll go get Lillian while you go and get Margret. Maybe they can figure it out. Red told me that Lillian said she has watched over their own for many generations. I will be back by nightfall. Do what you can for her."

"Okay, Daddy, but hurry."

Ernest and Lillian arrived back just at dusk. Meanwhile, Margret had been working with Sylvia, trying to help her keep food down. Margret and Lillian asked to be alone with Sylvia for a while. She needed to try to figure out what was wrong with her. Margret hurriedly came out of the cabin and was white faced. She told Lester and Ernest to fetch more water and keep it boiled. "Julio, cut up that sheet into small strips. We will need quite a few clean cloths."

"How is mama doing?" Nancy asked. "Is there anything I can do to help? I am so worried."

"Yes, you can get me your mother's medical bag, keep up your prayers, and encourage your father. She is not doing very well, but we have to keep the faith and stay encouraged. We are doing everything that we can to save her and the baby. I have to get back in, but knock when the water is boiling and the cloths are cut," Margret said.

Margret was back and forth, dumping buckets of cold red water, handing Nancy the blood-soaked cloths, and getting the clean hot water and cloths. Nancy wrung out and cleaned the red cloths to return them to Margret on her next trip.

Everyone was sick with worry and tried to deal with it themselves. Ernest went to the chopping block and began to chop the logs into kindling while Julio stacked the kindling. Lester kept the fire blazing under the pot of boiling water. When Nancy took a break, she pounded coffee beans to a pulp, poured some of the boiling water into the coffeepot, and poured the beans into the pot to make coffee. After the coffee brewed, she poured cold water into the pot to settle the grounds. She took cups of the steaming brew to Ernest, Julio, and Lester, who sorely needed it. She hugged her dad and told him that she loved him.

As the men were drinking their coffee, they heard a slap, then the bawling of a baby. Relief flushed over the men as they slapped Ernest on his, back congratulating him.

"I am still so worried about Red." Ernest told the men and Nancy while they were waiting for Margret and Lillian. "I remember her when I first ran into her aboard the ship. She was so beautiful, slim, and trim. She had a long red lock of hair that was tangled around her face. When she brushed it away and looked up into my eyes, I knew I had found the love of my life. I was so clumsy whenever I was around her. I just could not concentrate on what I was doing. Whenever I climbed the mast of the ship we were on to rig the sails, I would look all around the ship to see if I could spot her. She worked during the day, and it was late at night when she finished her long shift. She was tired and worn out from her work, but always bright eyed and friendly to me whenever I was around. She would flip her beautiful red hair to the back of her neck with the shake of her head. Sometimes she would just blow the lock back. She did not think she was too pretty, but she did not see herself through my eyes. I was called upon, day and night, to do some tasks aboard the ship, from rigging the sails to tossing a dead body off its bow of one of the diseased passengers. We were aboard one of those *death ships* that sailed from Ireland. Sylvia's job was to carry food and water to its passengers. She was very upset at the foul food and contaminated water she had to serve. She challenged the captain at every opportunity about how he was killing the passengers. He threatened her with bodily harm and told her he would throw her off the vessel if he ever heard her complain again. That may have stopped her complaining, but she began a campaign to carry clean water and good food to the children by stealing it from the captain's secret supply. She has always been headstrong about things like that. Whenever she sees an injustice, she tries to set it right. She never complains about her suffering and has been such a loving partner in my life."

"Daddy, Mother told me some of that story, but from her perspective. She saw you as a gallant, hardworking, and handsome young man. You were her knight in shining armor. You rescued her from the perils that befall a young single woman thrown aboard a ship in the middle of the sea. You fought for her and were willing to give your life for her. She loves you dearly, as I do." Nancy kissed her father on his cheek and hugged him.

When Lillian and Margret emerged a few moments later, Margret handed Ernest a wiggling bundle. "You have a strapping baby brother." She told Nancy. Nancy immediately started removing the blankets on him to see what her brother looked like. He had red wavy hair and an Irish face. She looked up at her father and said, "He looks just like you."

Ernest looked down at his boy. "He is an Irishman all right. He will make you a good brother and Red and I a good son."

Margret's face was ashen as she took the bundle back from Ernest and told them with tears in her eyes, "You and Nancy need to go into the bedroom and see your mother. She has suffered dearly and may not have much time."

Ernest looked immediately distressed. "What do you mean? Didn't she give birth to this child?"

"Yes, but she must have been bleeding inside for a long time. She is very weak, and I don't think she will last very long."

"I will ride to Boise and find a doctor. Surely he can save her."

"I am sorry," Lillian said, "but I think that it is too late. You must hurry in to see her. She is barely hanging on."

Nancy and Ernest went quietly into the bedroom and stood beside the bed, looking down at Sylvia. Sylvia looked at peace, but whiter than she ever had before. She opened her eyes and smiled a tired smile. "He is a beautiful boy," she said as her fingers laced through Ernest's fingers. "He will grow up strong and handsome like you." She turned her head and looked over into the pleading eyes of Nancy and said, "Nancy, he will be a little bit of a burden to you, but I know you will love him as I loved you. Please watch over him and your father. They will need much love after I am gone."

"Mother!" she cried. "Please do not go. I love you."

"I love you too, dear." With those last fading words, she closed her eyes and was gone as she breathed her last.

"Ernest and Nancy, I'm real sorry, but she must have been bleeding inside. We really tried, but she was too weak. We were only able to save your baby boy." Margret choked out, sobbing.

"I'm sure you did all that was humanly possible. We had such dreams for this place. Now I just don't know what to do."

"Ernest, you have two children who are depending on you. Nancy can pretty well care for the baby with just a little direction. I will take her to my cabin a couple of weeks and teach her what to do."

"Thank you, Margret. I don't know what we would have done without you."

"I'll come back over periodically to check on you so the baby and Nancy can see you. I'll also bring a cow over that we have to help feed them."

"I'll bury Red up on that hill overlooking our ranch and will build a stone hedge around it tomorrow."

"I'll stay through tomorrow, but I must get your boy some wholesome milk to drink shortly. By the way, what is his name?"

"I don't have any idea. What do you hink, Nancy?"

"Clay. Mama always said a baby is like clay, pliable and easy to mold while they are still soft."

"Claymore Walker. It has a good ring to it. Margret, thank you for everything you and Lillian have done. Tell Lester that when I get back on my feet, I'll repay him for the use of his cow."

It was a solemn, quiet ceremony around the grave plot encircled with a tall stone hedge. Ernest, Lester, and Julio had worked tirelessly building the stone hedge by hauling the rock from the creek. It took them all night and well into the next day to complete the walls. Ernest dug a deep grave himself while Julio fashioned a stone cross. Lester used a spare wooden spoke wheel from one of their wagons to make a gate in its entrance. It was a beautiful place atop a knoll in a meadow overlooking their three cabins and barns. The spring would bring out the colorful flowers that would surround the grave site.

Ernest stood hand in hand with Nancy. Lester, Margret, and Daniel stood to Ernest's right while Julio, Lillian, and Jeremiah stood to his left. Gray Elk and Babbling Brook heard about her death and stood behind the mourners.

Ernest opened the book Sylvia always carried with her. "She loved to read from the Bible in the morning and at night as she would tuck Nancy into bed. She especially loved First Corinthians." He read:

> Behold, I shew you a mystery; We shall not all sleep, but we shall all be changed, In a moment, in the twinkling of an eye, at the last trump: for the trumpet shall sound,

and the dead shall be raised incorruptible, and we shall be changed. For this corruptible must put on incorruption, and this mortal must put on immortality. So when this corruptible shall have put on incorruption, and this mortal shall have put on immortality, then shall be brought to pass the saying that is written, Death is swallowed up in victory. O death, where is thy sting? O grave, where is thy victory? The sting of death is sin; and the strength of sin is the law. But thanks be to God, which giveth us the victory through our Lord Jesus Christ.

1 Corinthians 15:51–57 (KJV)

"We loved her dearly. Please, God, take care of her until we meet up with her again."

In unison, they all said amen.

Ernest picked up a handful of dirt. "The Lord giveth, and the Lord taketh away. Blessed be the name of the Lord. Red, give Freda a big hug and thank her for the use of their wagon and its contents. Maybe you two can learn each other's songs and melodies now. You may also want to wander over to the Ute camp and give all our friends a big hug." He tossed the handful of dirt over the beautifully polished wooden casket Lester had fashioned from the lumber they had leftover from building their cabins.

Lester told Ernest, "I will finish the filling in of the grave if you will take Nancy back to the cabin where Margret and Lillian have fixed a little meal."

"Thank you."

"Since Nancy and Clay staying at Lester and Margret's for a couple weeks, why don't you join me and my brothers in mustang gather?" Gray Elk asked. "Sometimes a man must stay busy to break sadness." Gray Elk quietly departed to return to their camp across the river.

For the next few weeks, the pioneer families mourned the loss of Sylvia. Margret and Lillian were busy helping Nancy learn what to do with raising Clay. She was going to make a good surrogate mother for him.

Sylvia's death had taken its toll on Ernest. He had lost the love of his life and became quite haggard looking. He would go hunting but would not bring back much meat. He was very depressed.

Nancy returned to their cabin with Clay and told Ernest, "Dad, you need to get away from here for a little while to clear your head. We all miss Mother so much and still cry ourselves to sleep at night. Learning how to take care of Clay and watching over him has helped me the most. I think that you should take up Gray Elk's offer and go horse hunting with him and his brothers."

Mustanging

Ernest rode with Gray Elk and two of his tribesmen to meet their brothers from the west. They met them where the Payette River dumped into the Snake River. Then the ten men rode side by side south to where the mustangs roamed the semiarid scrublands of sparsely covered hills with sagebrush and tall grass. Gray Elk took the lead and motioned for the others to follow.

They rode hard and long across the prairie land and small creeks to the edge of a deep canyon. "We rest here for evening." He told Ernest. "Before sunrise, we need to be in position along rim. We spread out about a half mile apart so we don't miss seeing horses when they head down to canyon to hide during day. They go down into canyon at dusk to drink and drink again at dawn. They seem only to drink water twice a day, once in morning and once at night. That is why we want to be in position on rim before daylight. When herd comes up out of canyon, we will be able to watch where they head. We don't want to run herd but watch pattern."

"What if they do not take the same path every day?" Ernest asked Gray Elk.

"They generally do not. That why, when we find where they are going, we can determine how to capture them. Since they nomadic, we have to find them and then drive them into closest box canyon."

"The mustangs sound very smart and tough," Ernest stated.

"A tough stallion weighing around one thousand pounds will be leader of band of horses. Most of these wild horses weigh between five hundred to eight hundred pounds. Sometimes wild burros mix in with horse herd. If there is any danger to the band, the stallion will be first to sound alarm. That is why antelope and deer sometimes hang around a herd. They know that stallion will alert them if there are any predators in area. Once alerted to danger, stallion will position himself between herd and predator. Their main defense mechanism is to take flight. If that does not save them, they fight. It is also a mystery to me that stallions will not breed with their daughters and will not fight another stallion who intends to do so, but if that stallion tries to breed with one of the mares that are not his daughter, he will fight to death against foe."

"Don't the wolves cause these animals problems?"

"Not often. Neither wolves nor coyotes seem to bother them. However, mountain lion and bear kill a number of newborn and foals throughout year. The greatest danger to them is during springtime from March to July when they foal. It takes about eleven months for their pregnancy. We used to capture these feral horses and use them to kill buffalo just over into Bitterroot Mountains on other side of this mountain range, but then came the hide hunters that practically devastated whole bison population. We would spend days drying meat from buffalo so that it would keep. When hide hunters of east came, they would kill these great majestic animals just for their hides and let meat rot in sun."

The sun rose from the east and closed the gray shadows it carried with it. The ten horse hunters were hidden along the rim and were watching for any movement. As the sun climbed through the clouds, Ernest heard a whinny from below the rim and knew that the band was on the move. He signaled the other riders by using the mirror that Gray Elk had loaned him for that purpose. He directed the reflection along the rim on both sides of him to get the others' attention.

A herd of thirty mature mustangs raced up a canyon trail to burst out of its top right between him and Gray Elk. A beautiful jet-black stallion with a long mane and tail led them. It was a beautiful sight just to watch the wild animals run, but he had come for horseflesh, not the scenery. The ten riders converged into a line behind the running beasts. Gray Elk pointed off to his right, and the line moved to the right, causing the line of wild horses to swerve to the right. The horse hunters were running their horses flat out, hoping that their horse would not step into a hole and break its leg. The wild mustangs began swinging too far to the right, so Gray Elk's riders swung his riders to their right and pushed hard against the herd.

It seemed like hours had passed before the herd started slowing down after their morning run. It was not the first hunt that Gray Elk had been on; he knew exactly what he was doing and how to herd the running band. The herd approached several rolling hills and flowed over them. A shallow canyon emerged in front of them, and the running horses turned left into it. Gray Elk motioned for three of the riders to stay at the top of the hill and run along its ridge. Three other riders went to the opposite ridge while the four remaining rode behind the frightened herd. The canyon sides grew steeper, and the flat grew narrower. Suddenly, both sides of the canyon grew to a sheer cliff, and its floor became very narrow.

Gray Elk raised his hand and brought the chase to a halt. The riders on the rim rode back down to assist with the building of the barricade. The hunters began to make a large brush pile on the canyon floor to barricade the animals in the box canyon. While they were working, the black stallion came charging back to challenge the barricade. He lunged at the brush and pawed at the trees that blocked his way. "We need to let him and four of his lead mares go." Gray Elk lowered the barricade to let the black stallion run free.

"We just risk our lives capturing that beauty. Why do we want to let him and four of his best mares go?" Ernest questioned.

"When you plant field and harvest crop, do you eat all you harvest?" Gray Elk asked.

"No we don't, of course not. If we did that, we would not have anything to plant and harvest the next growing season."

"You answered your own question." Gray Elk smiled. "We have captured his herd, which are fine animals. However, if we keep all of them, when we come back, there will not be any more to take. We have to leave some for seed, just like you when you harvest your plants. When you keep seed for next season, it is best and biggest seed for next planting. Therefore, you strengthen your crop, not weaken it. If we took that great wild beast and left something less or his strongest mares, next crop of wild mustangs will not be worth capturing."

Gray Elk held up four fingers and sent two braves into the canyon. They did not have to go far before four great mares came busting through, challenging the barricade like their big black mate. When the four mares exited the canyon with their manes flying, the two braves helped block the path of the rest of the herd trying to break out. When the barricade was finished, they could see the horses milling back and forth, trying to climb the brush barrier to no avail. Other horses began trying to climb up one of the canyon walls or the other, just to fall back to its floor. The trapped horse herd had lost their freedom.

Gray Elk motioned to the horse hunters to gather around the campfire he had started in the middle of the canyon floor where they sat around eating their pemmican. Pemmican was the staple food for most all Indian tribes. Depending upon where the tribe was located, this determined what made up this ball of nourishment. For the Nez Percé, the squaws gathered various berries and nuts from the hillside in the fall and dried and chopped them. They especially enjoyed the huckleberries and currants that grew abundantly at the higher elevations. Pine nuts, sunflower seeds, or any other nut that a squirrel would eat helped give the pemmican its substance. They took dried venison or fish and pounded it into a powder. They mixed the berries with the powdered meat and rolled it in melted animal fat. They seasoned the substance with salt and assorted herbs and spices. The pemmican would last for a long time and was very nutritious and tasty.

Gray Elk handed a ball of pemmican to Ernest and told him, "We need to let our animals rest for a while. It was a hard run to capture this herd, and we need to rest up before we tackle our next task. Although we don't want to give wild horses too much time to rest before we begin working them. We have to rope and bind them to make them understand that they must follow us, not that stallion. While we take our break, that wild band will wear themselves out and find they are leaderless. When they are tired, exhausted, and have lost hope, we go back to work."

After the tribesmen rested and retrieved their ropes. They started roping and hobbling the wild horses. It was dangerous work, but they had done this many times before and were old hands at it. They worked the afternoon away, roping and hobbling the frightened horses. Ernest helped rope and hold the horses as the others hobbled the flaying hooves. Fully exhausted by the time the sun dipped low in the west, they had all the mature mustangs roped and bound. The yearling foals and younger ones they let run free. They would stay by their mothers like children hanging on to her skirt.

Ernest felt like he had been beaten to a pulp. He was sweating, bone tired, and bruised all over. He had been in many rough-and-tumble fights, but this was one he would remember for a long time. The only thing good he saw was that he had no time to mourn.

"We found three that have brands." A young brave told Gray Elk.

"Turn them loose. We cannot keep those with brands. We rest tonight and let horses get used to feel of rope. Soon they understand that rope is their master and that we master rope. As you can see, it is like training a child. You must first get their attention. They must know who to respect and who to fear. When we roped and bound them, you heard us talking in low, soothing tones. We did not yell or beat them, as some white men would have done. When they hear us whispering to them instead of yelling, and rubbing their coats instead of kicking them, they soon learn we are friend and to be respected. They will fear rope for some time, but soon, they learn that it also keep them safe."

"What of that black stallion? Won't he try to fight us and take back his herd?"

"He might, and I expect he will. However, he now has four of his lead mares. He not want to lose them. If we had taken all mares, he would have attacked us repeatedly until we would have had to either capture or kill him. He has start of a new herd. He will roam wide and far throughout this habitat to find other herds that he will try to steal. He may have to fight another stallion or two, but life is survival of fittest."

CARIE

The next morning, the feral horses were more docile. They had fought against the ropes all night and now understood that the ropes were mastering them. They worked with the new horse herd and tied three horses together. They unhobbled their rear legs, but kept their front legs tied together with a short rope. They let them get used to the ropes and loss of freedom. After some kicking and biting, they learned that they were still tied to the ones they were hurting. Gray Elk instructed, "We each lead one group of three back home. They fight us at first but learn to follow behind by time we reach river. They are tired and thirsty. They have fought hard for a day and a half. I think they enjoy getting away from this canyon. Keep rope tight, and watch that they do not try to bite or kick you or your horse."

"What if that black stallion tries to steal them from us?" Ernest asked Gray Elk.

"We will place a shot or two between his legs, and that will turn him."

Gray Elk led the way, holding the lead rope attached to three good-sized mature mares. One had a foal that was running at her mother's side. Two other Indians went ahead of Ernest. They handed him the lead rope and attached it to his saddle horn. He headed in line behind the three Nez Percé, leading two mares and one stud.

Ernest marveled at the little foals as they tried to suckle from their mothers even as they were moving. The ten tribesmen, including him, headed in a straight line back to the Snake River. At first, it was hard going as the wild horses struggled to break free.

Two of the tribesmen did not tow horses. The two removed the barrier and then caught back up to the string to help herd the horses into the corral. They rode alongside those that were leading a string and helped those whose horses were fighting the hardest. Ernest's horse was a strong bay, and whenever one of the mustangs got too close, it would let fly one of its rear hooves. Once it caught the mare he was leading under its jaw, practically knocking off its head. It soon quit trying to bite her and held her distance.

The string of horses were following along peacefully until the Snake River loomed in the distance. Then they began to fight harder on the lead ropes as their thirst took over any desire for freedom. When they reached the river, they lengthened the lead ropes so that the horses could drink their fill from the clear water. The horse hunters camped at the big river overnight and planned to move onto the main Nez Percé camp in the morning.

Around midnight, a galloping of hooves awakened the hunters. The feral horses tried to break free as a big black stallion whistled for them to rejoin his band. Gray Elk had ordered that they double-hobble the captured horses that evening, so the best they could do was to dance around and fall to the ground when they tried too hard to run after their stallion.

"Wow!" Ernest exclaimed to Gray Elk. "He sure wants his band back. He must have known that he was putting his own life on the line to come at us like that. We could easily have shot him if we wanted. Do you think that he will continue to make a play for these feral horses?"

"No. I think he wanted to try one last time to take them away from us before we crossed over Snake. He has reputation of stirring hearts of many horses in all ranches this side of Snake. Ranchers have lost a lot of horses to that ole black stallion. Sometimes they come into our camp, claiming that we stole them. They look over our herd to see if they can find any branded with their brands. If they ever found that we have captured one of theirs, they have threatened to hang us as horse thieves. That is why we release any with brands. We do not want to take a chance at one of their necktie parties."

They crossed the wide river the next morning. It was not too deep, and the horses kept their footing. They reached the Indian camp around noon. Then they steered the horses toward a large polled corral. Once inside, they remove their lead ropes, but left their front feet hobbled. Several smaller corrals opened into the larger one. Once all of the horses were inside the large corral and their mounts taken care of, Gray Elk directed that the men should open the smaller corral and move one mature horse into each of the three smaller corrals. Three men went into the smaller corral, roped the horse, and tied it tight to a snubbing post in the center of it. The horse twisted and turned around that post until it was quite exhausted.

"What do we do now?" Ernest asked.

"We let them fight rope and post. It is far easier to let them fight post than trying to hold end of that rope. Once they learn they cannot get free and are practically exhausted, we go to work talking smoothly to them and lay our hands on horse. We rub it all over with our hands, letting it get to know us more personally. By that time, it should know that we not trying to hurt it but become its friend. They are frightened and like a child. Rubbing them all over while talking quietly to them helps develop a bond. We do that several times before we even think about mounting them. I know several white men that think they need to just saddle horse and ride it into ground. We don't want to break spirit of horse but make bond with them."

"I can see that your way may lead to a horse that is more of a friend. When do you try to ride them?"

"On third rubbing of horse, we begin to put weight on backs. As you see, when they rub their backs, they apply their weight. Depending on the horse, they may even try to put a blanket on its back. Once horse accepts man's weight, we try to manually lead horse around snubbing post with someone on its back. The one on its back will use its legs to guide horse in the same direction as one leading it. When they accept that, we gently hand rope to one that is now astraddle of horse. We let him guide horse with his legs. A horse is a very smart animal and learns quickly. As long as we are gentle, they don't fight us too hard."

"Do you ever have a horse that is impossible to break?"

"Yes, we had three or four that just would not allow us breaking them. We solved problem easily enough by letting them return to stallion to produce foals for us to capture next year. Now, Ernest, why don't you take a turn at helping to gentle next horse?" Gray Elk smiled.

"Why not?" Ernest hopped into the ring next to a large mare and began rubbing her down. Several times, he had to twist aside out of the way of flying feet as she tried to discourage him. As he was leaning over, rubbing her front feet, she tried to nip him. He slapped her mouth as he had seen the other handlers do. He did not try to hurt her but just let her know who her boss was. As he was working the mare, he imitated the other handlers by speaking in soft monotones. Several times, he wanted to shout at the horse, but he held his temper even when she put her weight down directly on his toe. On the third rubbing, he put his weight onto her back. She jumped around but quieted down shortly. He took his weight off and placed a blanket onto her back, trying not to let it flutter in the wind. Once it settled, he leaned over her and straddled her back. She fidgeted and jerked around but did not persist. The lead man led her around the corral; Ernest used his knees to tell the animal which way to turn. The horse responded. Soon he found that he could maneuver the horse without the lead man pulling one way or the other. When he handed Ernest the rope, the horse continued to respond to his commands. Fifteen minutes later, Ernest slid off the horse. He tied it to a rail. She was green broke.

"Well," Gray Elk said. "You have just broken your first feral horse. She will make a nice gentle riding horse. Be careful you don't spoil her too much."

"You mean that you are giving me this fine mare?"

"Yes, of course. You earned her. I am sure you find she will be high-spirited and make a good companion. You need to ride her often and keep ight rope on her until she gets to know you and your home."

"Thank you." Ernest rode his bay away, leading the green broke mare. He crossed the Payette again and turned into the little valley. Nancy saw him coming and ran from the cabin to give him a big hug. She was full of questions and all smiles as she saw the young mare he was leading.

"I see you had some luck in your mustang adventure. I was so worried that you might get hurt that Clay and I prayed for your return every night. He is growing rapidly and pulls on my hair. He even tries to chew on it if I don't catch him."

"It sounds like you two have gotten to know each other. I am sure that Red would have been proud of you the way you have stepped up to take control. She loved you very much."

"She loved you too, Daddy. So what is the horse's name?"

"I have no idea. I haven't named her yet."

"Oh, so she is a mare. You know that you have to name her. It is your responsibility to name the animals that you bring home." She smiled.

"Well, I have not thought about it. She has quite a kick and put all of her weight onto my toe just to test me. Hmmm. I think I shall call her Carrie after my sister, Carieanne."

"Oh, I am sure my aunt will be pleased to find that you named a wild mustang after her. She might just come over here from Ireland and box your ears for that."

"I sure hope so. I would love to see her again. I miss all my family and wonder how they are doing."

"Why don't you write them a letter? Julio told me that they have a US post office in Boise now and that you can send mail anyplace in the world."

"That is a great idea. I will address it and start it, if you will finish it. The next time someone goes to Boise, let them mail it. I would like to send a note to the Reynolds family—John, Shirley, and their kids. Mary was especially close to Red. I am sure that they would like to know where we are and how we are doing."

The Letters

Nancy was busy with tending Clay and Ernest following Ernest's return from his wild horse hunt. Ernest rode Carrie every day and went hunting often on his new horse. He had to keep busy to hold his loneliness at bay. Whenever he was idle, his mind always drifted back to his days with Sylvia. Whenever he was in the cabin watching Nancy tend Clay, he thought of Sylvia. She was a great mother and cared for children. Sylvia was a wonderful mother and a great wife. *When will I ever be able to sit down and relax without thinking of Red? Will I ever be able to go to sleep and wake up without reaching for her just to find an empty bed? I smell her on my pillow, but she is not there. I smell her when I hug Nancy or Clay. I miss her so much I can hardly breathe.*

Ernest addressed the envelope, wrote his part of the letter, handed it to Nancy, and said that she needed to finish it. "I am going out to turn the ground to prepare for our spring crop. When you finish writing the letter to your grandmother and grandfather, just seal it and take it to Julio to mail it in that new post office."

He addressed it to Shane, Bridget, and Carieanne Walker. He wrote the following:

The Walker Clan Series: Bound for Horseshoe Bend

Dear Mom, Dad, and sis,

I miss you very much and wish you were here in this new land with me. I pray often that the conditions there have improved, and you are once again raising potatoes there. I did not know what to expect when I left. I felt unwanted and unloved but have learned that it was because you loved me that you sent me away. The trip across the Atlantic was deplorable. The drinking water became polluted and scarce. The food was rotten and sickening to eat. Indeed, this land is a land of opportunity and is in growing pains. In my travel to America aboard the ship, I fell in love with a beautiful spunky Basque gal from my homeland, Ireland. She brought joy to my life. Her name was Sylvia López. I nicknamed her Red, since she has red hair and reminds me of the fiery redheads in Ireland. When we joined a wagon train to cross the continent to the west, we asked the wagon master to marry us. We met many fine people on our journey and had a lot of harrowing experiences as we traveled across the new continent. We had a beautiful redheaded daughter when we lived in the Utah Territory for several years. Your granddaughter's name is Nancy.
We finally settled north of a settlement called Boise in the Idaho Territory with two other families. We get along well with them as well as our Native American Indian friends from the Nez Percé tribe. We have built a nice cabin, barns, and storage sheds. Our fields are green and raise nice crops. We raise sheep, cattle, and horses and trade with the local merchants for our needs. I am saddened to tell you, but I lost the love of my life, Red, when she gave birth to a strapping young Irishman. Your grandson's name is Claymore, Clay for short.

I miss the homeland but know that I will never be back there again. I hope that this letter finds you doing well and that your potato crop is once again free from the blight. I have asked Nancy to finish this letter and mail it to you.

Your loving son,
Ernest

Hi, you don't know me, but I have heard so much about you. My name is Nancy, and I am your granddaughter. Your grandson, Clay, keeps me very busy, feeding and changing him. He is walking now and speaking in broken English. He is playful, but sometimes a little ornery. He likes pulling on my hair and is always getting in my way. He chases our dog, Ole Shep, and loves to sling the wheat at the chickens.

Dad and I are still in mourning over the loss of Mom. I did not think that we could make it through one day when she passed, but one day has turned into another. Now it is almost a full year since she departed. Our neighbors are Lester, Margret, and Daniel Clark and Julio, Lillian, and Jeremiah Martinez. They are wonderful to us, and we share everything.

I have to tell you this. Right after Mom died, Dad went on a wild horse hunt. He brought back a nice mare. He named the wild mustang Carrie after my aunt, Carieanne. We all had a good laugh at her expense.

I sure wish you could come and see us even though I know it would be next to impossible. I would like nothing more than to see and wrap my arms around my relatives from Ireland and hear all your stories. Please write back when you can.

Missing you,
Nancy and Clay,
your loving grandchildren

Nancy did not take the letter over to Julio to take to the US post office but added to it a week later:

PS: I have to add another sad note to this letter before I send it.

She became saddened with teary eyes as she continued writing.

> When my mother died giving birth to Clay, I had to care for him while my father worked to put in our crops. He worked hard to pass the time of mourning. He had a bad accident right after we started this letter. He had just gone out to begin plowing when the mule bolted and dragged him all over the recently plowed ground. It bolted when a large jackrabbit jumped up and hopped between its legs. The mule finally quieted down but left my father with a badly broken leg. Its bone had punctured his thigh. I called on my neighbors, and we tried to set it, but it became infected and gangrene set in. The wounded area turned black and smelled awful. Dad died a few days later with the poison. I was so angry at that worthless rabbit that I took my father's old musket and blew it to smithereens.
>
> I am sorry to tell you this sad news about your son. My father was a brave man to the end. I wished that Mother would have been here to help. She was excellent at healing. She taught me a lot, but I needed to learn more. I'm sure that if I had more experience, I could have saved Father. However, I am now without a mother and father, but I know that they taught me well. I have some good neighbors that will take good care of us.
>
> We buried Dad next to Mom in a little plot that Dad created when Mom died. Their grave site sits overlooking our home and is landscaped with beautiful wildflowers. Dad built a stone hedge around the site. My neighbor, Julio Martinez, chiseled their names in stone and placed a headstone marker above their grave. It read, "Ernest and Sylvia Walker, loving parents of Nancy and Clay, would forever be missed."
>
> Love,
> Nancy

Nancy thought of the Reynolds family and decided to write them a letter as well. She wrote the following:

To the Reynolds family: John, Shirley, Mary, Harry, Edward, and Joseph,

I will have Julio or Lester try to find your address in Oregon. We hope you made it there and found everything that you were looking for. The Clarks and us have thought of you often and have missed every one of you dearly. We made a nice home in Utah with the Clarks. Both of our families have now enlarged. I now have a brother named Claymore. The Clarks had a boy by the name of Daniel. He is about six months younger than I am. We played a lot together in Utah Territory growing up. We had some wonderful Ute neighbors that had children as well. They were good to us, and we traded with them often. We had a beautiful place in Utah. Our cabins were next to a clear running stream with good soil for garden and other crops. Lester was a great farmer and grew a lot of crops for our animals. We had chickens, sheep, cows, and tried raising some wild turkey. It was fun while we were there. However, Mormons continued to cause us problems and finally run the Utes out of their homes as well as us. I am quite sure that Dad and Lester burned up our buildings after we left. They just did not want the bigots to use anything that we had built. We drove our wagons across to Idaho Territory and located a beautiful little homestead near Horseshoe Bend in Gem County. I do not think that you are very far from us, and maybe we can meet somewhere.

I have some sad news to share with you though. Mom died giving birth to Clay a few years ago. Dad just died from gangrene poisoning. They are buried in a nice lot Dad made for Mom overlooking our ranch. I have decided to stay here and continue with their dreams. I have good neighbors and will be okay.

Please write when you can, and let us know how you are doing and where you are actually located.

Love always,
Nancy and Clay Walker

Julio rode over to Boise and mailed their letters in the new US post office. Nancy hoped that the Walkers would receive it and reply. She and Clay were now orphaned as their mother was, and she stuck her chin out, flipped her red hair, and said to Clay, "We must look forward to the future and make it better than our past. Every day is just a new beginning, and we should take it one step at a time, little brother. We have a lot to live for, and there are great new frontiers to witness."

Afterword

As Nancy began to pray and think aloud, she spoke the Lord's Prayer to begin her talk with God.

> Our Father which art in heaven, Hallowed be thy name. Thy kingdom come, Thy will be done in earth, as it is in heaven. Give us this day our daily bread. And forgive us our debts, as we forgive our debtors. And lead us not into temptation, but deliver us from evil: For thine is the kingdom, and the power, and the glory, for ever. Amen.
>
> Matthew 6:9–13 (KJV)

Sylvia had taught her scripture and how it pertained to her life. She had her memorize many passages and said that when she departed, she would like her to think about what life would be like after death. Nancy recalled the following passage:

> What shall we say then? Shall we continue in sin, that grace may abound? God forbid. How shall we, that are dead to sin, live any longer therein? Know ye not, that so many of us as were baptized into Jesus Christ were baptized into his death? Therefore we are buried with him by baptism into death: that like as Christ was raised up from the dead by the glory of the Father, even so we also should walk in newness of life. For if we have been planted together in the likeness of his death, we shall be also in the likeness of his resurrection: Knowing this, that our old man is crucified with him, that the body of sin might be

destroyed, that henceforth we should not serve sin. For he that is dead is freed from sin.

Romans 6:3–7 (kjv)

Nancy remembered how her mama had taught her about God and watched as her Papa baptized her in the little creek where neighbors had gathered around to witness the blessing. It was a special place where both her Mama and Papa put on Christ before her as well as the Clark and Martinez family.

> Jesus said unto her, I am the resurrection, and the life: he that believeth in me, though he were dead, yet shall he live: And whosoever liveth and believeth in me shall never die. Believest thou this?
>
> John 11:25–26 (kjv)

"Mama, you and Papa are now freed from sin and never have to worry about earthly woes. God is with you, and you are with him forever. But, Mama, please look down on me and comfort me when I struggle. Help me find a life pleasing to you that will fill me with love and joy like you and Papa. I know that you will find someone brave and loving like Papa for me when it is time and that we will continue growing our family and this country that you loved so much."

> For if we believe that Jesus died and rose again, even so them also which sleep in Jesus will God bring with him. For this we say unto you by the word of the Lord, that we which are alive and remain unto the coming of the Lord shall not prevent them which are asleep. For the Lord himself shall descend from heaven with a shout, with the voice of the archangel, and with the trump of God: and the dead in Christ shall rise first: Then we which are alive and remain shall be caught up together with them in the clouds, to meet the Lord in the air: and so shall we ever be with the Lord.
>
> 1 Thessalonians 4:14–17 (kjv)

"Mama I know you and Papa are walking with Jesus and will stay with him until I am able to rise up with you. Please watch over me and wait for me while I dwell here."

> Let not your heart be troubled: ye believe in God, believe also in me. In my Father's house are many mansions: if it were not so, I would have told you. I go to prepare a place for you. And if I go and prepare a place for you, I will come again, and receive you unto myself; that where I am, there ye may be also. And whither I go ye know, and the way ye know.
>
> John 14:1–4 (KJV)

"Mama, I know that you and Papa are together, walking among your friends, and know that you are happy and helping me and Clay as we continue the journey that you started."

Note from the Author

This book begins a saga that depicts the beginning of the American frontier. It tells of the travels of many immigrant families and their struggles to find homeland. Their hardships, successes, and failures were typical of the history that made this nation great. The next story tells another side of the struggle—the struggle of those immigrants within the country striving to fight for what is right and to find peace and economy. I look forward to you reading my next story. Many of the characters like Louis Woods and Raymond Leigh in this story will be in that book. It is like that in life, like two ships passing in the night to find them looking at each other at port. The Walkers and the Woods begin a generation that strengthens this nation as their lives intertwine. The following books merge these two families into a new generation with new issues they must work through to find a life of their own.